The Mom-thing was f.
room lifting.

He could see Mary's face softening, her lips relaxing. Whatever had taken possession of her had let go.

"It *is* a very fundamental question," Mary said.

"What?" said Billy.

"How it found me," Mary said.

"Who?"

"Ordo," Mary said.

"There's no such thing as Ordo," Billy said.

"But there is. When it's here, it speaks to me. And why me? It could have chosen a thousand other people. It must have sensed my vulnerabilities, a perfect environment for hiding. It crawled through that sewer in search of a victim, and it found me."

"I don't think that's what happened," Billy said.

"What else could it be? I think I should ask it. Yes, next time, that's what I will do. When it comes again, I'll ask it."

In this fleeting moment of clarity, Mary for the first time understood the reality.

I'm not crazy, she thought. *It's not all in my head. It can get into my brain, into my body, take control, and I am powerless to resist. But try convincing anyone of that.*

"You need sleep, Mom," Billy said.

Mary did not protest. She turned onto her side, away from Billy. For a few seconds, she coughed. Then she was quiet. Asleep.

She would not wake until late the next morning, when she would recall nothing, not even when Billy timidly—fearfully—asked if she remembered what had transpired in the semi-darkness of her room.

"My memory these days," she would say, again, "is not working."

TRACES OF MARY

G. Wayne Miller

Dedication

To David Wilson and David Dodd, with heartfelt thanks for keeping my sci-fi, horror, mystery and fantasy torch burning brightly! And for all that both of you have done for so many other authors, too.

Cast of characters
In order of appearance

Tanya Audette, a young girl who lives in Boston.
Sophie Audette, her mother.
Zachary Pearlman, Boston shop proprietor and owner of Fluffy, a French poodle.
Billy McAllister, a young boy who lives in Providence, Rhode Island.
Jessica McAllister, his older sister.
Mary Lambert McAllister, their mother.
The Rev. John Lambert, S.J., "Uncle Jack," Mary's brother, a Jesuit priest.
Alice McKay Lambert, "Grammy," Mary and Fr. Jack's mother, of Blue Hill, Maine.
George Linwood Lambert, "Grampa," Alice's late husband and father of Mary and Jack.
Mr. Hawthorne, a mortician.
Amanda Leroux, a social worker at the homeless center Fr. Jack runs in Boston.
Stephen McAllister, Mary's estranged husband and the father of her two children.
Andre Washington, Billy's best friend.
Paul "Angel" Iannotti, 14, a school dropout and bully.
Ordo, leader of the Priscillas, the good species in a distant galaxy.
Alex Borkowski, Billy's and Andres's second-best friend.
Crimson Vanner, a drug addict and dealer.
Z-DA, last of the Lepros, an evil species in a distant galaxy.
Juan Sierra, a property owner in Providence, R.I.
Rudolph Howe Sr. and Jr., lawyers in Providence, R.I.

Mrs. Bartholomew, father of a boy burned in an amusement-park fire.

Lt. Perry Callahan, a Providence police detective.

Amanda Leroux's mother, an elderly woman who lives on Massachusetts' North Shore.

Erica Han, a reporter with the Bangor Daily News.

Charlie Moonlight, a Native American spiritual leader.

Prologue

Five years ago

i.

Page one, the Boston Globe, November 16, 2016:

Four-alarm blaze badly burns mother and daughter
Reports of gas explosion being probed
by James Soares
Globe Staff

BOSTON—A young girl and her mother were badly burned last night in a four-alarm fire that destroyed one apartment building and heavily damaged two others just outside Kenmore Square.

At least 23 families who lived in the three buildings, including several with children, were left homeless, and many suffered minor injuries. Seven firefighters were hospitalized for smoke inhalation and all were later released.

Listed in critical condition this morning at Massachusetts General Hospital were Tanya Audette, 11, and her mother, Sophie Audette, 34, according to a hospital spokesman.

"Both are expected to survive, but they face a very long recovery, given the extent of their burns," the spokesman said.

The blaze at 840 Beacon Street began in a fiery explosion at approximately 10:15 p.m. The possibility of a gas leak is being probed.

It was the first four-alarm blaze in the city in nearly a year.

The building was a four-story wood-frame structure and at least nine families were known to live there. The Audettes lived on the top floor of the destroyed building.

Eyewitnesses reported hearing an explosion before the apartments burst into flames.

"It was like the place was hit by a rocket," said one woman resident, who asked to remain anonymous.

"There was a screeching noise just before the place went up in flames," said Ronald Chang, 25, whose studio apartment was in the building. "I thought a plane had crashed."

Fire Capt. Steve Lewis said no plane debris or wreckage was found and an air crash was not a possibility. Federal Aviation Administration officials confirmed this.

"This is more consistent with a gas leak followed by explosion," Lewis said. "And this building was served by gas."

Nonetheless, arson cannot be ruled out, said an investigator who did not want to be named. Because of the explosion report, he added, officials will be considering the more remote possibility that some sort of bomb was involved.

The apartment was almost directly overhead a MBTA Green Line tunnel, not far from Fenway Park, but officials confirmed that no trolleys were near there at the time.

Fire Capt. Lewis praised firefighters and EMTs for what he called their "heroic" work entering the burning building and helping people to safety. They rescued several pets, according to Lewis.

"These were horrific conditions our women and men encountered," Lewis said. "But like true firefighters everywhere, they risked their lives to save others'."

The American Red Cross has arranged temporary housing for the displaced residents.

ii.

Unrecorded on November 16.

At 7:30 a.m., Fluffy, a French poodle owned by Zachary Pearlman, of 860 Beacon Street, went out the PetSafe Pet Door his master had installed in the bottom panel of the back door. Coffee in hand, Zachary, 78, was at the front of the apartment, checking the contents of the three rooms he had transformed into Zack's Bric-a-Brac, a Back Bay boutique with a steady clientele. It seemed the terrible fire at 840 Beacon had not caused any damage, save for the odor of smoke, which he could clear with fans. Good thing the windows had been closed when the fire had roused him from his sleep.

Fluffy peed on a trashcan, then sauntered over to a parked car, behind which he took care of number two. It was not until both responsibilities were fulfilled that he caught a whiff of a powerfully new and different smell: something burning, or recently burnt, like the smell in the fireplace after one of those rare occasions Zack used it.

Following his nose, Fluffy emerged from the alley and started down Beacon Street. There was a commotion a few buildings away—a major one, even by the busy standards of Kenmore Square, besieged by fans after every Red Sox game. There were cars, trucks, lights flashing, radios squawking, a saw sawing, a hammer hammering, people milling. Fluffy broke into a trot. The smoky smell got stronger and stronger until, having reached ribbons of police tape, it was everywhere.

The dog stopped.

Fluffy understood his cuteness, which usually could be counted on for a friendly pat or a hello from a stranger, but nothing doing today. These people were all business. Unnoticed, the dog passed under the tape, crossed a small garden now covered in broken glass and charred wood, and proceeded into the burnt shell of a building.

The dog poked here and there, sniffing, curious at these won-drous sights. Few things looked familiar in this dark new world. There was a blackened hulk of a refrigerator, a similarly blackened stove, a twisted piece of metal that might have been a lamp. There was a blackened TV and what might have been a sound system. The fire had been unusually hot, melting plastic and metal, incin-erating plaster and paint, and reducing furniture fabric and frame to ash.

There, next to the remains of a bed, was a waterlogged heap of what seemed, at first, to be burnt clothing.

But it wasn't clothing, Fluffy discovered on closer examination.

It was a pile of stuffed animals, one of which, prettier than the rest, appeared untouched by the fire, water and smoke. Fluffy liked stuffed animals. His master had a whole case of them in his shop, and on Saturdays and Sundays, the busiest days, that display was a hit with parents who strolled in with young children in tow.

Fluffy clamped down on the cat-like stuffed animal and lifted it from the heap. It was a pleasant sensation, that softness between his jaws. Unhurried, the poodle retraced his steps through the rub-ble and reemerged at the front of the building, passing unnoticed again under the sawhorses. The dog headed home, triumphant with its find.

Fluffy passed through the pet door into the kitchen. Zack was not around. The dog played with his new toy a short spell, but when the novelty had worn thin, he deposited it in a familiar place, the back of the Teddy bear display case, and hopped onto the armchair for a snooze.

In days to come, Zack—increasingly forgetful as he neared the end of his eighth decade—would be unable to recall buying the stuffed animal from the stream of vendors, mostly people clean-ing out their attics and basements, who came to him to sell or swap their precious finds. He would smell the smoke on it and send it off to be dry-cleaned.

When it had been returned, he would place it on the top shelf of the Teddy display.

Some two weeks later, a Rhode Island woman visiting her Boston-based brother, a Jesuit priest, would buy it as a Christmas gift for her youngest child, a girl who had a terminal illness.

iii.

Noon TV broadcast,
With meteorologist Denise Isaac.

"…and now, recapping your exclusive NBC-10 forecast: This afternoon, sunny and warm, highs near 60, with a light south-southwest breeze. Let's get out and rake those leaves! Tonight, clear skies, lows in the upper 40s, with those clear skies allowing perfect—make that perfect!—viewing of the meteor showers that began last night and are expected to continue tonight. We haven't seen such a sky spectacular as this in years and it won't last, so get out there with your phones and send us your photos! We'll post the best ones right here on NBCBoston.com…"

Chapter One: Heaven and earth.
Saturday, May 29, 2021

B illy McAllister's sister is dead.
Billy knows that.

But time cannot steal the young boy's memories. Time—four years, one month and 19 days of time—and still Jess appears in his dreams.

Sometimes in these dreams, she is calling to him.

She is someplace dark and cold, someplace distant and unreachable, no place he's ever been or wants to go. He sees nothing but Jess's face, illuminated softly by an unseen light. It's a sad face, not the face he wants to remember—not the face in that photograph Mommy keeps on her bedroom bureau. Tears cover both cheeks. Her hair is tousled, her lips cracked and dry, her eyes wide and dark and empty, as if not really her eyes, but fake ones constructed of cheap glass.

She is clutching her favorite stuffed animal, Baby Bear, the Teddy bear that Santa brought.

Baby Bear looks sad, too.

"Help us, Billy!" Jess calls in these dreams. "Me and Baby Bear! Let us out of here! We don't want to be dead! We want to be with you and Mommy and Uncle Jack!"

Billy reaches for his sister then—but always she's too far, and the distance to her is increasing, and Jess is shrinking, is getting smaller and smaller, until finally she is gone.

But in other dreams, it is summer—the summer of 2015, when they took that photograph so dear to Mommy's heart. The summer five years before the coronavirus pandemic, which devastated America and the world.

He was six that summer of 2015, Jess barely five. Her health had once again gotten better, and with every day, there was less talk of that "Pitts-bird" hospital, where she had spent so much time as the doctors fixed her one time and then, when she fell ill again, a second time.

Mommy was better, too. Mommy was not so upset all the time, wasn't short-tempered and grouchy and crying and yelling and screaming at him when he hadn't done anything at all.

Uncle Jack, who usually took Billy's side, said that after all the bad stuff involving Jess's health, the family deserved a good stretch—that it was always darkest before dawn, and now the sun was climbing high into the sky.

They spent June and July at Grammy's. Her house, larger than any house Jess and Billy had ever been inside, was in Blue Hill Falls, Maine, that magical seaside place where the mountain really was blue, at least when viewed from a distance. It was major fun, those two months, ice cream and corn on the cob and lobster and fried clams and staying up until ten or even eleven o'clock, way past regular bedtime. The ocean, cold as it was until August, when you might be able to handle a few minutes' swim without shivering, was the best.

Almost every day, they played on the little beach there at Blue Hills Falls, where Grammy's house overlooked Mt. Desert Narrows.

It was go-easy play because they had to be very careful of Jess. They had to keep the saltwater from those big zig-zaggy scars across her tummy, evidence of where surgeons had transplanted one liver into her, and then a second when the first had failed. They had to keep sunblock all over her, and she had to wear a straw hat and her Elsa sunglasses.

Jess tired pretty easily, but she had spurts of energy, too, and during them, they climbed rocks and hunted for periwinkles and fiddler crabs and built sandcastles and went sailing with Mom and Uncle Jack on Grammy's big boat.

"How big is the ocean?" Jess always liked to ask.

"Bigger than the biggest lake in the world," Grammy would answer.

"Wow, that's huge!" Billy would say.

"Almost as big as heaven," said Uncle Jack, a Jesuit priest who liked to shed his Roman collar on his occasional visits to Maine.

"Heaven is where Grampa is," Grammy would say.

"I want to meet him some day!" Jess would say.

"No you don't," her mother said on one occasion.

A dark memory had welled up within her and she said no more.

Grammy wagged her finger at Mary and quickly changed the subject, to the fairy-tale story of how her parents had met.

"My mother was a young girl living in Nova Scotia when one summer day, she and a friend drove to Burntcoat Head Park to see the amazing tides at the Bay of Fundy," Grammy said. "Do you children know about those?"

"No!" Jess and Billy said.

"Highest tides in the world," Grammy said. "One of the seven or eight or nine or ten Wonders of the World, I've lost count. People come from all over to see."

"Wow," Jess said. "Can we go there one day, Mom?"

"That would be nice," Mary said.

"So there was my mother, Miss Alice O'Reilly," Grammy continued, "when my father, George McKay of Blue Hill Falls, Maine, happened to be visiting there with friends. They'd taken the old steamer up from Bar Harbor to Halifax for a week-long holiday. And there was Miss Alice, watching the tide roll in with a rumble and a roar. Their eyes met, and both later said it was love at first sight. The rest, as they say, is history. They married, Alice and George moved in here, and along came I, their only child."

"Cool," Jess said.

"Neat," said Billy.

The question of what happened after that did not arise.

Not that summer.

Rainy days, they stayed inside Grammy's mansion and made mischief with her three cats and Tuggs the bulldog, a good-natured old hound that was Grammy's favorite pet. Once, when it was cloudy and cool but the heavens hadn't opened up, Jess and Billy snuck off to the family cemetery and mausoleum, which stood in a grove of pines on a bluff overlooking the ocean. Two hundred years of McKays and their spouses and other relatives were buried there— a few in the marble crypt erected by Grammy's great-grandfather, Samuel McKay, who'd made his fortune in the clipper trade and then, in a move that shocked his Yankee friends and associates, converted to Catholicism after a Jesuit priest who was said to possess the power of healing had laid his hands on his abdomen and cured him of the colon cancer that had been consuming him.

The burial ground and mausoleum, where Jess herself would be laid to rest in less than a year, was strictly off-limits and the one time Mommy found them nosing around there, she went ape. That was the only time they were punished that summer, although they got off easy, only one day without TV and no dessert.

The attic was also strictly off-limits, but there was no chance of them of getting up there, much as curiosity compelled them: the door was padlocked and nailed shut.

"But why?" Jess asked one time

The response remained as vivid as yesterday to Billy.

Grammy, he remembered, said "attics are no good for anything but collecting dust," and then she fought tears. Mommy convulsed, as if pain had pierced her body, and after screaming "do NOT ever ask again," she went into the kitchen, where she poured a tall glass of hard liquor.

"Grammy's right," said Uncle Jack, who visited as often as his busy schedule would allow. "Attics do nothing but collect dust, and dust does no one any good. Now come into the library, my precious niece and nephew. I have a new book I'd like to read to you. *One Morning in Maine* is the title. It's a classic I'm sure you will enjoy—more than the average bear!"

That was one of Uncle Jack's favorite lines, an ode to his niece's love of the Teddy variety.

In early August, as the Maine water was approaching swimming temperature, Uncle Jack drove up again from Boston. He stayed the weekend and on Monday morning, he took everyone back to Rhode Island so Mommy could apartment-hunt. The first place they visited was affordable, and near a school where Jess could start kindergarten and Billy, first grade.

So they took it. That night, they celebrated by visiting Ocean State Park, where they rode the merry-go-round and Ferris wheel, ate all the cotton candy they wanted, and had their picture taken in a booth.

By Labor Day 2015, Jess's health was deteriorating again.

In April 2016, she would die.

Sometimes, Billy still can't believe what happened Jess passed. He thinks it must have been a dream, but it wasn't.

He remembers that terrible night—the night before his sister's wake, which was the day before her funeral and burial. He is upstairs in the Blue Hill mansion, trying for sleep in a corner-post bed that had been his Grammy's great-grandfather's.

That night, Blue Hill's magic was gone. That night, Grammy's house was drafty and dark and forbidding, sounds carrying as if there were no floors, walls or doors.

That night, Grammy turned from loving grandmother to someone Billy did not recognize.

"Regardless of his age, he should say goodbye to his sister," she is saying to Uncle Jack.

They are in the library, directly underneath Billy.

"And he *shall* say goodbye," Grammy continued. "I see no need for further discussion, John."

"It will be too much for him, Mother," Uncle Jack protests.

Billy hugs the Transformer toy that Uncle Jack bought him, even though it wasn't his birthday or Christmas or anything, and he wishes desperately that Mommy could be here. As short-tempered as she could get, Mommy would set things right, Mommy would stop them from arguing. Mommy wouldn't make him go to his sister's wakes—there would be two of them—or her funeral.

But Mommy's not here.

Mommy's probably too bad off to even attend the funeral herself.

Mommy's at a hospital—and not the kind of hospital where they take X-rays and put broken legs in casts and give you your choice of lollipops for being such a brave little girl or boy. Not even the Pittsbird kind of hospital, with all its machines and tubes and stuff that helped his sister stay alive longer than some doctors said was possible.

Mommy's in the kind of hospital where people go when they've had what Uncle Jack calls a mental-health crisis.

"What's right for a boy isn't necessarily what's easiest or most convenient for him," Grammy is saying. "You should know that."

"He's six, for God's sake. *Six*, Mother! When I was six, the last thing you would have made me do was attend a funeral or a wake."

"No one important to us died when you were six, John. Some exceptionally fine psychologists write about how important it is for children, even young children, to be part of bereavement."

"And some other very fine psychologists have written of how emotionally scarring it can be. Think of Mary, Mother. If she finds out, she will never forgive you."

"Mary is in no position for judgments such as these," Grammy says. "And neither are you. May I remind you that I am your and your sister's mother. As such, it is I who am responsible for the family's well-being."

Billy begins to cry. For three days and three nights, he's been crying. Just when he thought there were no tears left, he's started again.

"But in this, you are right, John," Grammy says. "This is a terrible ordeal—for you, for me, for young William. Without question, bereavement is among the most unpleasant of life's experiences. May *be* the most unpleasant. But it is through these rituals that we begin to accept our tragedies and move on with life, as we inevitably must. You, John, ordained one of God's servants—a priest who has conducted his share of funerals and burials—surely understand what I say."

"And as a priest who took vows to speak truth," Uncle Jack says, "I must tell you you're making a mistake."

"And I think not. Will Billy be uncomfortable at his sister's final rites? Yes, he will—as will everyone who knew that precious girl.

"But deny him the experience, no matter how traumatic, and we will live to regret it. More importantly, *he* will live to regret it. It may take five years, or ten, or twenty, but there will come a day when he feels he's been horribly cheated. The psychologists are very clear on this point. Do *you* wish to explain to him come that day? I think not. Now I believe you should get some sleep, John. Tomorrow, as you know, will be a very long day. Goodnight. I am going to bed."

The memory continues.

On painfully to the next afternoon, the first of two wakes that will be held for Jessica McAllister, whose body has arrived in Bangor in the belly of a 757 jet that flew from "Pittsbird," where her final discharge from UPMC Children's Hospital of Pittsburgh was to the custody of a funeral home. Her body has been perfumed, her hair washed and set, and makeup applied in an attempt to bring color to her bloodless cheeks. She has been attired in her pink party dress, a Christmas gift from Grammy that she wore only once, on her final trip back to Pittsburgh, where her medical team gave it all they had until they had no more to give.

At 1:45, fifteen minutes before calling hours begin, they pull up in Uncle Jack's Honda Accord. The funeral home is surrounded by limos, long and sleek and black. There is a red carpet leading into the home. An awning over the door. A crowd of somber-looking men—wearing black, to match their limousines.

Until this week, Billy had never been to a funeral home before, never met a mortician, never seen a casket or a corpse, except in the horror movies he and his best friend watch when there are no grown-ups around to monitor their viewing.

"Hello, William," Mr. Hawthorne, the head mortician, says.

Billy hates being called that name, but he dares not correct the mortician, just as he would never dare correct Grammy.

Billy says nothing.

He takes off his glasses to dry his tears.

"Remember what I told you, William," Mr. Hawthorne says solemnly. "Jessica is with God now. Her suffering is over, and she is very happy."

It is the same message delivered with the same phony smile as yesterday, when Uncle Jack and Grammy came here to make the "arrangements."

As Billy and his family walk in, a man with a camera video-tapes them for a post on legacy.com, where his sister's obituary will be posted together with a link to the funeral-home website. In the background, a Rhode Island reporter Billy's seen on the evening news is live on Facebook covering the proceedings.

Billy holds Grammy's hand and they walk up the stairs into the foyer, where more morticians are gathered. It is not their presence that leaps out at Billy. Nor is it the organ music, so mournful and dark that it is palpable.

It's the smell.

A sickly-sweet smell, like one of those scented cards that come inside Mommy's magazines. The smell of flowers, but not flowers he's ever seen in any garden or florist shop.

In the big room to the left is Jess's coffin. It is covered and surrounded by lilies, of the cloying sort morticians prefer.

With so many flowers, Billy at first doesn't see his sister.

Grammy leads him forward and there she is, close enough to touch.

Jess.

A sort-of Jess.

Lying on her back, her eyes and mouth shut, her arms folded over her chest and her hands grasping rosary beads and Baby Bear, the Teddy bear that Santa brought.

Don't let them do this, he hears a voice plead. *The mission is not complete.*

The voice is high-pitched, squeaky.

It is not Jess's voice, not Grammy's, not Mr. Hawthorne's.

Except in movies, Teddy bears don't speak, Billy thinks.

But if they did, this would be the voice of Baby Bear.

Chapter Two: Adorable animals.
Wednesday, June 2

Other memories were more pleasant for Billy. Kinder.

Occasionally, images of his sister materialized out of nowhere. One minute, run-of-the-mill stuff would be going through his head, the next—shazam! He'd close his eyes and see Jess smiling at him, whispering, waving, as clearly as if she were standing there in front of him.

More often, the associations were situation specific. Billy could never hear mention of Blue Hill without remembering Jess. Nor when thinking about Disney World, which she, he and Mom had visited on a Make-A-Wish visit. Nor another of her wishes that had been granted: a basketball signed by Celtics player Isaiah Thomas, which now graced his bureau. He could never see a doctor, pass a hospital, or visit East Matunuck Beach, the last beach she ever saw, without remembering.

Jess adored animals—Grammy's cats, Tuggs the bulldog, the gerbils Uncle Jack bought just two weeks before that summer came crashing to an end, the polar bears at Roger Williams Park Zoo in Providence. They wouldn't allow live animals in her Pittsbird hospital room, not even tropical fish, but she could have *stuffed* ones—and she did, several dozen of them, gifts from people she'd never met but who'd read about her or seen her on TV or donated to her GoFundMe page.

"Do they have animals in heaven, Uncle Jack?" Billy asked a week after his sister's funeral.

"Well, let's see," said Uncle Jack. "Saint Francis is in heaven—and he was a lover of animals. So I imagine they do. And Jess is with them now—and with God."

Thus, it was not surprising—was perhaps to be expected—that on Wednesday, June 2, two days before his eleventh birthday, when Billy asked his mother for a pet, that he would think of Jess. Happy Jess, the one who would live forever in that magical Blue Hill summer.

"There's something I want to ask you, Mom," Billy said as he and Mary stood outside Cellar Stories, a used bookstore in downtown Providence.

"What is it?" Mary said.

"Can I have a pet for my birthday?"

"We haven't had much luck with pets," Mary said.

"But we could try again," Billy said.

"We'll see," said Mary. "Right now, we're book-shopping."

The sign on Cellar Stories said that masks were no longer required for people who were fully vaccinated against COVID-19. Mary was. Billy, too young to be eligible yet for the shots, had to wear his. He put it on and they walked in.

Save for schoolbooks, most of the books Billy and his mother read came from the library—but occasionally, usually after her monthly SSI payment had been deposited in her bank account, they came to Cellar Stories, where the prices were good. The pandemic had ruined many small businesses, but this bookstore had managed to hang on. With the pandemic subsiding in Rhode Island, which had one of the highest fully vaccinated rates in the U.S., sales were picking up.

"That looks interesting," Mary said, picking up a book from the science-fiction section.

The cover featured a bear-like creature, who, the back jacket copy said, was leader of a good group of people.

"It looks like Jess's Baby Bear," Billy said.

"It does, doesn't it," his mother said.

She handed the clerk ten dollars and said to Billy: "Happy birthday."

"Thanks, Mom," Billy said.

The two left the store and got back into their car, an aging Toyota Corolla, a gift from Grammy.

"Can we please go to Petco?" Billy said.

"I've already told, you, Billy, no goldfish."

"I don't want a goldfish," the boy said.

"No parakeets, Billy," the mother said.

"I know. I want a hamster."

"Nothing doing."

"Can't we just go *look* at them?"

"All right," Mary said.

They drove to Petco, on Providence's East Side, where Billy grew excited at the guinea pigs that were on sale.

"They look like rats," Mary said. "Ugh."

"Can't I *please*? For my birthday?"

"Have we forgotten what happened to our last one?"

"It died," Billy said.

"And why did it die?"

"Because I forgot to feed it."

"For a week."

"I was nine then. I'm going to be eleven."

Billy sounded confident, as if two years had imparted the maturity to own a racehorse, never mind a lousy old guinea pig.

"We'll see," Mary said. "That's the best I can say."

They moved along until they came to the hamster section

"What about them?" Billy said. "If I promise to feed them?"

"*Them*? You mean more than one?"

"Yes, you need at least two, so they won't be lonely."

"I suppose that's true."

Mary looked around and beckoned the clerk who had been standing nearby.

"Ma'am?" she said. "We've got some questions about the hamsters."

"Fire away," the clerk said. "But first let me say that the young boy is right: You need at least two. One alone can die of loneliness. Believe me, I've seen it happen."

"See, Mom?" Billy said. "Told you so!"

The clerk ran through the requirements for two hamsters to have a happy home: a tank with top, a water bottle, bedding, and a metal wheel for exercise and fun. Also, a copy of "The Complete Guide to Raising Hamsters." All of which, including today's special discount, would cost $195, money-back guaranteed.

"Ouch," Mary said.

She was thinking of the bills that had been piling up—bills for rent, utilities and her cell phone and land line.

"Believe me, you go anywhere else and you'll be paying twice that," the clerk said.

"So can we, Mommy?" Billy said.

"I think any decisions on birthday gifts have to be surprises," Mary said. "I think there's a state law to that effect. Sorry, Billy. You'll have to wait and see."

On their way out of Petco, Mary winked at the clerk.

Chapter Three: Behavioral health.
Thursday, June 3

The Rev. John Lambert, S.J., was serving lunch onto the trays of the homeless people who were moving through the serving line at Boston's Dean Street Residence when Manny, the site manager, called from across the room.

"Father Jack! Phone!" he said.

There was a time when you could count on one hand the women and children who needed Dean Street. But beginning in the 1980s, a decade when greed and selfishness had been consecrated the national religion, with trickle-down-economics Ronald Reagan anointed its High Priest, that had changed. The hate-filled politics of the Trump era had exacerbated the situation. Jack Lambert sometimes thought you had to look back to Jimmy Carter, Lyndon Baines Johnson, and John F. Kennedy to find an era when forgiveness, compassion and empathy—what Christ himself taught—were national values.

Now, Dean Street ran at full capacity year-round. Now, about half of its clients were mothers and their kids, with a disproportionate percentage from communities of color and immigrant neighborhoods.

The pandemic, of course, had worsened everything.

"Who is it?" Father Jack shouted back.

"Amanda."

"Amanda Leroux? My sister's social worker?"

"Yes. She said it's important."

"Tell her I'll be right there," Father Jack said.

He turned to the person next to him, an elderly woman who'd been volunteering for longer than Jack had been a priest. She'd drawn canned-peas duty today.

"Can you take over for a minute?" the priest said.

"Of course, Father Jack."

"I'll be back in a jiff."

Father Jack moved through the tables, greeting many of the diners by name. For more than a decade, he had run Dean Street. Some of his regulars had been with him that long—and longer. But sadly, most of the people he'd served were gone, many since early 2020 lost to COVID-19, which had been particularly cruel to people who were homeless, and to people of color and those who lacked economic means. If there was any long-term hope, Father Jack believed, it had come with science and the new administration of Joe Biden.

Father Jack closed the door to his office.

"How are you, Amanda?" Father Jack he said into the phone. "It's been a while. You're calling about Mary, I presume."

"I am."

"Is anything wrong?"

"I don't know," Amanda said. "That's what I want to talk to you about. You know your sister far better than I do."

"That's debatable."

Father Jack laughed. For five years—ever since his niece had died—Amanda had been Mary's social worker. Jack felt deeply indebted to her. He believed it was Amanda who had gotten his sister back on her feet, twice: after Jessica's death, and again two years ago, when Grammy—Mary and Jack's mother—died in her Blue Hill house.

After both deaths, Mary had been admitted to Portland Behavioral Health Center, a psychiatric hospital in Maine with a reputation that rivalled any in southern New England but was far enough from Rhode Island that word of her stays was unlikely to reach Providence, where stigma still held sway in certain circles. During both admissions, Billy had lived with Uncle Jack at his rectory.

Father Jack recalled her first admission to Portland Behavioral Health, the day after Jess died, when she suffered what the professionals called a "severe decompensation." He had driven to the center that day to provide the family history—and to see if there was any way his sister could attend her daughter's funeral, given her emotional state.

Meeting with the intake team, the priest had provided details of events that he knew had contributed to Mary's precarious mental health. Details of Mary as a young girl finding their father, George Linwood Lambert, hanging from a rope he'd tied onto a rafter in the attic of their home in Blue Hill, and of the counseling that had followed. It seemed to have helped her.

Because eventually, after the attic door had been padlocked and nailed shut and her nightmares had eased, Mary was able to return to school. Father Jack told the intake team how Mary had been salutatorian of her high school class, with early admission to Boston University. Graduating with honors, she had enrolled in BU's School of Social Work, where she earned her master's degree. And then she had begun a career as a Licensed Clinical Social Worker with Our Bright Future, a Boston-based behavioral health center that specialized in children and families. She had excelled there, winning employee-of-the-month awards and earning the affection of staff and clients.

Until now, his sister's childhood trauma seemed behind her, Father Jack said, although, he added, he had often wondered if finding their father dead by suicide had permanently altered her young brain. In his own ministry, he had met people with similar trauma histories who had been "fine" for years, and then experienced symptoms of Post-traumatic stress disorder. PTSD, he knew, could be a silent presence until some terrible event triggered it.

He himself had experienced PTSD, though moderately. He was much older when their father died, and when his symptoms surfaced—following the murder of a fellow priest and close friend—he had been quick to get professional intervention.

It had worked for him, at least so far.

On Mary's first admission, Father Jack gave the Portland Behavioral Health team details of his sister's life.

Of how she met Stephen McAllister, a young man from Boston, during her early days at Our Bright Future.

About the whirlwind romance that had followed and their wedding day, three months after she'd become pregnant with Jess, at a justice of the peace.

About the birth of Jess, a joyous event that brought her mother down from Maine bearing a carload of gifts.

About the hundreds of likes, loves and congratulatory posts made on Mary's Facebook page.

About the early plans for a christening, which Father Jack would conduct.

About how, four weeks after Jessica Mary McAllister entered the world, jaundice began to yellow baby Jess's skin. Biliary atresia, a rare liver disease of newborns in which the flow of bile from the liver is blocked, was diagnosed.

Medication initially controlled the disease, but by six months of age, Jess was failing.

By then, Mary was pregnant with her second child.

Jess was admitted to Boston Children's Hospital, where surgeons had hoped to perform the Kasai procedure, a curative operation with a high level of success. But X-rays and other tests had disclosed something more serious and rarer than biliary atresia. They found an associated hepatic vascular disorder: the vessels supplying blood to Jess's liver were narrow—and narrowing—by an even rarer form of artery stenosis.

"She will need a liver transplant to survive," the chief of surgery said. "I'm so sorry."

The chief was sorrier still to say that of the many liver transplants that had been performed at Boston Children's, only two had been cases involving the vascular disorder.

Both babies had died, the chief said, "but our team learned important lessons and we are willing to try again on little Jess."

Mary and Stephen heard this in shock.

And when the shock abated, they went online.

One hospital in America, they learned, had successfully cured more babies like Jess: UPMC Children's Hospital of Pittsburgh. With the help of Uncle Jack, who had friends at Duquesne University, a Catholic research-oriented school in the Steel City, UPMC Children's Hospital had agreed to see Jess. Eight months to the day after she was born, Jess flew with her parents to Pittsburgh, where she was deemed a proper candidate for a transplant.

"Now comes the worst part: the wait," a doctor had said as the family was leaving the hospital, bound for the airport and the trip home.

"But we are confident a donor will be found in time," the doctor said. "Around here, we hit home runs."

Six days after Jess's first birthday, her brother was born.

Six months after that, Stephen McAllister left for the West Coast.

"I need time," he said.

Mary was but mildly surprised. Mr. Right, as it had developed, was Mr. Wrong, a man with a nose for cocaine and an obsession with massage parlors.

"Don't ever come back," Mary said.

"But I have children," McCallister said.

"What you have is my fervent hope to never see you again," Mary said. "Now get the fuck out. My baby is crying."

That first time, Mary was released from Portland Behavioral Health after a long stay, during which staff had brought her to her daughter's funeral. In hindsight, given what happened during the service, that had been a terrible mistake.

Because Mary during her weeks at the center had only stabilized, not healed.

Heavily medicated, she went through the motions of life as an unemployed mother of a young boy. Returning soon to the staff of Our Bright Future was no option, as she and the director had agreed when the director offered her an open-ended leave of absence without pay. She needed time and no pressure, the director said; her own well-being and that of her son were what mattered.

As the weeks passed, Mary kept all medical and therapy appointments and accepted the help of a visiting nurse.

Income, however, was soon an issue.

Jack was in no position to pay all her bills, and while their mother had covered the co-pays from Portland Behavioral Health, that well was not bottomless: Grammy lived on a small inheritance, not a fortune, and she could barely manage upkeep of her mansion. If there was a bright spot, it was the fact that federal Supplemental Security Income had paid most of Jess's transplant costs when it was determined, before the first operation, that she fit the description of a disabled child. A GoFundMe campaign had paid for travel and other expenses.

Guided by the director of Our Bright Future, her brother, and Amanda Leroux, Mary enrolled in SSI under Section 12:15, "Trauma and stressor-related disorders."

The benefits were enough for her and Billy to maintain a

respectable existence as she worked toward the day when her recovery would advance sufficiently for her to return to work.

Jack continued his phone conversation with Amanda Leroux.

"It's been brought to my attention that Mary's missed two therapy sessions," Amanda said.

"You've talked to her about it?" Jack said.

"Yesterday."

"What did she say?"

"That she hasn't been feeling well. She said the last couple of weeks she's been really tired. She thinks it's probably some kind of low-grade bug."

"That's legitimate, isn't it?"

"I guess. But when someone's never missed a single session, it sticks out. And there's something else. When I saw her last, she had alcohol on the breath."

"Was she drunk?"

Jack's insides tightened a bit. He knew Mary's history of heavy drinking.

"No, she wasn't drunk."

"Thank God."

"But it was 11 o'clock in the morning, Father Jack. Eleven o'clock on a Monday morning. She denied she'd been drinking, but there was no question she had. I could smell it. Plus, there were empty beer bottles in the trash."

"I don't know what to tell you," Jack said. "I saw her two weekends ago. Everything seemed fine. She was hoping to return to work soon. Said she's sick of being on welfare, as she called it. Isn't that what she told you?"

"Yes. Which is why I called you—the fact that all year, she's been so determined. Has she mentioned anything bothering her lately? Something she'd want to keep away from me? Trouble with the rent or anything?"

Jack thought a moment and said: "Not that I can recall. In fact, on my last visit, I was thinking I haven't seen her this upbeat since right before our mother died. Certainly not since my niece passed away."

"Nothing with Billy?" Amanda said.

"No. And I spoke to him by phone on Sunday. He's looking forward to his birthday and summer vacation."

"Well, something is going on, Father Jack," Amanda said. "I'm sure of it."

"Do you want me to pay her a visit?" the priest said. "It's only an hour's drive to Providence."

"No," the social worker said, "I don't think that will be necessary, at least not yet. I'll just keep a closer eye on her for the next couple weeks."

"And I'll do the same Saturday. It's Billy's birthday. Mary's throwing him a party."

"Which I won't be able to attend, unfortunately," Amanda said. "I'm taking a three-day weekend. Going camping."

"Have fun," Jack said.

"But I'll check in on her first thing Tuesday morning. Can I call you that afternoon?"

"Please do. You know where to find me."

Jack hung up the phone and went to his computer, where he composed a letter to his sister. He'd lost track of how many letters—hand-written and word-processed, for delivery by email or Facebook message—he'd written to Mary over the many years.

Dear Mar, he wrote.

> *You always were the sensitive child. The one who cried at movies, the one who couldn't bear to be alone, the one who couldn't go to sleep unless the light was on, the one Mother always said would need watching over, no matter how old you got. And Mother was right. You still need that light and, as always, I am happy to be there with it.*
>
> *Mother always said it was losing Dad that made you that way. You were nine, and it was easier for me, being almost 10 years older. But nine—what a terrible age. You were daddy's little girl, the one he brought into the observatory after the sun had set to peer into his telescope and talk about the life he was convinced was out there in the universe. "Friendly" is the word he always used to describe what he imagined extraterrestrials' nature and intent, should they ever reach earth. Nothing like the*

evil aliens in so many science-fiction movies and books, going back to at least The War of The Worlds, which Dad always talked about. How many times have we said your love of science fiction began with those nights looking through Dad's telescope?

I won't get into Stephen again except to say a most un-Christian-like thing, which is that the man is an ass-hole. Being charitable, I hope he gets the help he needs for his addictions—but if he does, pray God he stays in California.

It hasn't been easy for you Mar, has it? After five years of heartache with Jess, it all caved in. And just when it seemed Jess's death was as far behind you as maybe it's ever going to get, just when you and Billy had carved out a space for yourselves, when the depression and the drinking that accompanied Jess's last days were only bad memories, Ma dies. What a cruel blow. What a test of faith.

But against the odds, you passed that test. It's been a tremendous struggle, but you've fought heroically. The last six months—we've seen you turn the corner. Why else has Amanda been so enthusiastic about Mary, her favorite client? Why have I been so optimistic?

Why am I beginning to believe my prayers for my dear sister are finally being answered?

The strength you've found, Mar. That's why.

Love,

Your brother.

Jack said a silent prayer for his sister, and returned to the Dean Street Residence cafeteria, where staff and volunteers were cleaning up after lunch.

Chapter Four: Death Alley.
Thursday, June 3

"Whatcha ask for your birthday?" Andre Washington said to his elementary-school classmate and best friend, Billy McAllister, as they walked home on an afternoon heavy with the threat of thunder.

"Hamsters," Billy said.

"Ooo-eee! My mom won't let me have hamsters!"

"Yeah, and I don't think mine will either," Billy said. "But it couldn't hurt to ask."

"What else?"

"A skateboard."

"I told you could borrow mine," Andres said. "Anytime you want."

"I know. But I want one of my own."

They rounded Elmwood Avenue and headed down Forge Road, where Billy and Andres lived in identical old Victorians six doors apart. This was Providence's Armory district. Culturally, racially, and economically it was a diverse neighborhood, with whites, Blacks, Latinos, Southeast Asians and undocumented immigrants. With last year's killing of George Floyd by Minneapolis police officer Derek Chauvin, it had become a center of the Black Lives Matter movement. This year, Billy, Andres, and their mothers had attended a demonstration hailing the conviction of Chauvin.

"What else you want?" Andres said.

"A Nintendo Switch and a mountain bike and an iPhone."

"Whew! That's bad, man. Think you'll get all *that*?"

"Nah. But I figure the more stuff you ask for, the better the chance you get at least *some* of it. It works at Christmas for me. Doesn't it for you?"

"Yeah, baby!"

Billy and Andres exchanged high-fives.

They were more than best buddies, this bespectacled white kid and his Black friend. They were blood brothers—and not some just-messing-around phony blood brothers, but the real thing. They'd pledged themselves to each other last summer by holding a burning match under a pin, pricking the middle fingers of their right hands and mingling droplets of their blood, a ritual Andres's older brother, whose idea it was, swore went back to the time of Roman gladiators.

The bond between the boys went beyond ritual. Andres walked with a limp, the lingering effect of a badly fractured leg he'd suffered when he was run over by a hit-and-run driver, and Billy had felt empathy for him virtually from first meeting. Andres's empathy for Billy began a few months later, when Billy shared the story of the death of his sister—and it deepened when Billy revealed the impact of her death and then the death of his grandmother on his mother. Until Andres, Billy kept those secrets from peers and Andres was still the only kid who knew.

The boys rounded a corner and there was Paul Iannotti, a fourteen-year-old boy nicknamed Angel. He was a school dropout, a bully known as a "street kid" who lived, rumor had it, in an empty old mill after his family had thrown him out. Iannotti supposedly was using crack cocaine.

At the sight of Billy, Angel cowered.

"Tell her to leave me alone," he whimpered. "Tell her I didn't mean no harm."

And then he ran off.

"Wow, that's weird," Billy said.

"No kidding," Andres said. "He looked scared shitless. Who was 'her'?"

"I have no clue," Billy said.

He soon would.

Angel had been a different kid two days ago, the day of The Fight. That day, Billy and Andres had been walking near this very spot when they'd heard his voice:

"Hey gimp!"

Billy and Andres stopped.

"Let's see how fast you can run" the voice said.

Angel's voice was coming from the back of an abandoned house Billy and Andres had just passed. They couldn't see him.

"Don't call my friend that word," Billy said.

"You gonna stop me?" Angel said.

"I sure am," said Billy.

He sounded defiant, but actually he was petrified. He knew the only way to stop Angel was with a fight, and he'd been in a fight exactly once in his life. It had left him with a bloody nose and a vow to avoid fights at all costs.

But this—this was Principle. Every adult he'd ever admired, from Uncle Jack and Mom on down, had drummed into him the importance of standing up for Principle. Principle meant not calling a person with a physical disability names.

But this was Angel, who shot off his mouth and did drugs— but had the rap of being a Major Wimp when backed into a corner.

"Why don't you come back here?" Angel said.

"Why don't you come here?" Billy said.

Still, he and Andres could not see Angel. Black clouds were draping the city in shadow and a light drizzle was falling. The thunder and lightning weren't far off now.

"If you're so brave, you'll come back here, gimp-lover!" Angel shouted.

Billy started down the drive, cluttered with the rusting skeletons of cars. There was a boarded-up garage back there—a garage and a mountain of trash left by midnight dumpers.

"Don't," Andres implored. "What if he's got someone with him? What if he's got a gun or a knife?"

"I don't care."

"Billy—"

But Billy was on his way. Principle and honor at stake.

For half an instant, Andres considered leaving, but that wasn't what blood brothers did. Pansies or Major Wimps, maybe, but not blood brothers. As they'd mingled their blood last summer, hadn't they gritted their teeth and sworn "ultimate allegiance" to each other, "for better or for worse, in sickness and in health," just like wedding vows?

Andres followed his friend.

They spotted Angel behind one of the junkers, an old VW bus that had been cannibalized. He was a tall kid—but not a strong

one. He was scrawny and pale, like no one had ever fed him right.
And maybe no one had.

They were facing each other now, Billy and Angel, almost—but
not quite—close enough to reach. Or punch.

Or shoot, Billy thought.

Billy swallowed.

"Well, gimp-lover?" Angel taunted.

"You apologize."

Billy cast about for a weapon—a piece of wood, a two-by-four,
a bottle, a brick, anything. But he saw only fast-food wrappers and
soiled Pampers and rotted fruit rinds and battered hubcaps and a
coil of frayed clothesline.

"Come on, Billy," Andres said. "Let's go."

"He's gonna apologize," Billy said.

It was as if Billy had made some mighty boast—said he could
drive a car or get a date with a junior-high girl, say, and now, the
moment of truth, he felt hot and sick. What if Angel *did* have a
gun or a knife? What if three of his scum-ball friends were waiting in ambush behind the garage? What if he were high and he
was seeing snakes or something, like crackheads were supposed
to, and he was mistaking them for vipers that had to be slayed?
Crack could weird you out in unpredictable and violent ways, or
so Billy had heard.

"Say you're sorry," Billy managed.

"I ain't sorry for shit," Angel said.

Billy took a tentative step. His face was in Angel's now and
he smelled smell booze and something smoky and sweet and it
wasn't cigarettes.

"Say you're sorry."

Angel sucker-punched him in the face, shattering his glasses.
The frame slid down the end of Billy's nose and dropped to the
ground.

Angel ran.

"You OK?" Andres said.

"I'm… OK," Billy said.

"You sure?"

"Yeah."

"Let's get out of here," Andres said.

"You lead the way. I'm having trouble seeing."

"You coming?" Billy said two days later when they spotted Angel again.

"Would you just forget him, Billy?"

"He's gotta learn his lesson."

"He did learn his lesson. Didn't you hear him? He's scared shitless of you."

"Not me; he said *her*. Whoever *she* is."

"He must've meant you."

"You coming or you gonna stay?" Billy said.

"I think—"

"You do what you want. I'm going after him."

Andres hesitated. Then he set off after his friend.

Angel had disappeared down an alley.

Death Alley it was called—no one knew why, that was just its name—a narrow thoroughfare that ran between the backyards of Forge and Firepond, parallel streets. In another era, horse-drawn lorries had traversed Death Alley to deliver coal and ice to customers. Now, the alley was overgrown. Dark—even in fair weather—and strewn with tread-less tires and orphaned shopping carts. The rear windows of Billy's and Andres's apartments overlooked Death Alley. Both their mothers had declared it off-limits, a prohibition neither son obeyed.

"He went that way," Billy said, pointing right.

They started running in that direction.

"Gimp-lover! Fuckin' gimp-lover!"

The voice was distant but distinct.

And then, there he was, some 200 yards away. Billy could see him—fuzzy but sufficiently in focus to make a positive ID, even with the old pair of glasses Billy wore. His mother had not gotten around to buying new ones after the fight.

Angel hurdled a fence behind a triple-decker whose first-floor windows were covered with plywood.

"He must have gone inside," Billy said when they'd reached the fence.

"You going in?"

Andres figured he was; in the last few minutes, he'd concluded that his friend had lost his marbles.

"With or without you, I'm going in," Billy said. "He's gotta say he's sorry, Andres. No one calls my friend the N-word."

Billy cleared the fence.

Resigned, his friend followed.

The inside of the triple-decker was gloomy—but no gloomier than the afternoon, which had turned ugly since school dismissal, twenty minutes before. Except for some leaky spots on the third floor, at least the house was dry, but outside, the rain was steady, the wind gusting. Last summer, when a tornado had ripped through Providence, tearing roofs off buildings, the weather had this identical feel. Billy might have been alarmed if he hadn't been so obsessed.

"That leaves the basement," he said when they'd scouted the second and third floors and found nothing but pigeon shit, ratty furniture, and empty wine bottles.

"I tell you, he ain't here," Andres said. "He got away."

"We have to check the cellar."

"But it's locked," Andres said as they stood by the door. "From this side. He *couldn't* be down there."

"I wanna check anyways," Billy said, and now Andres was really worried.

It wasn't Angel anymore—Angel, it was abundantly clear, had slipped away. It was Billy, and the rain outside, and the cellar, that creepy cellar in this boarded-up building that winos and junkies used... might reuse, at any minute.

Once again, Andres thought of bolting.

Once again, his blood-brother oath flashed through his mind.

"This is it," he said. "Then I gotta go, Billy. I told my Mom I'd be home right from school."

Billy slid the bolt to the door and opened it.

The view down was darker than anywhere else in the house, and having old glasses didn't help, but it wasn't hopelessly murky: feeble daylight penetrated through the cellar windows, and as Billy's eyes adjustted, he could make out boxes, a broken baby carriage, a wheel-less bicycle frame, a variety of shadowy shapes.

He started down.

The stairs creaked as he descended, but they did not give way.

His foot found concrete and he stopped.

"It's OK," he called up to his friend.

Andres padded down after him, his hand groping for a rail that wasn't there.

"I don't like it here," Andres said. "It smells bad."

"I told you, it's OK."

"Angel ain't here," Andres said. "See? Nothing but spiderwebs."

"We just have to check in there," Billy said. "Then we can go."

He was pointing at a wooden door—the door to the old burner room, he supposed.

"Billy..."

"Come on."

Billy crossed the damp cellar floor. Andres was right. It stunk down here. Like a really bad case of mildew... or something worse. Something rotting. Something...

dead.

He kicked the door open.

Nothing but an old oil burner and a pile of coal, remnant of an earlier chapter in the Fossil Fuel era. No Angel. Nobody.

Outside, a dog howled and a peal of thunder rattled the house. Dust showered down on the boys, blackening their hair and faces. In the distance, they heard the wail of a siren. There was another sound, too, one neither immediately placed.

A whooshing, like water running slowly down a drain.

"What is it?" Andres said.

"What?"

"That sound."

"I don't know," Billy said.

The boys listened intently.

Most definitely, it wasn't rain.

It was a gurgling.

"I think it's coming from here," Billy said. "Here, by my foot. See the sewer pipe?"

"Yeah," Andres said.

"See where it's supposed to go into the wall?"

Billy tapped the pipe with his foot.

"It's broken. There's a space there where there should be pipe. An opening."

"So?"

"So that must be making the sound. Water must be going through the sewer—on the other side of the foundation. It's probably the same sewer that's hooked up to our house."

That sewer hookup, in fact, was next to his mother's bedroom.

The McAllisters lived in a basement apartment, and except for the bars on the windows—"to keep us safe," his mother said—it was an OK place, with new floors and walls and appliances and no smell, even on rainy days. Six doors down, Andres's apartment was also in the basement. It also had bars on the windows, but it wasn't any big deal for him, either. "That's life in the big city!" Andres's mother once joked

"Gross, a sewer," Andres said. "That's why it stinks in here."

"I wonder if you can see it—the big sewer, I mean. Main lines are supposed to be wicked big. Some you can even get inside. Like on *Beauty and the Beast*."

Billy knelt to get a better look.

"Whaddya doing?" Andres said.

"I wanna see if I can see anything."

"Like what, shit?"

Andres chuckled—a flat chuckle that lingered in the air.

Billy did not reply. It was impossibly dark inside that hole… or was it?

Wasn't that a pinpoint of pink light that he saw?

Wasn't that another, right next to it?

Two pinpoints?

Two *eyes*?

They seemed locked on Billy.

They seemed to blink at him.

And then they were no more.

Outside, the dog howled again.

A new smell filled the area—an almost electric smell, the smell of an old transformer or something. Or was it more like the sulfurous smell that hangs in the air after lighting off a pack of firecrackers. Billy and Andres couldn't place it. They only knew it had to be bad news. What if a gas line ran through here and there was a spark?

As they were about to leave, the boys heard a single word.

Much closer, a single word was uttered.

The pronunciation was perfect, if the meaning was not:

"Ordo."

Billy stared at his friend.

Andres hadn't moved.

Andres hadn't spoken.

Again, the word was uttered.

"Ordo."

Bravado had been carrying Billy, but now his courage was gone. Andres's, too.

Now Principle seemed a silly concern.

Now their circumstances seemed dire.

They were in an abandoned building, and there was thunder and lightning outside, and a smell here that could be something burning, and there were probably rats, there had to be rats, and no one knew they were here... no one. Someone could come and brick them up, like in that Edgar Allen Poe story, and no one would find them... ever.

"*Ordo.*"

This time, the voice was high-pitched.

The boys froze.

"You heard that, right? Billy whispered.

"Yes," Andres said. "What the heck?"

"Come on!" Billy said, grabbing his friend's hand. "We gotta get home!"

Without another word, they scrambled up the stairs, clamored down the hall and burst outside, into a raging thunderstorm with torrential rain and clouds as black as night.

Dear Jess, Billy wrote into his journal that night.

> *Sort of got in a fight a couple of days ago with Angel. You don't know him. He's the kid who sells crack. That's a bad drug. He called Andres a gimp. He called me a gimp-lover. That's a very bad word. It made me mad. When I wasn't really even looking, he hit me in the face. My glasses broke. I have a spare pair. They don't let me see too good, but that's OK. Mom says we can get a new pair real soon.*

> *We saw Angel today again and chased him. Andres didn't want to but I did. I hate kids like Angel. He's not too big, plus there was two of us. He ran down Death Alley. That's the alley that runs in back of the houses. We thought he went into one of the empty buildings. We went in, too. We looked everywhere but didn't see him.*

The cellar was smelly and spooky. There was a strange smell, like an overheated blow dryer or something, and then a weird voice called out a weird name, Ordo, three times. No idea what THAT word means or what made it, but we didn't wait to find out. So we ran like crazy. There was a thunderstorm outside and we got soaked. Mom was mad. Of course, I didn't say anything about what happened. She's always telling me to stay out of abandoned buildings and back alleys.

I hope Dad calls on my birthday. But he probably won't. He didn't call last year or the year before. I don't remember any year he's called. He didn't even call much even when you were sick. But he did visit you in Pittsbird. Mom says he's in California now, but I don't know if she really knows or is just saying that. We don't even have a picture of him. Wherever he is, I do wonder what it's like in California. If I ever go, I'd like to see the Lakers play. Maybe Scarlett Johansson would be there. I love her superhero movies!!!

I got a little homework to do so that's it for now. Goodnight, Jess.

Love, Billy, your brother.

Chapter Five: That word.
Friday, June 4

Uncle Jack came to Billy's birthday party. So did Andres and a bunch of other neighborhood kids, including Alex Borkowski, Billy's and Andres's second-best friend. They pigged out on ice cream and cake and chips and soda and then Billy opened his presents. The biggest surprise was the hamsters from Mom. Billy got two of them, along with food, bedding, a tank and all the accessories. Uncle Jack gave him five $20 bills—with explicit orders to start a bank account. Andres's gift was a skateboard. Billy also got a Wiffle ball and bat, a telescope, three books, and a Red Hot Chili Peppers T-shirt, the latter from Alex, who shared his tastes in music.

"Did you have fun?" Mary said when everyone, including Uncle Jack, had left.

"Did I have fun? Does a bear shit in the woods?"

"Billy," she scolded. "Remember what we said about language like that?"

"Sorry. Of course I had fun. Thanks!" he said, kissing his mother. "You know, you didn't have to get the hamsters."

"Don't you like them?"

"I *love* them, but they're expensive. Can we afford them, Mom?"

"We'll manage somehow," she said. "We always have. Besides, that's not your worry. It's mine. And we'll make it."

"But I could help."

Mary polished off her beer. During the party, she'd been careful to have only one—and even that one had elicited looks from her brother, who did not seem satisfied with her assurance that, yes, everything was under control and, no, she wasn't drinking heavily again, just a couple of pops every now and then.

Now, with Jack gone, she'd suddenly discovered one heck of a thirst.

"Help? What do you mean, Billy?"

"I could give you twenty dollars. Even forty."

Now she got it.

"No way," she said. "Uncle Jack was very specific: That's for a bank account, and a bank account alone. And that's where it's going to go."

The evening wore on. Mary settled onto the sofa with a book, an old Ray Bradbury novel she'd borrowed from the public library. Mary read. Mary polished off her six-pack. Billy played with his hamsters and watched TV. It turned nine o'clock, then ten. Mary fixed a rum and Coke and, slurring her words, told Billy she was "zonking out," he could stay up until eleven if he promised to be good.

At eleven, the news came on. Billy's eyes were closing. Mary's were closed. She was snoring, her hands tucked under her head, her pocketbook at her feet.

Billy got up, went to the bathroom, then continued down the hall to his bedroom. He slipped into his PJs and scanned his bureau, assessing how his new acquisition—the hamsters—fit in.

The boy was proud of his bureau. He was not an overly fastidious boy, but he was naturally tidy and neat, someone who'd early on grasped that old dictum: a place for everything and everything in its place. There was a certain reassurance, looking at what was on his bureau. A certain soothing effect, as if here, in his own little corner of the universe, everything was under control.

The centerpiece was a photograph of him, Mom and Jess that Uncle Jack had taken that final wondrous summer in Maine. Next to it was a giant plastic spider Billy had won at Ocean State Park. There was a Red Sox pennant, thumbtacked into the wall. His latest report card, which had mostly Bs. A mirror, on which Billy had taped every ticket stub to every Patriots, Red Sox and Providence College basketball game he'd attended with Mary and Uncle Jack. Posters of Red Hot Chili Peppers, Linkin Park and Guns N' Roses. A model Stealth bomber he'd built and painted. A Baby Ben alarm clock, a Christmas gift from Amanda, the social worker.

Billy brought pen and paper out of his desk drawer.

Dear Mom, he wrote.

> *Thank you for the hamsters. They are my very favor-*
> *ite gift. I know how much they cost (I think). That was a*
> *lot! So I want you to have this $20 dollar bill. Don't say*
> *no. You have given me lots of things so now it's my turn.*
> *You can use it. Maybe for the phone bills, which I know*
> *are late because I saw the bills (I didn't go in your purse.*
> *They were on the table).*
> *So don't say no. Please! I won't tell Uncle Jack. This*
> *is our secret.*
> *Love, Billy.*
> *P.S. I still have 80 dollars! A bank account with $80*
> *dollars is still good.*
> *P.P.S., I promise to take good care of the hamsters.*
> *You can watch me. You won't believe it!!!!!*

Billy folded the twenty into the letter and stuffed it into an envelope. He sealed it and went into the living room.

It was dark there now.

Some light from the kitchen penetrated, but the lamp by Mom—either a bulb had blown, or she'd stirred long enough to turn it off. Because he'd left it on, he was sure of that. At night, a light always burned in their apartment. Since he was a baby, Billy had never been able to sleep without some lights on. Sometimes he wondered if he would ever outgrow it.

But now... now all was dark.

Mary had shifted position on the sofa. She was facing the TV when Billy had gone into his room, but now her face was toward the sofa back, her features hidden from view.

Billy tiptoed across the floor and reached for her pocketbook. How many times had Mom told him not to go near her pocketbook? But this—surely, she'd understand this. Surely, once she'd thought about it, she'd accept his generosity—like she accepted Uncle Jack's frequent generosity. He unzipped her bag, dropped the envelope inside, then re-zipped it.

He started back toward his room.

The smell hit him.

Not the booze on Mary's breath—although that was there, a sweet-sour smell like spring lilacs gone by. This was sharper.

This was hot and electric, like an overheated iron.

The same smell he and Andres had found in that basement.

The TV flickered off.

And his mother muttered a word.

The word.

"Ordo."

That same word from that basement.

Pronounced with that same high pitch and clarity.

Ordo.

Mary's body tensed, then went limp, as if a powerful but non-lethal current had passed through. She burrowed her head further into the sofa.

"Ordo."

This time, the word was muffled.

This time, Billy could not be sure it had come from his mother—and not from under the couch, or in the couch, or even inside the wall. This time, he could not be sure he'd really heard a word and not just some kind of sleep-generated sound.

But the first time—no question, she'd uttered that word. He could still hear it, echoing in his head.

"Mom?" he called. "Are you OK, Mom? Do you want the TV back on? Do you wanna go to bed? Can you hear me, Mom?"

But he could not rouse her, not with words. And he did not dare to shake her. For reasons he could not articulate, he did not want to touch his mother. Didn't want to be near her.

Especially didn't want to hear that word ever again.

Billy was shivering.

He stood, aware of how terrified he would be if he heard that word again.

Sleep eluded Billy. He lay in his bed, a single sheet covering him. City sounds made their way to his room, but like most urbanites, tuning them out was easy. His interest was the next room: the living room, dark as the inside of a coffin.

Billy was afraid.

Afraid Mom would awaken—and she did, once. Slowly, she made her way to the bathroom. The toilet seat slammed, a door banged, and Mom shuffled into her bedroom, where for the last two hours there hadn't been another sound—nothing but that same belabored snoring.

Ordo.

Absolutely, that was the word he'd heard.

But what did it mean?

Was it a verb?

A noun?

Was it English?

Sure didn't seem so. Billy didn't know any foreign languages, at least none that he could really speak, but he'd heard enough Spanish and Cambodian and Portuguese at school to suspect it wasn't one of those. And it sure as heck wasn't French, which they'd started studying this year in school.

So what was it? Some kind of name? Some kind of *code*?

Had he only imagined he'd heard it?

No way, he thought.

Imagination isn't that vivid, he thought. *Imagination doesn't leave an echo inside your head hours later.*

Besides, what reason could there possibly be for his imagination to associate Mom and that word and that cellar?

The TV, he thought. *Probably she hit the remote. Or maybe there was a surge or something and the set got shorted. That would explain the smell.*

But that word...

For about the millionth time, Billy checked the green luminescent hands of his Baby Ben. Two-ten in the morning. Far away, he heard a siren. Closer, maybe three or four buildings down the street near Andres's place, he heard a man and a woman arguing. But otherwise, it seemed no one else in the city was awake.

No people, that is.

In their cage, the hamsters were busy with their wheel.

Every once in a while, one or the other would squeak—their way of talking, Billy supposed. Hamsters were nocturnal—Uncle Jack had taught him that big word, which he intended to try out on his teacher Monday morning—and that meant they were awake at night and slept all day, the exact opposite of people. Most people, anyway.

Suddenly, the hamsters stopped their play.

There was momentary silence and then it was shattered. Both of the hamsters—he was sure it was both—started squealing. It was a wounded squeal, like pain was being inflicted on them, pain like needles being stuck into their eyes or their tails being cut off or...

The squealing stopped.

Billy took a breath, waiting for—whatever. But there was nothing, no movement he could detect, no sound from the cage or anywhere else in the apartment.

He padded across the floor to the bureau. The light was not good, but he could still discern the shapes of his new pets. They were huddled together in the corner. There was no blood on either animal that Billy could see, no scratches or visible injuries. Both animals were breathing. Both seemed pretty much OK, just temporarily paralyzed, as if the most frightening thing that could happen to a hamster—being threatened by a giant cat or dog, maybe—had just happened.

One at a time, Billy patted his hamsters: first He-man, the brown-spotted male, then Wiggle, the white female. Slowly, they responded to his hand.

"It's OK, guys," he said. "Everything's OK."

It was another hour before Billy was asleep.

Chapter Six: The Culvert.
Saturday, June 5

Billy tumbled out of bed the next morning at 10:30—the latest he'd ever slept on a Saturday. Mary was in the kitchen, fixing bacon and eggs and listening to a radio talk show.

"Kind of late for you, isn't it, Tiger, for a Saturday?" she said when he came into the room, went to the refrigerator, and poured himself orange juice.

"I guess so," Billy said.

"Andres called. An hour ago."

"What did he say?"

Billy rubbed his eyes, trying to get the sleep out, and put his old glasses on.

"Said to call him when you get up. He wants to go skateboarding. Want some breakfast?"

"OK."

"Fried or scrambled? Cook's serving both today!"

"Scrambled."

"Scrambled eggs it is, coming right up!"

Billy couldn't believe it—how cheerful his mother was, how bright-eyed and bushy-tailed, as she herself would say. She'd had so much to drink last night, had gotten... well, *drunk,* or darn close to it, and here she was, practically dancing around the kitchen. It had been more than a year since his last experience, but Billy knew about hangovers. This didn't fit the description.

The questions—they seemed to float in the air, demanding to be asked.

Why did you drink so much, Mom? You know you shouldn't. Do you remember being on the couch like that? Snoring so loud the walls

*almost shook? Do you remember that gross smell? Do you remember
saying that word, Ordo? Do you know what it means? Where it comes
from? Or what it has to do with that sewer line in that cellar?*

But he did not ask those questions. Maybe, deep down, he
didn't want the answers. Worse, maybe he worried that she might
not know them.

And where would that leave him?

Or *them?*

"Awesome!" Andres whooped.

"Wicked!" Billy agreed as their friend tore past on his
skateboard.

Encouraged, Alex Borkowski did it again. He jumped, spun
720 degrees, then landed back on his board, which roared down
the back slope of the parking lot of Food Chain. The market was
located about a half mile from Billy's apartment, at the point where
Death Alley ended at Mashpaug Pond.

"There," Alex announced when he'd stopped. He was at the
edge of the lot, at the top of an embankment that led down to the
water, oily and murky, even on a sunny day.

Andres and Billy skateboarded toward him.

Alex was 12, a year older than them, but maturity hadn't made
him a skateboard star. Athletic ability had. Some kids excelled at
one sport, maybe two sports. Andres, for instance, was a mean
enough hoop player; Billy showed promise at football. But Alex—
Alex outperformed at any sport. Soccer. Stickball. Street hockey.
Roller blading. He'd been gifted with one of those bodies in which
strength, stamina, balance and hand-eye coordination meshed
perfectly to produce the standout athlete. He was a nice kid, too.
Friendly. Not given to bragging, like most kids in his league.

"How long did you have to practice learning that?" Andres
asked.

"Not long," Alex said, and his friends believed him.

"What's the secret?" Billy said.

"No secret. Just a coupla simple rules. First, you gotta be going
downhill. You have to have a good head of steam. When you're
really moving and you've got your balance, all you do is jump and
spin." He pronounced the last word as if it were magic—and to
Andres and Billy, at least, it might as well have been.

"I don't know if I can do it," Andres said. "My leg."

"Maybe try?" Billy said. "But only if you want to."

"Let me see you first," Andres said.

"OK," said Billy.

"Just remember to have your board under control before you jump," Alex said, "and everything'll be cool."

Billy tucked his skateboard under his arm and walked to the crest of the hill. All of Food Chain's customers were parked on level ground, closer to the store. All except two old wrecks—one that had been torched, the other stripped to the frame—that were halfway down the parking lot. He'd have to be careful to avoid them, once he got going.

"Here goes nothing."

Billy pushed off.

"Remember: you gotta be going *fast!*" Alex said. "Otherwise, you won't have time for two turns."

Two turns? Billy thought. *I'll be lucky if I can do one.*

He was gaining speed now. It felt exciting and good, the wind rushing at him, ruffling his hair and whistling past his ears. He'd skateboarded before, countless times—Andres had let him borrow his board whenever he'd asked—and so he had the basics, the balance, down pat.

Jumping was another thing.

"Do it quick," Alex said, "or you're gonna be in the pond!"

Billy took a deep breath, crouched, sprang into the air and swiveled.

And when gravity reclaimed him, he landed on his ass. His skateboard shot away from him, rolling down to the bottom of the lot, across the embankment and into the pond.

"Shit! Double shit!"

"You alright?" Andres said, rushing toward him.

"Yeah," Billy said, standing. "But my board's in the water."

"We better get it," Alex said, "before a snapping turtle gets it first."

"There aren't any turtles in Mashpaug Pond," Andres said. "No fish, either, except for carp. I know, 'cause I seen some guy catch one once."

The boys scrambled down the embankment to the shore of the pond. Like much of the landscape in this part of the city, the pond was a forgotten place, a dirty place, a place where Native Americans, the first inhabitants of the area, had encamped centuries before, but by the twenty-first century had become a cesspool.

The boys had watched the skateboard go under, but now that the ripples had subsided, they couldn't see it. The water was too filthy.

"We need a stick," Andres said.

"It'd be faster if we wade into it," Alex said.

"*You* can wade into it," Billy said, "but not me. You can get sick from Mashpaug Pond. That water is wicked gross."

"Yeah, you're right," said Alex. "Let's find sticks."

They found three and began poking around in the sludgy bottom. Cans, bottles, car parts—in the first few minutes, they fished out a bunch of junk, but no skateboard.

They were moving in a westerly direction, toward Death Alley.

Soon, they'd reached The Culvert.

And that's how they considered it—with a combination of mystery, awe and fear—and in capital letters: *THE CULVERT.*

The Culvert went under Food Chain's parking lot and connected to an elaborate system of storm drains and sewer lines that honeycombed the Armory District. During a heavy rain, water discharged with a vengeance into Mashpaug Pond from The Culvert and it was something to see, an inner-city Niagara Falls. During hot spells, The Culvert was down to a trickle, if that. With a diameter of four feet, it was possible to walk into it—and some kids, armed with flashlights, had done just that. Rumor had it that if you got hold of the blueprints, you could go all over the city of Providence. Billy, Andres and Alex didn't know anyone who'd tried.

But its size and darkness weren't what had made the culvert The Culvert.

Margaret Bucci had.

Seven-year-old Margaret Bucci, who had gone missing last spring. Posters nailed up around the neighborhood and newspaper stories, Facebook posts, and police pleas for public help had turned up nothing, for three weeks.

Until a city sanitation worker on an inspection several hundred feet inside The Culvert had found her decomposed body, which bore unmistakable wounds of a vicious assault with a sharpened object and whose body had been decomposing even as the K-9

Squad was combing her neighborhood, which included Andres and Billy's homes and Death Alley.

Homicide had been ruled the cause, but no arrests had been made. The cops didn't even have a person of interest to interrogate.

Billy stood by The Culvert, his head echoing with his mother's admonition, delivered the same evening that the late Margaret Bucci's face had been on the six o'clock news.

Stay away, Billy, she'd said. *It's no place for kids. Not little kids, not big kids. No good can come of going down there.*

The three boys stood, the same thought going through their minds.

The same phrase, "seven-year-old Margaret Bucci."

Billy spoke first.

"It didn't come down this far," he said. "It's gotta be back there."

"Yeah," Andres agreed.

"Whatsa matter, you guys chicken?" Alex said.

"Nah," Billy said.

But in truth, a shiver was dancing down his back. He could see into The Culvert—only a few feet—and it was dark the way he imagined a cosmic black hole must be. Cold air was coming out of it, carrying was a faint trace of an odor.

It wasn't the smell you'd expect from a storm line.

Not a sewer smell, either, but a hot smell... the smell of wires burning.

The same odor from that cellar and his living room last night.

Billy wondered if the storm drain followed Death Alley... whether it might have been the black nothingness of The Culvert they'd peered into that afternoon in the cellar.

What if it goes by my house? he thought with alarm. *What if the line into our cellar is connected?*

"'Fraid of Margaret Bucci's ghost?" Alex teased.

"Nah," Billy said.

"Me neither," Andres said.

"Well, her ghost's in there," Alex said.

"No way," said Billy.

"Way, and trapped forever," Alex said. "They say in rainstorms, you can hear her. She's calling her Mommy."

Alex cupped his hands and lowered his voice.

"'Help me, Mommy!' she says. 'Freddy Krueger's got me! He's cutting me with his knives!'"

Andres's eyes widened.

"That's bullshit," he managed, before his voice broke.

"Yeah," Billy added. "Perfect total bullshit."

"Is it? Then how about you walk in and prove it."

No one spoke.

Suddenly, it was put-up-or-shut-up time.

"How... far in?" Andres said.

"Without a... light?" Billy said.

But Alex had taken his prank far enough. There was always the risk they'd turn the tables on him—dare him to go, either alone or with them—and then the situation could get complicated. Not that Alex was scared. It's just that The Culvert was gross. Besides, he was already tired of this. He had better things to do, like skateboarding.

"Only kidding," he said. "We gotta find Billy's skateboard. And if there's one thing we know, it's that it didn't go in there. I think we must've passed it. We'll have to double back. We'll have to be more careful this time."

Billy started to relax. He was almost comfortable again, was walking back toward.... when he heard it.

"Ordo."

He stopped, the taste of bile in his throat.

"Did you hear that?" he asked his friends.

"Hear what?"

"That... voice."

"I didn't hear nothing," Andres said.

"Me neither," Alex said.

Billy strained to hear.

But there was nothing, only an overworked imagination, echoing from last night. For an instant, he was tempted to blurt out what had happened. The smell, that word again, hadn't he been dying to tell Andres?

And hadn't a part of him thought *no, no, no, that'd be the worst thing to do*?

That maybe Andres would think he was a fruitcake?

They were looking at him funny now, Alex and Andres.

"Must've been the wind," Billy mumbled.

He laughed nervously, hoping that would pass it off.

It did.

Alex had been busy with his stick, and he'd found Billy's skateboard, grimy and wet, but otherwise unharmed.

Chapter Seven: Our bright future.
Monday, June 7

Mary was at the kitchen table when Billy came home from school.

Two bottles stood within arm's reach: one of Coke, and another of rum. That bottle was half gone.

Billy approached his mother, stopping when there was still some distance between them. Mary tossed back what was left in her tumbler, swished the ice cubes around and eyeballed her son. It was an empty look, as if his presence would take some time to register. As if she couldn't decide if his presence mattered.

"I'm home, Mom," Billy said.

Mary fixed him with that odd look and said: "Yes you are, aren't you? Home sweet home. Home. Where the heart is."

"Are you all right, Mom?"

That took a while to percolate through her brain.

"I suppose it depends on what you mean by 'all right,'" she said finally. "What *do* you mean?"

"I mean do you feel OK?"

Mary pointed to the wall behind her.

"Did you see that?"

He hadn't—but now he did. There was a ragged hole where the landline had been. The phone lay in smashed pieces on the floor.

"What happened, Mom?"

For an instant, Billy thought someone else was in the apartment. Someone strung out on crack who'd broken in, demanded money, and not getting it, had roughed up Mom and started dismantling the joint.

"What happened?" Mary said. "What *happened*? I smashed the phone, that's what happened."

"But why, Mom?"

"Because the bastards disconnected it. And if they were going to disconnect the phone, then by God I said *let's really disconnect it! Let's permanently disconnect it! Let's rip the mother-fucker from the wall.*"

"But you still have your cell phone," Billy said.

"A lot of good that will do," she said. "They cut that service off, too."

"Cable TV and the internet still work," Billy said. He could still go online, with the iPad his school had given him early in the pandemic, when all learning was remote.

"Those are from another company," Mary said. "We're luck they haven't shut them off, too."

Mary poured more rum, topped it off with Coke, and drank. Her hands tremored and she was perspiring.

Billy felt sick. It was like waking up one morning only to find they'd been transported back in time two years, to that traumatic period following Grammy's death.

"Didn't you find my twenty dollars?" Billy said.

"I found it, but how far do you think it went against *this*?"

Mary waved an envelope.

"*This* is a $435 phone bill. This is four months of non-payment. This is America, where Big Business has a constitutional right to ruin your life!"

"But you could have called Uncle Jack," Billy said. "He would have paid it."

"I wouldn't be so sure about that," Mary said. "Only so many times you can go to the well."

And then, Mary broke. She began sobbing.

"Oh, Mom."

"God knows I tried, Billy," Mary said. "But there comes a point where excuses don't count. When… there's no excuse for screwing up."

Billy took the last steps toward his mother.

"That's OK," he said, putting his arms around her. "We don't need a phone."

"Yes, we do," Mary sobbed. "We need a phone, just like we

need a car that runs better, and... a better place to live, and new furniture, and... and..."

She couldn't finish, couldn't bring herself to tell Billy that it was more than telephone service—that they were four months behind on the rent and the landlord, as understanding as was, had dropped by to beg for his money... and gone away empty-handed.

"It's hard," Mary said when she'd composed herself. "Some days are better than others."

"I know, Mom. I understand."

"I love you, Billy."

"I love you, too."

"You're all I've got."

"And you and Uncle Jack," Billy said, "are all I've got."

When Jess's first liver transplant began to fail, the Pittsburgh team vowed to give the girl a second chance if she could survive the wait for a second donor.

She did. During the wait, Mary—with the help of her brother, her mother and visiting nurses—was able to continue working at Our Bright Future.

The second transplant was a success, surgically.

Then her immune system began to reject this liver, as it had the first.

Jess's Pittsburgh medical team wanted to try once more—"third time's the charm!" a surgeon said—but the case, unprecedented in the hospital's annals, had to clear the ethics committee.

Citing the scarcity of donors and the remote chance a third transplant would succeed, the committee after deliberation refused to give the green light.

Mary was crushed.

Jess's team, who had come to see the girl as "one of the family," as a nurse put it, revolted. They took their case to the hospital president, who happened to be a good friend of the president of Duquesne University, who happened to be a friend of Father Jack, and the search for a third donor was on. One was found a week later.

"A miracle," Father jack said. "God bless the family and may their loved one find eternal peace at the side of The Lord."

Stephen McAllister visited his daughter before the third operation and Grammy did, too, and with Uncle Jack having offered a Mass for his niece, Jess was wheeled into the OR.

Mary's clean slate had begun with her discharge from Portland Behavioral Health Center. It was May. Mary was alcohol-free and, thanks to the marvels of modern chemistry, she was able to function. She and Billy stayed the remainder of the spring in Blue Hill. That summer, at the urging of both Grammy and her psychologist, they returned to Providence with several thousand dollars from Grammy and her old Toyota, which Grammy never used.

Mary found the apartment where they lived and while she didn't return to the staff of Our Bright Future, she was able to serve as a sort of consultant-on-call. She drew emotional support from her mother, her brother and Amanda. Billy returned to school and slid smoothly into a new circle of friends.

Then Grammy died, and the bottom fell out again.

This time, Mary's recovery was slower, the pharmaceuticals heavier, the rehab more intensive, the prognosis less certain. For six weeks, Billy lived with Uncle Jack. Mary looked older when they were reunited. Paler and thinner and different, in other ways Billy didn't understand.

But it was Mom.

Mom, the person he loved more dearly than anyone. Mom who, despite everything, would go to the ends of the earth for her surviving child.

So what if she couldn't work right away? If the only apartment they could afford wasn't very big, wasn't in the best part of town? So what if Amanda checked in every other day instead of every other week, like before?

Mary was making it. They were making it.

At 5 o'clock in the afternoon, an hour after Billy got home, Mary went to her bedroom to "take a nap," as she phrased it. At 6:30 p.m., when she showed no sign of rousing, Billy scrounged around in the cupboard and came up with a box of macaroni and cheese and a can of tuna. He made dinner and ate it, refrigerating the leftovers in case Mom woke up and was hungry. Then he washed his plate and silverware, toweled them dry and put them away.

His only homework was math and he made quick work of that. Outside, the day had grown long. He heard voices, mostly kids' voices from a game of basketball, but he was not tempted to join them. Mom might need him—when, or for what, he could only guess—and duty demanded that he remain with her. Didn't she always stay with him whenever he was sick?

After double-checking the lock and turning on every light in the apartment but the one in her room, he went into the living room to watch TV. He watched episodes of *Teenage Mutant Ninja Turtles*, only half tuning in, his attention focused on the reassuring purr of his mother's sleep.

His anxiety concerned something else.

Will I hear it? he wondered. *Will I hear that awful word? Please, don't let there be that awful word.*

With the TV droning on, Billy said an Our Father and a string of Hail Marys, just as Uncle Jack had taught him when, as a little boy, he'd wanted God to help him with something, or watch over and protect him, like his guardian angel.

But there was no word.

No sounds, only car brakes and horns and grownups arguing outside.

Dear Jess, he wrote into his journal after he'd fed his hamsters and turned down the covers on his bed—but not turned off a single light.

> *Mom acted weird again today. Well, maybe not exactly weird. More like angry. She broke the phone. Smashed it with a hammer. I had to clean it up because she went to bed before dinner. I think it's all about money. Mom tries very hard, but since before my birthday there hasn't been enough money. That's why the landline and the cell phone were disconnected. It happened before and Uncle Jack helped out and they turned them back on. Maybe Uncle Jack will help us out again. I hope so. I don't want Mom to do more smashing, like the TV or the stove or anything. At least the Internet is still working.*
>
> *When Uncle Jack and I have our private talks, which we do pretty often, Uncle Jack says that some people don't have good luck, no matter what. He says clouds follow them around, like it's always raining, or just about to.*

Mom's like that.

It was real bad after Grammy died. I already told you about that. Mom started drinking again and had to go back into that special hospital in Maine. When she got out, things got better. The way Uncle Jack explains it, even the cloud people get to have sun, especially if they try. And Mom really tries.

Like this class she's been taking. It's about her license, which she needs to get back so she can work again at Our Bright Future. She's gonna graduate by the end of the summer. Then we'll get off Supplemental Security Income, SSI they call it, and SNAP, the fancy name for food stamps. I hate being on those, 'cause if people knew, they'd make fun of us like I see on TV. So I don't tell anyone, except Andres,' cause he's the only kid I know who can keep a big secret like that.

When mom gets that job, first thing I'm gonna get is a Nintendo Switch!!!! Then maybe contact lenses (at least new glasses, I'm still wearing my old ones after my others got broken by Angel). Mom wants a new car because the one Grammy gave her doesn't run too good any more. Me and her both want a new apartment or maybe even a whole house. This place is OK, but it would be neat to live in the country. Like up in Blue Hill, where we don't go any more, not since Grammy died.

Well, Mom's still asleep and I'm tired, too.

Goodnight, Jess, I will always love you.

Chapter Eight: Only meanness.
Friday, June 11

When Billy thought of it—and since the shit with Angel Iannotti, he'd been thinking about it a lot—you couldn't find a better blood brother than Andres Washington.

Andres was fun to play with, Andres never spilled secrets, Andres always took Billy's side in schoolyard arguments, Andres had a healthy fear of girls, Andres liked Ocean State Park, Andres loved They Might be Giants, and someday (they both fancied) Andres was going to play pro basketball, just like Billy was going to be a professional football player.

But there was a deeper connection.

A socioeconomic tie that neither boy was old enough to fully comprehend, except viscerally. Andres's family, like Billy's since Jess's death, had gone the so-called welfare route. Andres's mom, like Billy's, had vowed to get off the dole—and in Mrs. Washington's case, eventually had succeeded, after eight long years. Andres's dad, like Billy's, was absent. The only difference there was that Andres's dad was MIA, while Billy's wasn't missing, just mostly out of touch and living in Los Angeles.

As the blood brothers sat outside Billy's apartment this second Friday afternoon in June, the treat—Andres's—was Popsicles. The topic was dads.

"And he never came back?" Billy was saying. "Never even wrote a letter?"

He'd heard the story before, of course. But there was solace hearing it again.

"Nope," Andres said. "I was still a baby. Ma says he might be in New York, 'cause he had a girlfriend there. An actress or model or something. But she doesn't know. He never came back, never called or anything."

"Mine hasn't been much better," Billy said, but he could not be as harsh as Andres. Despite the hurt, the years of indifference and neglect—Billy was nine the last time Stephen McAllister had checked in on his oldest child—Billy would welcome him back in a second. It was probably fantasy, but he imagined that having his dad in the house would make things better.

"He didn't send you nothing for his birthday, did he," Andres said.

"Oh yes he did," Billy lied. "Twenty bucks. It came today in a card."

"Wow! Next Popsicle's on you, dude!"

"You got it."

"Your dad's in California, right?"

"Yup."

It was a point of pride with Billy, his dad being in California, the Promised Land.

"Still a pilot?" Andres said.

"Yup!"

Truth be told, Stephen McAllister—according to the last conversation with Mary, which occurred the last time she'd tried once again to get child support from him, a year ago—was a baggage handler with United Airlines. Or maybe not. Pathological lying was another of his personality traits.

"I don't know what my dad is," Andres said, "if he's even alive. If he is, Mom figures he's probably in jail, thinks he's tied up with a drug cartel. Maybe it would be better if he were dead. He treated me and mom and my brother like shit when he was here."

"In his card," Billy said, "my Dad said he's gonna fly me to California with him someday!"

"Wicked!"

"Wanna come?"

"Is Angel Iannotti an asshole? Of course I wanna come. When's he gonna do it?"

"I don't know," Billy shrugged. "He didn't say."

They were down to their Popsicle sticks when the voice rang out: "Well if it isn't old Billy-Boy!"

The man in the new Mercedes killed the ignition, left his sunglasses on the dash and stepped out onto the sidewalk. He was a tall man, mid to late thirties, balding, mustachioed, wore a muscle shirt and two gold chains. And black leather pants.

It was those black leather pants Billy remembered best.

Those signature leather pants, which he'd never seen anyone else wear, and the nickname by which Crimson Vanner, Mommy's boyfriend for a short while, always addressed him—a nickname Billy had loathed from the moment Crimson had used it.

"How are you, Billy-Boy?" Crimson said.

"OK, I guess."

"What's the matter, too good to shake my hand?"

Crimson had his outstretched, but Billy hadn't reached for it.

"Nah," Billy said, limply extending his hand.

"That's better, Billy-Boy! That's great! You can judge a man by the way he shakes your hand. And don't you ever forget it, dude. Who's your friend, Billy-Boy?"

"His name's Andres."

"Crimson Vanner, Andres. Pleased to meet you."

Andres mumbled something and offered his hand.

"Now *that*," Crimson exclaimed, "is a young man who's being raised *right*! Speaking of being raised right, Billy-Boy, is your momma home?"

What do I say? Billy thought. *No way does Mom want to see him again. Crimson's bad. As bad as they get. How many times has she said that? How many times has Uncle Jack said dropping him was the best thing she could have done?*

But here he is. Somehow, he tracked us down, and here he is, leather pants and all. Do I lie? Say she's not home? And if I do—will he believe me? Will he force his way in? Will he hurt Mom if he does?

"Mom's... at the Laundromat," Billy said.

He was trying to sound cool but failing.

Crimson mulled that over.

"Laundromat?" he said.

"Yeah. She just left. She won't be back for... hours. She hasn't done laundry in... weeks. You should've seen how much there was!"

"Which Laundromat, Billy-Boy?"

"Geez... I don't know."

"Not lying to me, are you Billy-Boy? Not telling a little story because you think you should protect your momma for some silly reason, are you?"

"Oh, no, Crimson."

"What floor do you live on, Billy-Boy?" Crimson said. "Top? Middle? First? Basement?"

The smile had evaporated from his face and now there was only meanness, the kind of meanness that had lashed out at Mary more than once during the fleeting time she and Crimson Vanner were together.

"The... ah... basement."

How could he lie about that? Crimson would look at the mailboxes and know.

"Thank you, Billy-Boy," the man said. "I think I'll have myself a look-see. Nice meeting you, Andres. And nice seeing you, Billy-Boy."

Mary was done vacuuming Billy's bedroom when she turned around, stepped into the hall, and nearly bumped into Crimson Vanner.

"Oh, God!" she said.

"Hello, Mary," Crimson said.

"What the hell are you doing here?" Mary said.

"Do I sense hostility, Mary?"

"What do you want?"

"Why, nothing more than to say hello. You sound uptight, Mary. I don't like it when you're uptight. It puckers up that pretty face of yours in ways unbecoming to you."

"How'd you find me?" Mary said.

"How'd I find you? Let's just say we have our ways."

"I want you to leave."

"But I just arrived."

"Get out, Crimson."

"Such hostility."

"Out. Now. Or I call the police."

"But that would be so rude. You wouldn't do anything like that, would you, Mary? It's not in your nature. And certainly not in your best interests, given your record. You do remember your arrest for possession of cocaine, don't you?"

"No charges were ever brought," Mary said. "And it was your cocaine, not mine."

"Ah, but that was never proven. Nor even suggested. I am *very* careful in how I conduct my business. Staying off the radar has been my secret to success."

"I'm calling the cops," Mary said.

Crimson contemplated that a moment—seemingly, with great delight.

He smiled.

"Really?" he said.

"I mean it, Crimson. Get out or I'll call the police."

Crimson held his response—just long enough to raise a barely perceptible quiver on Mary's upper lip. He'd seen it before—a distinctive sign that she was starting to feel fear.

And fear was an emotion Crimson Vanner fed on.

"Call them with what, Mary? Certainly not the phone. I tried reaching you yesterday, and do you know what happened? I bet you do. I got a recording about service being temporarily disconnected. On both phones. That's their polite way of saying: no cash, man. So I hardly think you're going to call. You could send your Bill-Boy running for them, but I don't think it's possible you'll call them. Nor do I think Billy-Boy has the balls to rat me out."

"Please," Mary said, and later, when the crisis had passed, she would be ashamed for using that word. "Please leave. I don't have anything to say to you."

Mary looked at Crimson—scrutinized him for the first time in two years. Age hadn't seemed to have touched him.

On the surface, he was all Hollywood Boulevard gloss—those gold chains and leather pants and suffocating aftershave, Brut or Musk or one of those awful scents. But there was something beneath the tinsel and shine. A powerful eroticism, especially in those eyes... those bottomless brown eyes that, she'd often kidded him, belonged to some Italian Renaissance poet, not some twenty-first-century operator whose passion was nose candy, not verse.

The way he'd made love... so slowly, caringly... as if the laws of the universe had been boiled down to pleasing her.

They'd met—in the paper goods aisle of Food Chain, of all places—a month before Mary's mother had died. For most of that month, she'd believed his yarn about being an IT consultant. She'd believed those cryptic calls he got on his cell were computer related. She'd believed that cocaine was his recreation, not vocation.

Just like when she'd fallen in love with the father of her

children, she'd bought a bill of goods… believing, again, in White Knights and Prince Charmings.

Believing that finally, incredibly, the man of her dreams had materialized right here in Providence, Rhode Island.

Then Mary's mother died. The dark clouds returned and the occasional snort became the hourly high, and Prince Charming revealed himself as a Big-Time Dealer, and before Mary could see her way through things, before she could get past the sex, Uncle Jack and Amanda had checked her into Portland Behavioral Health Center for the second time.

When Mary got out, mercifully Crimson was gone.

"I've missed you," Crimson said. "A day hasn't gone by that I haven't thought of you."

"Bullshit," Mary said.

"No, the truth. I thought we could have dinner and a bottle of wine or two. My guess, Mary, is that it's been some time since a man has treated you well."

There was a pull—no question, there was a pull, Mary could feel it, like a heavenly body caught in the gravitational field of a distant planet.

Save for Billy and Andres, she might have been drawn in.

But there they were, behind Crimson.

They'd crept down the stairs, through the door and across the kitchen, where they had eavesdropped long enough to get a handle on things.

Now it was three of them and one of him.

No one said anything as everyone processed how the balance of power had shifted.

These kids are punks, Crimson thought, *but even punks can be witnesses.*

"We want you to go," Billy said.

Crimson ignored him.

"Touching, aren't they?" he said to Mary. "Billy-Boy and Black Sambo, leaping to your defense."

"You fucking pig," Mary said.

Crimson's processing was complete.

Not worth a quick one, he thought.

Turning and brushing past the boys, he said "I can see that I have outworn my welcome. Shall I try another time, Mary?"

"No."

"Not some fine moonlit night?"

"I never want to see you again," she said.

"Let me leave my card in case you change your mind," Crimson said as he went for the door. "I've moved. Into someplace very nice. Someplace I think you would appreciate. Goodbye, Mary. Shake, Billy-Boy?"

Billy only looked at his outstretched hand, and then he was gone.

Chapter Nine: House of horrors.

Saturday, June 12

"Mom, if you don't feel good, we don't have to go," Billy said as they waited for the bus that would take them to Ocean State Park, a few miles south of Providence on the coast of Narragansett Bay.

"A promise is a promise," she said.

"But you have a headache."

And she did—a pounding headache that had been with her since midnight, when, locked in insomnia, she'd given up on sleep and embarked on a cleaning binge that had ended in exhaustion after 3 a.m.

What troubled Mary was that her headache—clinically, she supposed, a full-blown migraine—had no apparent cause. She'd had no taste for alcohol yesterday, so hangover was not suspect. She hadn't hit her head, wasn't coming down with a cold, hadn't loaded up on carbs or sugar.

Her best guess was that somehow it must be traceable to Crimson. His sudden re- appearance in her life had dredged up festering emotions.

Time had hidden, but not healed.

"I took Tylenol. My headache's better," Mary said, not truthfully. "And you've waited all week."

"But we could go tomorrow."

"Nope. Here's the bus. We're going."

They put their mandated COVID masks on and boarded.

On the bus, Billy couldn't get his sister off his mind.

The last time you came here, Jess, you were feeling so much better, he thought. *Even Grammy, who always read the worst into every-thing, was sure you were gonna make it.*

A tear was descending his cheek.

How long does it go on? he wondered, once again.

It was a question no one—not Mom or Uncle Jack or Amanda or Andres, the only kid who knew much about his sister—had ever satisfactorily answered.

How long does someone miss someone so bad? How long before the memories don't seem so real, don't seem like they happened yesterday, not four or five or six years ago?

Over and over but with patience, Uncle Jack had told Billy that it would get easier, but it would have to take time. Over and over, Mary had said the same.

And they were right, for a while.

It *was* finally getting easier when Grammy died. Grammy's death had brought everything back, but then months passed when Jess didn't weigh so heavily on his thoughts, didn't visit him nightly in his dreams. When he thought of her now, it was less about her sickness and death and more about the happy mem-ories, the, summery ones, memories of occasions like going to Ocean State.

So what was it lately?

Why was this spring so different?

The last few weeks, he'd thought more about Jess than at any time since Grammy died and Mom had had to go away again.

He'd even started writing in his journal again, after over a long time without an entry.

And his dreams—the last two weeks, Jess had taken over his sleep, every night.

Not the nice dream, either.

The terrifying one, where she's entombed in that dark place and talking to him.

Only what she's saying now doesn't make any sense.

Now, she's no longer calling for help.

She is speaking in a strangely even voice and using grown-up words in a vain attempt to explain something complex, something Billy doesn't understand, something Jess herself seems barely able to grasp but feels powerfully compelled to inform her brother.

This was the gist of her communication:

Light years... crave the darkness... a year is but a day... the mission is not complete... beware Z-DA...

Only one phrase was recognizable:

The mission is not complete...

Billy has heard that in his nightmare, the one where they're about to seal Jess's coffin.

The bus stopped, the door opened, and a morning appreciably warmer than when they'd boarded flooded in, carrying with it the carnival sounds of Ocean State Park.

Billy clapped his hands.

"Our first visit of the year!" he said as thoughts of his sister receded.

After a string of rainy weekends, this Saturday had dawned clear and warm and dry, and like a bear from hibernation, Rhode Island had lumbered alive—not just here but throughout the state. And not only because of the weather. Rhode Island had one of the highest rates of people fully vaccinated against COVID-19, and the governor had lifted restrictions on most gatherings, indoors or out. The pandemic was easing.

Closed in the summer of 2020 because of the pandemic, Ocean State had reopened with fireworks and continuing large crowds. It was packed again today.

Mary considered Ocean State a great cultural mixer. A demographic snapshot on any given day would have found Native Americans from South County, Italians from North Providence, swamp Yankees from South Kingstown, French Canadians from Woonsocket, Colombians and Guatemalans from Central Falls, Hmong and Cambodians and Blacks from Providence. All-day admission to Ocean State was relatively cheap, the food was tasty, it had bus service, and on days when cities sizzled, a sea breeze kept the temperature tolerable.

"It's all some of these people can afford," Mary had explained to her son.

"Sort of like us," Billy replied.

"Only for now," Mary reminded him.

They bought two books of tickets and made a beeline for the Corkscrew, the over-and-under loop-de-loop ride that was featured in Ocean State's TV and online advertising. Mary wouldn't go near the thing, but it was the highlight of Billy's day, and he began and ended every expedition to Ocean State on it—preferably, riding in the first or last car. Ordinarily, Andres would have been his partner in crime, but Andres this weekend had aunts and uncles up from Philadelphia and his mother had refused to relieve him of family duty.

From the Corkscrew, Billy moved on to the Roundup, then to the Yo-Yo, then the Tilt-a-Whirl and Free Fall. The line for the Free Fall was the longest—the ride was Ocean State's newest—and against her better judgment, Mary left Billy to board on his own and crossed over to the Beer Garden, where she bought a 16-ounce cold one. It quickly smoothed the edges of her migraine.

But the brew had another effect, too.

Suddenly, the amusement park seemed unnaturally bright—as if the sun's strength had increased, and her sunglasses had lost their dimming power.

Dizziness swept over Mary.

Her breathing was suddenly labored, her pulse elevated.

A feeling of apprehension had been unlocked.

But of what?

The House of Horrors, that's what, Mary thought. *He's going to want me to go on that.*

They'd passed the ride on the way in and Mary had felt a twinge of panic then, setting eyes on it. But she hadn't made much of it.

Now the feeling was strong.

It's not that I'm afraid of anything in there, she thought. *I've been on that ride a dozen times and it's always been a hoot. No, it's not fear at work here. What's at work is compulsion. There's something in there I want, something I need. I'm being drawn in and I don't know why.*

Except, she *did* know why.

The darkness.

I crave the darkness.

I could be very comfortable in there, with all that darkness.

But that was absurd.

Mary ordered a second 16-ouncer, intending to down it before Billy finished his ride. The beer further smoothed her migraine—only a few manageable bumps and burrs remained—but it did not touch her anxiety. Her stomach was cramped, and even though the mercury was nearing 80, she was cold. She was not feeling herself.

She wanted to go home.

She was finishing her beer near the video arcade when the games suddenly went dark.

"What the F?" the attendant shouted.

He went to the arcade control panel.

Nothing amiss there.

A moment later, the games were back online.

"OK, folks, we're back in business!" the attendant said. "Don't know what happened, but it's all OK now."

Mary had been watching.

Now she smelled something burnt, like a broken appliance.

The smell dissipated into the air.

"Had enough for today?" Mary asked Billy when he'd taken a ride on the Free Fall.

"Are you kidding?" her son said. "There's ten more rides I want to go on! There's Bumper Cars and the Tempest and the Flume and—"

"How about a hotdog?"

Maybe she could coax him toward leaving with food.

"Na," Billy said.

"Fried Dough?"

"Later," he said. "I want to go on more rides. And I want you to go with me."

Mary breathed deeply.

"That's OK," she said. "I'm fine just watching you."

"Oh, come on," Billy insisted. "I'm tired of going on everything alone. You said your headache's better. Pretty please? Just one ride? The Corkscrew?"

"Uh-uh," she said. "You know I hate that one."

"Free Fall, then."

"Too high," she said.

And she thought: *House of Horrors. He's leading up to that one.*

He was.

"How about the House of Horrors?" Billy said.

"I don't think so," she said.

"Why not? It's not high. It's not even fast. And you always enjoy it."

"I just… don't want to."

"Ah, come on, Mom. There's no line."

So bright out here, I need another beer, Mary thought.

But Billy was leading her by the arm toward the turnstile, tended by a young man.

"Don't be a poop," Billy said.

"Wouldn't be fair to disappoint your boy," the young attendant cut in, grinning. He activated the foot pedal and Car Six lock-slammed into starting position. After handing over the tickets, Billy clambered aboard.

"Ma'am?" the attendant said. "We've got some people behind you. Please get in."

Taking Billy's hand, Mary did.

Car Six lurched forward, through swinging doors and into cool, musty darkness.

"Awful dark in there. I'd take off your sunglasses if I were you," the attendant said.

Mary did not.

The House of Horrors was among Ocean State's oldest rides, and it showed. Weather had opened cracks in the walls, and the cracks had never been repaired, and daylight seeped in at a dozen points. The backdrops needed paint. The black-light banks had missing and broken bulbs. The car springs had lost their flexibility and riders felt every turn, every stop, every joint in the rails. The exhibits had fared worse.

And the mannequins—those supposedly terrifying figures were like The Scarecrow in *The Wizard of Oz*, tired and frayed. In the competition with Six Flags and other national amusement-park chains that offered far more than any small family-run park, Ocean State had shrunk its maintenance budget in hopes of finally turning a profit after almost a decade of losses. Last summer, with the state in lockdown, had sent the owners begging to banks and the federal government for relief. Maybe with COVID fading now, this would be the year.

Car Six advanced deeper into the darkness.

Past the great white shark, it went. Past the hanged man, the drowned man, the guillotine, the skeleton from the grave, and the vampire. Now they were on the bottom floor, where the darkness was more complete.

"Like it?" said Billy.

"Very much," Mary said, sounding sedated.

"Told you so! Take off your sunglasses so you can see!"

Mary mouthed four words:

"I crave the darkness."

But with the clang of the car, Billy did not hear her.

The House of Horrors was, of course, more joke than horror: Only the youngest kids, kids younger than Billy, for whom parental guidance was advised, were ever genuinely afraid. From behind, Billy and Mary heard teenaged giggles mingling with the tired recording of the vampire victim's tortured screaming. More distant still, a match flared, and the sweet smell of marijuana mingled with the must.

Car Six rounded a turn, passed a red EXIT sign, and stopped. Ahead was a monster, one Billy remembered well—because, while not scary, it was weird, the weirdest thing in here.

It was difficult to guess what the designer of this one had in mind—if indeed this were the original design, and not the patchwork product of years of cheap repairs. The creature was non-human—that much was clear. It featured a huge head, blinking red lights for eyes, what had at one point probably been a thick coat of fur, and four arms with four hands, each of which had eight fingers with sharpened fingernails.

The monster roared, waved its arms and took a step toward Car Six.

Billy laughed and made a face as the monster opened its mouth.

Out popped its tongue.

Billy froze.

He remembered the tongue, more vividly than anything else about the House of Horrors. Everything else in here, he and Andres had agreed, was... well, boring. You'd get 50 times more scared watching a Friday the 13th film—and they'd seen several of those at Andres's, when Mrs. Washington was out.

But the monster's tongue—it wasn't any ordinary tongue darting toward your face, but a long thick tongue with eyes and ears and teeth and skin like a snake's. A creature inside a creature. A very nice touch, Andres and Billy agreed.

But it was not the same tongue this year; apparently, the old one had worn out and whoever had replaced it had missed the mark. This thing looked like they'd gone to the mall and bought nothing resembling a tongue but a familiar-looking stuffed animal.

Mary dug her nails into her son's forearm, and he looked at her and what he saw in the bleached starkness of those pulsating black lights wasn't the woman who'd seemed to enjoy her beer, or the woman who'd put up token resistance to this ride, or the woman who'd just conceded she really liked it, after all. This woman's face was contorted, and her teeth were bared and her eyes were wild and wide and red.

"Mom, what's wrong?" Billy said.

Mary did not reply. Did not seem aware her son was there. Struggling against the safety bar, she squeezed out of the car and hurled herself at the chicken wire protecting the creature.

"Don't Ma! You'll get electrocuted!"

Mary ripped the chicken wire away. For one endless moment, she stood, her face an inch from the monster's. Its tongue—that stuffed animal, or whatever it was—darted in and out as its eyes flashed red.

"Mom!" Billy screamed, and he was about to go after her when the House of Horror's controls clicked onto the next cycle and Car Six jerked and started moving again.

Billy turned.

And watched as his mother ripped the tongue from the monster's mouth.

"Mom!"

"Ordo!" she screamed. "Bring me Ordo!"

Billy had all but forgotten that word.

All but forgotten the cellar and that night after his party, when Mom had lain on the couch in darkness like this and the word had escaped her. All but concluded that none of it was worth worrying about because over a week had passed and everything had been OK.

So *it's someone's name*, he thought in the microsecond before Mary really went mad, really started tearing the monster display apart, really set in motion the chain of events that would injure a dozen people and prompt those who knew Mary to suspect that this time, she might be permanently losing her mind.

The state fire marshal's office—which would take months to conclude its investigation, and whose report would be cited in the flurry of lawsuits that would be filed—would record the moment of power loss at 1:14 p.m., Saturday, June 12.

The cause of the fire which leveled the House of Horrors and the adjacent arcade would be recorded as sparks from said horror house's "Main Monster Exhibit."

The cause of the sparks would go down as the "unexplained but violent" actions of one Mary McAllister, listed address 125 Forge Street, Providence, R.I., who, in the words of the fire marshal, "attacked the display, pulling it from its mount, severing and short-circuiting its 120-volt AC power supply."

The short-circuit had overloaded Ocean State's main power panel, killing electricity to everything at the park but the Free Fall, which had an emergency generator, and the administrative offices, which were on a separate feed.

Twelve injuries or fire-related complaints would be noted by the marshal, including the aforementioned Mary McAllister, who sustained smoke inhalation and minor burns; two children treated for mild shock; a man who experienced severe angina; a woman who suffered multiple bruises in a head-over-heels tumble down the slippery slope of The Flume, a water ride; a teenager who broke a leg jumping from the Ferris Wheel; and a woman who suffered a concussion when she fell and was nearly trampled by a crowd rushing to get out of the Beer Garden. The most badly injured was a boy whose shirt caught fire as he escaped the House of Horrors.

The state fire marshal would also record how Billy McAllister had saved his mother's life.

The fire had started easily and spread fast.

The monster's fur caught first. Made of some synthetic material manufactured in the days before strict fire codes, it smoked, then crackled, then burst into orange flames. Mary screamed and dropped the object of her wrath. It was fully consumed now. Fingerlets of fire licked at the wooden wall. It went up like crumpled newsprint.

From the wall it was a short distance to the ceiling.

There were more wires in the ceiling—wires feeding the House of Horror's lights and electric track. They shorted, sending off a fireworks display of sparks. A fuse malfunctioned at the main power panel. The panel arced and the smell of electricity was strong. The main breaker blew. The park's electricity went down, taking with it every ride but the Free Fall.

At first, no one seemed to care.

Like any park its age, Ocean State had its infirmities, occasional power outages and mechanical malfunctions among them, and Ocean State regulars—they were in the majority today—accepted that, almost as a precondition of admission. Sure, the park had died—but it would spring back to life soon! The authorities would take care of everything. Meanwhile, it was a sunny day. There were worst fates than being suspended for a few idyl moments from the Tempest or stuck on the starting incline of the Corkscrew roller-coaster. What a story to tell! Maybe it'd make the six o'clock news!

Ted Freeman, co-owner of the park and today's supervisor, was doing next week's staffing schedule when the phone rang, and his foreman barked: "Power's out."

"No fire, right?" Freeman said. "God knows we don't need that now. Or anytime."

"Not that I see," the foreman said.

"Good."

Freeman knew what to do. He called the fire department, the standard precaution, and then National Grid, the utility, then ordered his electrician to fast-foot it to the power shed. Thank God Ocean State's public-address system was wired into the office—the park's public-address speakers would work. You didn't want folks freaking out. The insurance company could refuse a settlement if he didn't follow the emergency drill, A to Z.

"Ladies and gentlemen, children of all ages," Freeman said into the microphone, "we're experiencing a minor power shortage which we expect to fix momentarily. If you are on a ride, we ask that you stay where you are and not attempt to climb out. Attendants will answer any questions you have. Thank you for your cooperation."

Once the ceiling went, the House of Horrors was fully engulfed. Flames broke through the roof. Smoke that would soon be spotted as far away as Newport rose into the cloudless sky, riveting the attention of most of the 2,145 people at Ocean State Park that day, as enumerated in the investigations that followed.

It took forty-six seconds before pandemonium was unloosed.

The first few moments were a period of horrified discovery. No one knew what to think. No one knew what to do. The people stranded on the Corkscrew looked over at the folks stuck on the Ferris Wheel, who peered down at the crowd marooned on the

Tempest, who were gazing at the kids dangling from the Yo-yo. People quickly realized:

Something is wrong.

Radically wrong.

It's not just that the power's out.

The place is on fire!

At the thirteen-second mark, the roof of the arcade caught.

At the sixteen-second mark, the first person panicked.

She was a mother who had accepted her daughter's dare to ride the Flume, which carried riders along a twisting water concourse that ended in a grand finale down a 45-degree slope. Mom and daughter's car had stopped three-quarters of the way up the chain-driven ascent to the slope top. Mom did what Ted Freeman had asked everyone not to: She stood, apparently in an attempt to see if help was on its way and lost her balance. She teetered a second, then toppled, crying in blind terror as she thudded down the watery incline.

Several hundred people watched her go.

Many started to scream.

But the screaming was worse in the crowd that had built outside the House of Horrors.

People were pouring out of it, stumbling directionlessly, their hands over their eyes and mouths. One boy's shirt was on fire. He looked like an actor on the set of some Vietnam War movie, a boy bundled in napalm.

The blaze was creating a draft that only fueled itself—and the fire that was eating away at the arcade, next door.

At the 46-second mark, as approaching sirens could be heard, people started to run. And jump. The emergency gates opened and Ocean State Park began to empty.

If the House of Horror's emergency lights had failed, Mary McAllister probably would have died. The ten other people inside with her likely would have, too. Miraculously, the batteries were charged and the lights and EXIT signs enabled those ten to claw their way out, just as they enabled Billy to locate Mary when the power died and Car Six stalled.

"Mom!" he yelled as he progressed through the smoke. "Mom, where are you?"

Billy started to cough, and his eyes started to tear, and he remembered what they'd been told in school two weeks ago when Officer Bob, the fire-safety guy, had come around for his annual talk. *Stay low. Crawl if you have to. The good air's on the bottom.* The only bit of advice Billy disregarded now was: *Get yourself out first. Don't go back into a burning building.*

"Mom! Where are you Mom?!"

He found her on her knees, doubled over.

She was coughing violently and clutching at her hair. One side of her scalp had been singed. Somehow, she'd managed to back off from the worst of the heat and flames—but not the smoke. She hadn't heeded any fire-safety guy's advice; head up, she'd tried to run to safety. The smoke had penetrated her trachea, her bronchi, reaching down deep inside her lungs to choke off her air. She was incoherent and on the threshold of unconsciousness.

"We gotta get out," Billy shouted.

Above them, the smoke roared like helicopter downthrust.

Mary was a slight woman, but there was no way Billy, even filled as he was with adrenalin, could carry her. He might have been able to drag her, but time was against them. Columns of flame were shooting up, the smoke pressing lower and lower, compressing the good-air zone. Eventually, Officer Bob had warned in that part of his talk dealing with the need for speed, the good-air zone would narrow to inches... and then disappear.

"You... gotta... crawl!" Billy shouted.

Billy shook his mother.

"Mom... crawl..."

This time, Mary responded. She began to move, first one knee, then an arm, then the other knee. Billy was looking for one of those red EXIT signs—and, incredibly, he spotted one, on a wall mere feet away.

"Mom... crawl..."

They were almost at the door when it was flung open from the outside. The attendant had watched, horrified, as people had come pouring out of the house. But that boy... that boy and his mom... the women who'd gone in there with her sunglasses on... there'd been no sign of them.

Fire extinguisher in hand, he'd come looking for them.

Chapter Ten: No memory.
Sunday, June 13

"Here, Billy," Uncle Jack said to his nephew as he handed him dollar bills.

"What're these for?"

"You looked thirsty. The soda machine's in the lobby."

"You want to talk to Mom alone, don't you," Billy said.

"Do you mind?"

"Are you gonna be long?"

"No."

Billy started off.

"Thanks, buddy," his uncle said.

"You owe me one."

"Yeah? See if you collect! Now scoot, pal!"

Jack watched as his nephew disappeared into the elevator that would take him down to the lobby of Rhode Island Hospital, where Mary McAllister had been kept overnight. Billy, who'd suffered minor smoke inhalation, had been treated in the emergency room and released to the custody of Amanda, who'd taken him home with her last night. They hadn't been able to reach Jack until this morning. After a call to Mary's doctor—he'd learned never to walk in on a scene like this uninformed—he'd sped down Route 95 to Providence.

The priest closed the curtains around him and his sister.

"The doctor says you're probably going home tomorrow," he said. "You don't know how relieved I am, Mary."

Mary nodded but made no effort to speak. The doctor had warned Jack of the Demerol haze he might find his sister in.

"You were lucky," Jack said. "Your burns aren't very serious. Your hair will grow back and the doctor says there shouldn't be any scarring. It could've been a lot worse. You could've... died. If it weren't for Billy, you probably would have."

"I know," Mary managed.

"He could have died, too. Or been badly burned."

"Yes."

"I don't say this to be mean," Jack said. "Only to say that your guardian angels were watching over you both."

Jack showed Mary *The Providence Journal* he was holding and drew his sister's attention to the front-page story on the Ocean State fire. Mary and Billy were mentioned a few paragraphs in, next to a photo of a young boy being loaded into an ambulance against the backdrop of the still-blazing arcade. Inside the paper, two full pages had been devoted to the incident.

Police Chief: "Miracle no one died," read the headline to one sidebar story.

Could have been like Station fire, read another.

It was a reference to The Station nightclub fire, which killed 100 and injured hundreds in West Warwick, Rhode Island, in February 2003.

"The paper quotes the fire marshal as saying you may have caused it," Jack said. "'Attacked exhibit, setting off sparks.' "

"How would he know that?" Mary said.

"Because according to this account, that's what you told the EMTs in the ambulance."

"I have no memory of that," Mary said.

"What happened in there, Mary?" Jack said. "Do you remember that?"

Mary struggled to raise herself higher in her bed.

"I know you're in pain," Jack said, "and I won't press it. But what happened, Mary?"

"Like I told the police: I don't remember. One minute I was getting in that car... the next I was... here."

Jack was silent.

"You don't believe me," Mary said.

But he did.

"You're like... them. You think I'm covering something up."

He didn't.

He'd talked to the doctors, who were convinced that whatever had happened inside, Mary McAllister genuinely couldn't recall.

Trauma of the magnitude Mary had experienced can cause amnesia, but before confirming that, the doctors had run a barrage of tests: a CT scan, X-Rays, EKG, EEG, some heavy-duty toxicology. They'd had the staff shrink do a preliminary psychological profile. A staff social worker did a workup. There were signs of a possible underlying depression, but as for what had triggered her outburst—that was the word Billy had told the staff in the ER, "outburst"—there was no major abnormality, none that was coming to light, at least. There was no indication of drug use, no convincing evidence of intoxication. An hour after admission, Mary's blood alcohol level had been .06, a not insignificant reading, but below the legal level of drunkenness and consistent with Billy's account that she'd only had two beers.

The doctors were tempted to believe the precipitating factor was nothing more mysterious than a bad case of sunstroke—Mary had been complaining of the sun, Billy had told them, had actually gone into that ride with her sunglasses still on. But they could not embrace that hypothesis until they had ruled out some darker possibilities: epilepsy, organic brain damage with roots in some childhood head trauma, tumor, late-onset psychosis.

With a report from Portland Behavioral Health in hand, they were recommending Amanda keep a close watch on her client over the next few days and that Mary McAllister undergo further testing sometime soon. Perhaps, they said, another admission to Portland would be appropriate, though it was nothing they could order.

For the moment, Mary seemed in no danger of harming herself or others.

"I believe you, Mary," Jack said. "That doesn't mean I'm not worried."

"Do you think I'm not?" his sister said. "I'm scared, Jack. One minute your life's OK... the next you're in a hospital and they're saying you did things—crazy things—you don't have the faintest memory of. And... I don't. Honest to God, I don't."

"No one is accusing you of anything," Jack said gently. "It's just that lately, you've been under some stress."

Mary cringed at that word. It was a euphemism, one that had fluttered in and out of virtually every conversation in those days that followed Jess's death, and then her mother's.

"What's that mean?" Mary said.

"It means I've been planning to talk to you about... *things*."

Another euphemism. Its history was even more painful.

"Now I get it," Mary said. "You think I was drunk."

"I didn't say that."

"The hell you didn't. It came through loud and clear. Just like with the police."

"No one's blaming you," Jack said, "not me or the police or anyone. But you have been drinking again, Mary, you can't deny it. You've missed two therapy sessions, too."

Mary flopped back on the bed.

"I give up," she said, raising her hands to her temples, which not even Demerol could numb. "You win."

"Oh, God, Mary," Jack said, stooping to hug her. "I'm sorry. The last thing you need right now is an inquisition."

But Mary didn't hear him. She was crying and wishing it was dark, wishing it was night, when surely the throbbing in her temples would stop.

Chapter Eleven: Mom-thing.
Monday, June 14

Mary was discharged Monday morning at ten. Amanda and Jack drove her home, fixed lunch for her and Billy, and made a run to the market, where they stocked up on soups, sherbets and ginger ale.

Except for a Tupperware container of leftover American chop suey that was growing mold in the refrigerator, there was no mess in the apartment, no dirty dishes piled up, no clothes awaiting the wash—peculiar, considering the chaotic circumstances of Mary's life. Or so Amanda remarked to Jack out of earshot of Billy and his mother.

At one o'clock, Amanda left, promising to check in tomorrow. At two, Jack followed. On his way back to Boston, he was stopping at AT&T, where he would pay Mary's landline and cell balances and have both services restored. Jack had not inquired why there was a hole in the wall where Mary's kitchen phone had been. There would be time for that and related matters later when Mary's recuperation was further along.

"Can you get me my medicine?" Mary asked her son as the dinner hour neared. She was in bed. Even though the day had been hot, and their basement apartment was warm, she was huddled under a blanket, with the windows closed and shades drawn.

"Sure," Billy said. "Where is it?"

"In the bathroom. In the medicine chest."

It was not the Rhode Island Hospital attending physician's policy to prescribe Demerol on an outpatient basis, but he had no compunctions about Tylenol with codeine and he'd sent her home with a bottle. The prescription wasn't as potent as Demerol, but it would smooth out the headaches Mary still complained of.

The last thing Mary McAllister needed just now, the doctor had confided to Amanda, was more fuzzy edges.

"Do you need a new bandage or that ointment stuff?" Billy shouted from the bathroom.

Mary felt the back of her head, where her hair had been singed and her scalp had sustained only first-degree burns.

The bandage was dry.

"All set," Mary called back.

Billy brought her the bottle. Mary shook out four pills, twice the recommended dosage, swallowed and chased them down with water.

"Can I ask you something, Mom?" Billy said.

"Aren't we all talked out?"

Mary attempted a laugh.

"Just one little question," Billy said.

Since Amanda and Father Jack had departed, Mary and her son had dissected Saturday again—relived it, reveled in Billy's heroism, thanked God they'd both made it out alive and no one had died or been seriously hurt. Mary's drinking hadn't come up and she hadn't tried to explain her behavior Saturday afternoon at Ocean State Park—nor had Billy prodded her. On both points, there was an unspoken agreement that, at least for the time being, certain things were better left unsaid.

"OK," Mary said. "Fire away."

Even before Saturday, Billy had been rehearsing this question, pondering how best to phrase it, wondering in what context he should—could—raise it. Saturday had made the matter urgent. But now, when he thought he'd finally gotten his courage up, he was faltering.

"Well?" Mary urged.

"Does the word… 'Ordo' mean anything?"

There, he was out with it.

"The word what?"

"Ordo."

Ordo

Ordo…

The word reached familiar neurons somewhere in Mary's brain, but it was with faint resonance, like a childhood memory that had been buried for years. For a moment, Mary tried concentrating—tried focusing on that wisp of a memory, hoping something solid would materialize.

Nothing did.

"I don't think so," she said. "Should it mean something?"

"You've said it a couple of times," Billy said.

"When?"

"When you were... asleep. And again Saturday, inside the House of Horrors."

"When I was... not myself?"

The sentence seemed to shame her.

"Yes."

"But I don't remember," Mary said. "I keep telling everyone, I don't remember. When will you believe me?"

"I believe you, Mom," Billy said.

He looked at his mother lying there in the gathering darkness, her head bandaged, the lines on her face long and deep. He stared, but it was not her features that struck him most. It was her size. Mom seemed small—smaller than before the weekend, if that was possible—small and fragile and weak. For the first time in his life, Billy realized there would come a day when he would be bigger and stronger than his mother. He realized that day would be soon. That thought scared him.

Supper was chicken soup from a can. Mary managed half a bowl and then, proclaiming tiredness, she announced her intention to get what the doctor had ordered: sleep. She'd barely finished speaking when she was dozing.

It was a school night. Andres wasn't allowed out after supper on school nights, either, and so Billy went to his room, where he started re-reading a Harry Potter book and played with his hamsters.

"What's it like to be so little, anyways?" he said as he held He-Man.

The hamster sniffed and ran a circle in the palm of Billy's hand. They were simple creatures, hamsters—simple but perpetually happy. Food, water, a fistful of fresh shavings every now and then, and everything was A-OK with those little guys.

"Huh, He-Man?" Billy said. "Do I look wicked big to you? Do I look like a giant? I think if I was you and you were me—you were the person and I was the hamster—I'd be afraid. But I'd never hurt you, He-Man. You know I'd never hurt you, don't cha? Huh?"

The hamster stopped circling for a moment. Whiskers twitching, it looked at the boy, seemingly acknowledging that Billy was indeed benevolent.

"Yeah, you know that," Billy said. "You know you're safe. No dog or cat gonna get at you, not while you're living here. Nope. We don't even have a dog or a cat."

Billy was absorbed in his thoughts when he thought he heard something.

A scratching kind of sound, seemingly coming from inside the walls, where maybe a mouse was loose. Hopefully, not a rat. Along with the sound came a blast of air.

Billy was spooked. He flashed back to the day Angel Iannotti had sucker-punched him.

The boy returned He-Man to his tank and listened intently. But all he heard now was his Mom's measured breathing.

Billy brushed his teeth, set his alarm, and bid his hamsters goodnight. He'd just crawled into bed when he heard:

"Get in here."

The voice shocked him.

It was his mother, speaking as she had inside the House of Horrors.

Heart racing, Billy waited to see if she'd speak again.

Maybe I only imagined it, he thought. *It's late and maybe the weekend is finally catching up on me. Maybe it's only my mind, playing a nasty but harmless trick.*

"I'm calling you," the voice demanded.

"Mom?" Billy said. "Is that you, Mom?"

"Get your ass in here!"

On ghost feet, Billy crossed his room to the door. The air in the hall was colder than in his room, but that wasn't what Billy noticed.

It was the smell.

That same seemingly source-less electric smell.

Billy swallowed.

"One more chance to get your ass in here and then I'm coming for you! You'll wish I hadn't!"

Mary's room was dark, but he could see the outline of her body under a blanket. Her face was veiled by shadow.

"Closer," the voice demanded, "so I can see you better."

Billy approached, his mother's features taking on definition as he moved in. Her lips were curled back from her teeth, and he could see her tongue, darting along her lower teeth.

He could not see her eyes, because she was wearing sunglasses.

"I want answers, not bullshit," snarled the voice, the voice of the Mom-thing as Billy would call it from now on.

"Mom, what's wrong?" Billy said.

"You fucked with me."

"But what did I—"

"It wasn't Ordo in there, as you led me to believe in luring me onto that ride," the Mom-thing said.

Billy thought: *Do I call Amanda? Andres's mom? The police?*

Then he remembered: *There's no phone. Uncle Jack said it probably won't be reconnected until tomorrow.*

The voice rose in volume.

"It wasn't Ordo! It was a fake! You fucked with me!"

"You're just upset, Mom," Billy said.

"Don't call me Mom!" the Mom-thing screamed. "Stop the bullshit! This is Z-DA you're talking to! Do you think I don't know who you are? Is that it? Do you think I believe you're just some boy named Billy? Do you think I have not learned you were a member of Ordo's party when he came to earth in search of me? Do you think I do not know you are not some stupid human boy but Theus, first lieutenant of the Priscillas' Security Forces? Answer me!"

Do I run?

"Do you want more medicine?" Billy said.

He was terrified and grasping at straws.

"I want Ordo," was the reply. "I want Ordo so that we may have it out, once and for all."

"You need sleep, Mom," Billy said. "In the morning, everything will be better."

"My patience is wearing thin," the Mom-thing said. "I'm tired of your lies. I want Ordo."

"But I don't know what Ordo is," Billy said. "You don't either, Mom. We talked about it. Remember?"

"You will lead me to Ordo or you will die," the Mom-thing said. "Deliver him, and you will be free to return home. I give you my word, Theus. It is not you who are my enemy. It is your leader, Ordo.

Deliver him and you shall be unharmed. And if you are troubled by loyalty, rest assured that no one but you and I need ever know."

The TV was on a local station in the background, but neither Mary nor Billy had paid any attention to it.

Now, Mary did.

The ten o'clock news was on, and various officials were discussing the report soon to be presented to Congress about the Director of National Intelligence's findings about the government's knowledge of unidentified aerial phenomena, as they are known in military parlance. Congress in December had ordered the director to disclose what was known.

"There is stuff flying in our airspace," Florida Senator Marco Rubio was saying. "We don't know what it is. We need to find out."

"Right now there are a lot of unanswered questions," said California Representative Adam Schiff. "If other nations have capabilities that we don't know of, we want to find out. If there's some explanation other than that, we want to learn that, too."

Rubio continued: "I mean, some of my colleagues are very interested in this topic and some kind of, you know, giggle when you bring it up. But I don't think we can allow the stigma to keep us from having an answer to a very fundamental question."

The Mom-thing was fading, and Billy felt the tension in the room lifting.

He could see Mary's face softening, her lips relaxing.

Whatever had taken possession of her had let go.

"It *is* a very fundamental question," Mary said.

"What?" said Billy.

"How it found me," Mary said.

"Who?"

"Ordo," Mary said.

"There's no such thing as Ordo," Billy said.

"But there is. When it's here, it speaks to me. And why me? It could have chosen a thousand other people. It must have sensed my vulnerabilities, a perfect environment for hiding. It crawled through that sewer in search of a victim, and it found me."

"I don't think that's what happened," Billy said.

"What else could it be? I think I should ask it. Yes, next time, that's what I will do. When it comes again, I'll ask it."

In this fleeting moment of clarity, Mary for the first time understood the reality.

I'm not crazy, she thought. *It's not all in my head. It can get into my brain, into my body, take control, and I am powerless to resist. But try convincing anyone of that.*

"You need sleep, Mom," Billy said.

Mary did not protest. She turned onto her side, away from Billy. For a few seconds, she coughed. Then she was quiet. Asleep.

She would not wake until late the next morning, when she would recall nothing, not even when Billy timidly—fearfully—asked if she remembered what had transpired in the semi-darkness of her room.

"My memory these days," she would say, again, "is not working."

Chapter Twelve: The finest casket
Wednesday, June 16

Billy remembers the events that followed Jess's death with searing clarity. He is at the funeral home, alone in a hall at a table with a coloring book and a box of crayons and a lollipop the mortician made a big show of handing him. Grammy and Uncle Jack are in the mortician's office. They've closed the door so Billy won't hear what they're saying, but when he strains, he can. The voices are muffled, but he can make out the speakers and their words.

He is horrified.

"And that model," the undertaker is explaining, "would cost twenty-five thousand dollars, a significant markdown from the list price we are delighted to offer. It does, of course, carry a 50-year warranty, unique in the business. Naturally, for such an investment we would be willing to arrange suitable terms for you."

"That is the one we want," Grammy says.

"But mother," Uncle Jack implores, "We don't need anything like that."

"I think her choice is a wise one," the mortician says. "The Batesville Promethean Bronze is truly the world's finest protective casket, built to withstand the elements. It is designed with not only your beloved's needs in mind, but yours as well—the peace of mind that comes of knowing that in this time of grief, you did your very best."

"We'll take it," Grammy says.

This is Jess *they're talking about*, Billy thinks, numbed by what he's hearing. *It's like they're talking about a toaster or sofa they're going to buy.*

"Can we be alone a moment?" Uncle Jack says.

"Certainly," the mortician answers. "I'll be in my office. Take all the time you need."

The soft tread of footsteps.

A door opens and shuts.

"I know how upset you are, Mother," Uncle Jack says. "And I believe your grief has affected your thinking, understandably. But I feel it's my duty to tell you how badly you're being had."

"With my choice of casket, I presume you mean?"

"Yes. Twenty-five thousand dollars—it's Jess's soul we must be concerned with, not her earthly remains. And that soul is safely with God, we can be sure."

"Mr. Hawthorne is a lovely man," Grammy says. "An upstanding member of the community. He was such a comfort when your dear father died, John."

"And he's pressuring you into something we don't need. Something *Jess* doesn't need."

"It is my money, my decision," Grammy says. "I want that casket."

"Listen to us," Uncle Jack says, "haggling like it was a used car purchase we're contemplating. But I feel very strongly about this, Mother. Dust to dust, ashes to ashes—the Lord teaches us the temporal nature of the human body. Remember how Jesus was laid to rest: in a simple tomb."

"I shudder to think of Jess," Grammy goes on, "in just any old wood casket. Wood cracks, John. Wood rots. Wood lets in the cold and wet. You heard Mr. Hawthorne. The casket I want is guaranteed to be airtight and watertight."

"She will be in a granite mausoleum," John says.

"And mausoleums do not leak? Mausoleums do not get cold?" Grammy has turned angry.

"You've been inside that mausoleum," she says. "Mold and mildew—even mushrooms—grow in there. Not to mention the bugs. Granite can't keep out ants."

"You weren't worried like this when Dad died."

"Your father was a grown man. Jess is a baby."

Grammy starts to cry, and as he listens out in the hall, Billy starts to cry, too. He wished they hadn't brought him. He wished Uncle Jack had gotten his way when he'd implored Grammy to leave him at home while they took care of "the arrangements."

("There's no need for him to come to the funeral home for this,"

Uncle Jack had said. "We should leave him home.")

("All alone in this big old house at a time like this?" Grammy had replied. "Please, John. Let's not be ridiculous.")

("I don't mean alone. We could get a sitter.")

("And that's the very last thing he needs: to be left with a stranger at a time like this. First, he loses his mother. Then us. Shame on you, John. He's coming.")

Inside the office, a door opens and shuts again. Billy, nearly blinded by tears, makes his way back to the table. He cannot finish his drawing. It was a drawing of a stick-figure girl and boy. The boy has no eyes or mouth.

"Have we reached a decision?" Mr. Hawthorne says after handing Grammy a Kleenex from a dispenser that shares his desktop with a pen set and leather-bound appointment book.

"Yes," Grammy says. "The Batesville Promethean Bronze."

"You will not regret it," Mr. Hawthorne says. "As the years go by, you will understand only more deeply the lasting value of your investment in your dearly departed."

Billy's memories fast-forward, everything passing in a soundless whir.

Past that night, past the wake the next day, past the second night, when his father, just off the plane from California, takes him out for a burger and fries at McDonald's.

Finally, the morning of Jess's funeral. The casket has been sealed, a rosary said, the guest book closed. Some of the flowers have gone out a back door for placement on the altar, and now they are in the first of a procession of black limos, crawling toward the church. Billy is between Grammy and Uncle Jack, his hand in his uncle's. No one speaks. No one cries. It's past the point where anything seems real.

An assistant undertaker—attired, like his boss, all in black— leads the immediate family to the front pew on the right-hand side of the church, which is filled to overflowing.

As they move toward their place, Billy scans the crowd, this vast sea of faces. He recognizes almost no one and wishes he could blink them all away. He holds Uncle Jack's hand more tightly and fights back the tears welling up inside him again. He will not cry in front of them, this ocean of strangers.

Uncle Jack settles Grammy and Billy in the pew—Grammy on

the aisle, Billy next to her—and then disappears into the vestibule, where he will change into his vestments. Uncle Jack is concelebrating the mass with Father Benoit, pastor of Saint Joseph Church.

Billy turns to eye that crowd again.

The same undertaker that brought them in is escorting Billy's father to a seat on the other side of the aisle—a move that, like choice of casket, Grammy negotiated during conclusion of "the arrangements." Grammy's dislike for William McAllister predated her daughter's brief marriage to the man and harden into hatred when he left before Jess could walk. During his stay in Blue Hill, Grammy has refused to let him into her house.

Billy cannot know it yet, but this morning is the last time he will see his father. When the funeral is done and Jess has been deposited at the McKay/Lambert family mausoleum, he will plant an impersonal kiss on his son's forehead, take down Uncle Jack's phone number, say nothing to Grammy, return his rental car to the airport, and head back to the West Coast.

The organ stops.

Uncle Jack has appeared at the rear of the church to greet the casket containing the body of Jess.

"The grace of our Lord Jesus Christ and the love of God and the fellowship of the Holy Spirit be with you all," the priest says.

His words are uttered with solemnity.

Billy cannot see the casket yet.

"I bless the body of Jessica Mary with the holy water that recalls her baptism," Uncle jack continues, "of which Saint Peter writes: 'All of us who were baptized into Christ Jesus were baptized into his death.'"

The liturgy continues. Holy water is sprinkled, incense burned. Uncle Jack turns and heads up the aisle, followed by pallbearers pushing the bier.

Now Billy can see the casket.

It approaches, soundlessly, the pallbearers looking neither left nor right. Doctor Cooke, Jess's doctor from Pitts-bird, is a pallbearer. A distant cousin Billy's only met once is a pallbearer. The chief of staff for the governor of Rhode Island is, too, along with three undertakers. But not Billy's father. Grammy was firm on that.

White gloves, Billy thinks—another of those Mad-Hatter thoughts that have become common this week. *Those guys are wearing white gloves, like the rabbit in* Alice in Wonderland.

"Why are they wearing gloves?" he whispers to Grammy.

"Shhh!" Grammy whispers back.

Uncle Jack and Father Bennett are about to start the funeral Mass when the head mortician, sitting next to McAllister, signals to the altar. Uncle Jack nods. Heads turn. A buzz spreads through the congregation.

Mary has made it, after all.

Staring straight ahead, she moves up the aisle supported by a counselor from Portland Behavioral Health Center.

Mary's presence had been the biggest question mark. Yes, they would do what they could to get her here, the center staff had said. Adjust her medication and drive her here and immediately back, to lessen the stress. Send her in the custody of a veteran counselor.

There was no guarantee she could make it without decompensating, but the staff understood the mother's grief and insistence. So they had decided to risk it.

But no one had told Billy there was even a chance Mom might make it. No need to get his hopes up like that. On that point, Grammy and Uncle Jack, who'd handled communication with the center, had agreed.

The counselor steers Mary toward her mother and her son.

Mary looks old and emaciated. The dress she's wearing no longer fits and you can see bone beneath the skin of her arms and legs. It's not only weight loss that bears testimony to Mary's ordeal. Her eyes are bloodshot, her lips bloodless and stiff, as if they were plastic glued to her face.

But it's Mom.

"Mommy!" Billy shouts as Grammy rises to let Mary into the pew. "Mommy!"

If it's possible to experience ecstasy in this nightmare, Billy does—if only momentarily. *Mommy's here! Mommy's come!*

"I love you, Billy," Mary says flatly.

"I love you Mom," Billy says. "I missed you so much."

"Shhh," Grammy says. "Both of you."

The Mass begins. They are barely into it when Billy's joy slips back to sorrow… and past sorrow to the horror he experienced at Jess's wake… and past that into something worse. Because they have parked the bier in the aisle next to them—so close he could touch it if he traded places with Grammy.

Thoughts so cruel that they might persist forever fill Billy's mind.

They've closed her casket.

Closed it for good.

Never to be opened.

With Baby Bear in her arms.

The church begins to spin. Slowly at first, like a ride starting up at Ocean State Park, but then with increasing speed, everything blurring together. Even sound is twisted: the incantations of the concelebrants, the strains of the organ, the soloist singing the High Mass.

Through that centrifuge of sound and motion something emerges steady and clear.

An anchor.

A voice.

Not his sister's, but a squeaky voice, not unfamiliar. He heard it yesterday, viewing Jess laid out in her casket.

Don't let them do this, it said. *The mission is not complete.*

He stares at Jess's casket, the voice begging him to intercede for a task he does not comprehend.

He stares at his sister's casket, expecting something to happen.

In the nightmare he will have later that day, something does.

The lid opens.

Jess sits up.

Stands up.

The bier rocks and Jess struggles to maintain her balance. She looks around, disoriented. She seems to recognize no one.

She seems to care only about Baby Bear, clutched firmly to her chest.

"Mommy," she says. "I love my Baby Bear."

A collective gasp escapes the congregation and then the mayhem begins.

People scream. People utter startled prayers. At the rear of the church, where those who know Jess only through the news media are concentrated, a woman panics. She flails her arms and bulldozes past the two people between her and the aisle and lumbers out of the church. Others follow her. An older man faints.

"Satan!" a man shrieks.

Uncle Jack and his priestly sidekick are paralyzed, as are Grammy and Mary.

Jess starts to climb down from her casket.

Somehow, she manages to get onto her feet without falling.

She takes a step.

Only Grammy separates her from her brother.

"Please, Billy," she says, "take my Baby Bear. Baby Bear doesn't want to go where I have to go. Baby Bear has to complete the mission."

Billy does not remember passing out at the funeral Mass or being brought to Grammy's house and tucked into bed. He does not know how long he's been asleep or what happened after he passed out, that terrible scene Mary caused.

"Where's Jess?" he asks Grammy when he awakens.

She is leaning over him, smoothing his brow and smiling angelically.

"She's with God now," Grammy says.

"But… she opened her casket and… and…"

"No, Billy, that was only a nightmare. I'm so sorry you had it. But Jess is dead. Jess is happy, because she's with God."

"But I… saw her… open it…"

"You fainted, Billy," Grammy says, arranging the blanket around him. "And now you need your sleep. We'll be downstairs if you need us. Now you must sleep. Here. Take this. The doctor said this will help you get better."

She spoons him a capful of cherry-flavored liquid. As he drifts off, he hears two voices downstairs: Grammy's and Uncle Jack's. Uncle Jack's is loud, Grammy's soft. Uncle Jack is berating Grammy for what she put her grandson through.

Chapter Thirteen: Increasing problems
Tuesday, June 22

"Ladies and gentlemen," Billy began, his voice quivering, "children and parents, honored guests, teachers, Mr. Monson, welcome to fourth-grade graduation at Carl Lauro School."

Billy looked out at the auditorium and understood—with more poignancy than was possible during rehearsal—how small and alone he was up here on stage.

Worse was the size of the crowd. The auditorium was packed. Not a spare seat anywhere. People were standing in the aisles, overflowing out the back doors, lined up like tin soldiers against the walls. There were 205 fourth graders at Carl Lauro, Providence's largest grammar school, and it seemed every kid had used his or her quota of four guest invitations for today's end-of-school assembly, a Lauro tradition.

Billy was older than a majority of his classmates—just turned eleven, not ten. He should have been wrapping up fifth grade. But the chaos of Jess's final year, when Billy had bounced between Pittsburgh and Massachusetts and Blue Hill, had set him back so severely that his teachers had recommended he repeat first grade. And he had.

To good end.

By second grade, Billy McAllister was beginning to realize his potential. By then, he was in top reading and math groups. His recent essay on "What School Means to Me" had won Lauro's annual contest; his prize was a medallion and today's address. What school meant to Billy McAllister, he'd written—and was about to recite to the graduation assembly—was "the chance to be whatever I want, even president."

Billy cleared his throat—there was a tickle he couldn't seem to dislodge—took the huge breath Miss Matthews, his teacher, had suggested and continued on.

"The subject of my essay is What School Means to Me," he said. "What school means to me is teachers who are very kind and very good. When you have a math problem, they help you out. Or when you don't know a word in reading, they help you look it up in the dictionary. If you... if you..."

So far, he'd been reciting from memory—but memory, he was discovering, can be fickle when you're on stage, the spotlights bright, the audience big.

"If you..."

His head was swimming.

If you... If you...

The rest wouldn't come.

Billy reached into his pocket for the written copy of his essay. He'd promised Miss Matthews he had it memorized, but she'd insisted he carry a copy just in case. Billy unfolded it, laid it on the podium, and scanned his handwriting. Everything was a blur. Mom still hadn't gotten around to buying him new glasses.

"If you get good grades," a voice whispered, "and just say no!"

It was Miss Matthews, standing behind him with the other teachers and Mr. Monson, the principal, who would be handing out the certificates when Billy finished.

Billy bent over.

Now the words were in focus. He found his place and took a breath.

"If you get good grades," he read, "and just say 'no' to drugs and alcohol and cigarettes, you will do well in school. After school, you could get a job as a fireman or a plumber. Or you could go to college and become a lawyer.

"Or you could run for office. You probably would want to start small, and mayor might be a good idea. As you get older, you could run for governor or senator. Then you would be able to run for president and maybe you would win. But to even have a chance, you would need good grades. That's what school means to me, the chance to be whatever I want, even president someday. Thank you."

The auditorium burst into applause, and only now—now that he was through it and his head wasn't swimming—did Billy dare to look again at the crowd. He couldn't see them with 20/20 definition, but he could make out the most important part of the assembly: the front row, where his mother, Uncle Jack and Amanda sat. That was part of the prize-winning essay package: the best seats in the house for the essayist's guests.

Leaving for school this morning, Billy was afraid Mary wasn't going to show up—or worse, was going to do something that would embarrass him.

Mommy hadn't acted crazy for a whole week, but neither was she back to her old self again. She complained of headaches, and she'd left the apartment only once, to do the laundry and buy a wig that matched her real hair.

Now, there she was, sitting in the front row and applauding just like everyone else. Billy was more relieved over that than having gotten through his essay. The only thing that looked off kilter was her sunglasses, which she was wearing most of the time, even in the apartment. But Billy could handle that. He could convince himself wearing them indoors was really cool.

"Thank you very much, William, for those uplifting words," Miss Matthews said. "They should serve as an inspiration to us all. And now Mr. Monson will pass out this year's certificates, starting with Mrs. Pritchard's class."

When the certificates had been handed out, the Pledge of Allegiance recited, and an a cappella rendition of "God Bless America" sung, the ceremony was over. Congratulations were in order, particularly for Billy, who had comported himself with the poise of an eighth grader. The handshaking and back-slapping and hugging took the better part of ten minutes, and then the crowd began to thin.

"I can't believe I heard no one say anything about Ocean State Park," Mary said. "Just a few dirty looks."

"You got lucky," Uncle Jack said, "and thank God you did. Some people are such vicious gossips. Last thing we needed was a scene."

Walking toward Uncle Jack's car, the conversation shifted.

"As impressive as you were," Jack said to his nephew, "I couldn't help but notice how close you had to get to your essay to read it. Are your glasses OK?"

"Oh, sure," Billy said.

"Really?"

Jack's tone suggested he suspected otherwise.

"You sure they're not giving you a little trouble?" he said. "Speaking as someone who's worn glasses since I was your age it looked like you were. Didn't you get a new pair a couple of months ago?"

"Yeah," Billy said, "these are my old ones."

"What happened to your new ones?"

"They got broken. But these are fine," he said.

Having been chastised by his mother for getting them busted in a fight, he wasn't about to tell the whole truth and risk her ire again.

"Mary?" Uncle Jack said. "Why is he wearing his old glasses?

"His new ones broke," she said, giving no further detail.

"And you didn't bring him to get new ones?"

"Have *you* ever been on SSI?" Mary said. "Or are you even aware of the paperwork and forms and delays required to get reimbursed for pretty much any expense?"

"Yes, I'm aware of the bureaucracy," Uncle Jack said. "I see it every day at Dean Street."

"Then you know what I'm up against," Mary said. "It's not like I have a money tree growing outside my apartment."

"But you have me and mother," Uncle Jack said.

"Like I haven't caused you both enough trouble," Mary said.

"That's what a brother is for," the priest said. "I'll drop you off at your apartment. Billy and I are going shopping."

Father Jack drove with his nephew to Providence Place Mall. At Lens Crafters, Billy was examined and fitted for glasses that would be ready in an hour. In the food court, the boy and his uncle ordered burgers, fries, and shakes and repaired to a private corner table.

Uncle Jack had finally pried from Billy the story of how he'd broken his glasses. Now that it was out, Billy wondered why he'd been afraid to tell him. Uncle Jack didn't sanction fighting, but he seemed relieved—no, pleased—that Billy's fight had been over Principle.

"You know I don't condone fighting," Uncle Jack was saying.

"Does condone mean approve of?"

"Yes. And under most circumstances, fighting's bad. It's not a civilized way to resolve differences."

"It's how wars start, right?"

"Right. That's exactly how wars start, with fighting that keeps escalating—getting worse and worse. But in this case, that kid never should have called Andres what he did. Words that make fun of disabilities don't belong in the language. They're disgusting."

"Angel's disgusting, too."

"It sounds like he's got some problems of his own," Jack said, "but that's still no reason for him to go around calling people bad names. I'm not saying what you did was exactly the best route you could have taken, Billy, but I do understand. There are plenty of people I wish I could take a pop at. The SSI bureaucracy, for starters. To keep a kid waiting this long just so he can see right—it stinks."

"You can say that again!"

Billy polished off his main course and Jack sent him back to order desserts.

"I have another reason for wanting to be alone with you," Jack said when he'd returned. "I think we need to talk about your mom. Just between the two of the us."

Billy was not surprised.

They'd started one of their private talks at the hospital but had been cut short by Amanda's arrival.

"I already told you," Billy said. "I don't know why she did what she did in there. She just wasn't feeling so good."

"She wasn't feeling too good even before Ocean State, Billy," Jack said. "I was worried. Of course, I'm a lot more worried now."

"She's getting better," Billy offered.

"Is she?"

His uncle's skepticism came through loud and clear.

"Oh, yeah," Billy said. "She is."

"She's not drinking? Or taking drugs? I know it hurts to talk about things like that, but if there's a problem, it's better we do. You understand that don't you, Billy? You understand that it's you and your mother I'm concerned with?"

"She's not drinking or taking drugs," Billy said, wondering if it was true—as Uncle Jack had once said—that grownups often have a sixth sense about when kids, especially ordinarily honest kids, are lying.

"Only the medicine they gave her at the hospital," Billy said. "The special Tylenol."

"Do you know what depressed is, Billy? It's the state she was in after Jess and then your grandmother died. Staying in bed a lot. Crying sometimes. Not eating."

What about calling me weird names? Billy thought. *Thinking I'm somebody else? Is that depressed? Does that have to with alcohol or medication? Or something even worse, a really bad mental illness, something worse than depression?*

Bill had read about some of those illnesses online and seen YouTube videos. Schizophrenia was a really scary one, an illness where you hear voices and see things that aren't there.

But Mom can't have that, Billy had concluded. *She wouldn't have good days along with the bad. Schizophrenia's only bad, all the time.*

"Mom's getting much better," Billy repeated. '

Uncle Jack considered this a moment and then pushed on.

"You know," he said, quietly, "it wouldn't do anyone any good not to be truthful with me. It wouldn't be good for you. And it wouldn't be good for your mom. If she needs help, we should get it for her. By thinking you're helping her you really could be hurting."

"She just had a couple of bad days, that's all," Billy said. "But everything's much better now, Uncle Jack. Scout's honor."

But of course everything wasn't much better.

And the truth was, Billy was scared.

Scared of Mom—the way he'd been scared of her right after Grammy died, when she'd been both drinking and doing drugs.

First, Ocean State.

Then that night a week ago.

Billy had never seen anyone act so angry, so intimidating, so strange.

Calling herself Z-DA. Calling me Theus. Throwing around that other name, Ordo. Screaming and swearing like I was her enemy. Like she wanted to kill me.

Maybe it IS schizophrenia.

The only thing he could relate it to was one of those movies Andres's older brother rented and he and Andres liked to sneak onto the Washingtons' channels afternoons Mrs. Washington at work. Like *Friday the 13th or Nightmare on Elm Street* or *The Exorcist* or *The Conjuring* or *Halloween*. Or TV shows like *The Haunting of Hill House* or *Castle Rock*, that sort of Stephen King stuff. Those were what Mary's behaviors resembled.

Except this wasn't a TV show or movie, which is what made it doubly scary.

It was his mother, and she wasn't pretending or horsing around or putting on a show. If Billy had come to any conclusion in the last week, this was it: Mom's brain was making things up and she believed them, just like they were real.

How many times the last week had he replayed those two crazy scenes: Ocean State and that night? How often had he turned them over in his own mind, hoping to make some sense of it all, desperate to find the clue that would explain everything?

As upside-down as it seemed, he wanted to believe that drinking or drugs *had* been at fault. He wanted to believe because drinking and drugs had caused problems before—and those problems had eventually been solved. Only she hadn't been drinking that much, at least not the two times when she'd been craziest. No drugs, either, none that he saw—except for the stuff she came home from Rhode Island Hospital with.

But she wasn't on that stuff yet when they went into the House of Horrors. And the week and a half she had been on it, there'd only been that one night of madness. If that stuff was the problem, wouldn't she have flipped out every night and day? Why would a doctor give someone something that would make her go bananas, anyway? Wouldn't that be against the law?

One question after another, all wrapped up into one humungous and growing problem.

There must be something wrong inside her head.

Must be schizophrenia.

What else could it be? Maybe the burns she'd suffered at Ocean State had made things worse, but they couldn't have caused her to flip out. Mary had been weird before going into the House of Horrors.

How do you fix something wrong inside someone's head?

Can you even?

There was some comfort knowing that during the last week, there'd been no more instances of bizarre behavior—nothing, at least, of that magnitude.

But there were limits to that comfort. If you looked at things closely—something Uncle Jack said wise people always did—you couldn't miss all the multiplying problems. Mom was more and more drifty, as if it anything you said to her took two or three times longer than it should have to get through. When she wasn't in bed or watching TV, she was tidying, even when there wasn't anything to tidy. Day and night, she kept her curtains down and wore those sunglasses. Billy was doing most of the shopping now. The newly reinstalled phone was off the hook half the time, and she never looked at her cell, that he saw.

And while for the most part she wasn't drinking much—or at all—there had been a couple of days when she'd gotten drunk, no doubt about it. So drunk her words came out wrong and she wobbled when she walked. Billy wondered how Jack knew. Maybe some adults had a sixth sense about drinking, too.

Should I tell someone?

How often had he asked himself that?

Who would I tell?

He'd ticked off the list of possibilities.

There was Andres—and Billy had come close to telling him, many times, but had never quite gotten up the courage.

Alex? He probably would've just made fun of him.

There was Mrs. Washington—but she was always busy, always at her jobs. You could forget the people who lived upstairs—they were new to the neighborhood, and Billy barely knew them.

You could also forget his teacher or his guidance counsellor, who called Billy into his office once in a while. They were very nice, but Billy had this feeling you couldn't trust them, that whatever you told them would somehow get to the principal, who wasn't so nice. The same went for Amanda. As good as she'd been to him and especially to mom, she had to write up reports to send to SSI or child welfare.

That leaves Uncle Jack.

If I tell anyone, Uncle Jack will be the one.

But I can't.

Because there was no predicting what he might do. As close as he'd been to Billy over the years, he'd been just as close to Mary. More than close, *concerned.* If Billy let on what was really happening... no way could he keep it to himself. He'd go straight to Mary, or maybe to one of those doctors who'd recommended a whole bunch of other tests anyway.

Mom would be sent away again.

Billy knew that.

Billy was more terrified of that than what was happening to his mother.

"Promise me something?" Uncle Jack said.

"Sure."

"If your mom's not feeling good, you'll come to me?"

"I promise," Billy said.

"Even if she's not feeling good only a little. OK?"

"OK."

"There's an old saying about nipping problems in the bud."

"I don't know that one," Billy said.

Jack laughed.

"Geeze. I thought I'd hit about every aphorism in the book by now."

"What's an aphorism?"

"A fancy word for an old saying. Nipping a problem in the bud means you address it before it becomes too big. In other words, early on. That's what I want you to do with your Mom. Little things—they have a way of becoming big things if you let them get away from you. And that's where you come in. Sometimes people don't know themselves when they're heading into deeper waters. They need someone else. Understand?"

"Understand."

"It wouldn't be snitching, Billy. Not when you love someone as much as you love your mom. It would be the right thing to do. And you have a finely tuned sense of right and wrong. The fight over calling Andres names is the latest demonstration of that. Now, it's been over an hour. But before we go get those glasses, promise me one more thing?"

"Sure."

"You won't break *these* in a fight?"

"Promise!"

"Now slap me five."

Chapter Fourteen: Something about Billy.
Tuesday, June 27

Another week passed. The West End municipal pool opened and Billy and Andres went every day. After, they played pickup basketball or touch football or skateboarded with Alex, steering clear of The Culvert. At home, Billy made his bed every morning and prepared supper every night. He kept his dirty clothes off the floor, cleaned the hamsters' cage, took out the trash Mom had so neatly bagged and piled in the corner of the kitchen floor that she obsessively washed and waxed.

Mom said she really appreciated all that.

Mom said he was being the best big boy.

With Jack's encouragement and Amanda's intervention with a teacher who'd been intent on dismissing Mary for her spotty attendance, Mary returned to the class she needed to complete so that the state Health Department would reinstate her social worker license, which had lapsed. Recertification would be delayed, but it would happen by summer's end and then she'd be able to work again at Our Bright Future, which had been so good to her through it all.

Physically, Mary was coming around, too. Her burns were healing nicely, the doctor informed her on a follow-up visit. There would be no scars. It wouldn't be too long before the wig was history.

Yes, on the surface, Mary was doing a tolerable job of going through the motions.

Underneath, she was coiled.

She found herself dwelling on Jess's death, and her mother's—how far she'd fallen both times, how steep the climb back had been. She was trying desperately to avoid parallels with the last few weeks, but increasingly, those parallels were impossible to avoid.

Except for those crazy spurts of energy, which roared up on her unbidden, then dissipated in mindless tidying binges, she was fatigued. No amount of sleep seemed capable of refreshing her—and some nights, she was getting 12 or 13 or 14 uninterrupted hours.

Because Jack had laid it on the line, she dragged herself to class, but her heart wasn't in it and she found herself drifting away half the time.

And she was hitting the bottle again—and finally feeling guilt over it.

When she'd started this spring, she'd convinced herself she could handle it.

It was just a couple of beers, after all. What was the problem with that? Didn't millions of people drink responsibly? Hell, her brother was usually good for a brew, and wasn't he a priest, praise the Lord and pass the altar wine? Even when a couple of beers had multiplied into a six-pack, and the six-pack had begged for rum chasers, and the combination of the two was producing blackouts and hangovers, as it had several times, she'd told herself she could handle it. Told herself everything was cool; everything was under control.

Only it wasn't.

Deep down—and not so deep down just lately—she knew the monkey was on her back again. She wasn't getting drunk every day, but the compulsion was growing stronger. On days she didn't drink, it was only because she consciously—constantly—summoned the willpower to abstain. Many days, that willpower was a shaky thing for Mary McAllister. Very shaky indeed.

But temptations of demon alcohol were child's play compared to what was in her head. Lately, it was like the ocean in the sixteenth century: uncharted, unfriendly, treacherous. Sail too far and you really might fall off the earth.

Even before Ocean State, she'd been getting headaches.

Mild at first—ibuprofen-treatable and infrequent—by late spring they'd developed into migraines once or more a week. She'd read about migraines online, at trusted sources like WebMD and the Mayo Clinic, and she confirmed the symptoms: the nausea, reminiscent of morning sickness; the pounding, as if the lining of her brain were the skin of a kettledrum; the extreme sensitivity to light; the auras; the sounds of noise and music and voices.

A migraine would explain all that, Mayo and WebMD assured her. It would explain why a conventional painkiller couldn't completely deaden the symptoms. It would explain sunglasses and keeping drapes drawn in a basement apartment, where direct sunlight penetrated but a few moments a day. It would explain the facial tingling, the confusion, as if consciousness would soon fade.

But what would explain Ocean State, when consciousness *had* faded, not returning until she was in a hospital bed, amnesiac, burned and the subject of an arson investigation for behavior so bizarre it had put her on the front page of the newspaper?

What could explain Billy?

Billy, this child she loved with an intensity defying description.

Billy, who, along with her brother, was all she could had left on this earth since losing Jess and then her mother.

Billy…

Something's different about him now, she kept thinking.

Not that there was anything concretely different. Her son didn't look different, didn't have questionable new friends or strange new tastes in music. He wasn't sick, hadn't suddenly developed some pre-teen chip on the shoulder.

In fact, using a reliable yardstick by which a parent can measure an 11-year-old's attitude—performance on chores—he was gliding right along.

But he just isn't…

him.

The first time the thought had occurred to her—scouting the hamsters before his birthday, oddly enough—Mary had dismissed it as nonsense. Just a momentary blip on her mental screen, as harmless and fleeting as a line from some forgotten song.

Only it wasn't fleeting. Once the thought was planted, it had grown into unshakeable conviction. She could hardly look at her son any longer without believing…

Something's different, in a bad way.

He's doing a good job of hiding it, but something's definitely not the same.

Her dreams lately only buttressed the conviction.

Her dreams—these sweat-soaked affairs that she couldn't articulate on wakening, couldn't recall in focus, only believed were unhealthy and insidious.

But this she knew beyond doubt: Billy appeared in them.

And when he did, the sleeping Mary talked to him as if he were…

A stranger.

A stranger with a terrible secret.

But it was worse than that wasn't it?

Because Billy wasn't just suddenly a stranger.

He was actually an entity, if that was the word, that she'd known for hundreds, maybe thousands, of years on a long space-time journey that had begun in a distant part of the universe.

And that entity, by whatever name, was her enemy.

Mother-fucking crazy, that's what that *is*, the still-rational part of Mary's brain thought.

But once she'd latched onto it, she couldn't let go.

One of my sworn enemies… sworn to defeat me, regardless of how long it takes or where the journey leads.

And in the year 2021, it had led to Planet Earth, where by late spring the United States and some other countries seemed to be finally emerging from a pandemic. Many survivors had endured stress and suffered great loss and their mental health had been affected. Those with pre-existing conditions were especially vulnerable.

Mary knew she fit into that category, and more than once, she had found herself on the verge of confronting Billy.

But what would she say?

How could she phrase such questions without looking loonier than she already did?

How could she be sure it wouldn't get back to Jack or Amanda or her doctor? Or the investigators leading the probe into the Ocean State Park fire?

She was already in it deep; Ocean State had seen to that. The last thing she needed to do right now was hand anyone more ammunition.

And she was scared, more than she herself could acknowledge.

The truth is, it's nothing so simple as a migraine, she thought.

And if it is a space-time journey, what proof do I have that anyone else would accept?

Mary obsessively cycled through other possibilities. A brain tumor. A particularly savage return of the depression that twice had proven its power to crush her. During her post-Ocean State hospital stay, the doctors had recommended further testing. They had made the appropriate referrals but had left the scheduling to Mary.

So far, she hadn't made an appointment. Clinics and doctors' offices weren't places she could handle just now.

Right now, it felt like the top of her head was about to blow off.

In a manner of speaking, it was.

Chapter Fifteen: Ambulance chasers.
Wednesday, June 30

The fiftyish man was seated at his computer in the inner office of Sierra Properties Inc. The concentration on his face, the smoothness with which he segued from the letter he was writing to answering the phone and back to his laptop—everything about the man bespoke competence. Juan Sierra, one might guess, was successful. And confident. And, judging by the absence of jacket or tie, down to earth as well.

In truth, Juan Sierra was all of those things.

As a young man who owned nothing, not even a crude knowledge of the language of the land he was adopting as home, he'd made passage to America from his native Panama 32 years ago with dreams—and a trade by which to achieve them.

Sierra was a carpenter, and he had what the best of them do: a true eye, a steady hand, a keen mind, and the desire to keep working while others take to the local bar come quitting time. He also had what only true craftsmen do: synergy with his chosen material. Sierra and wood—together, anything was possible. Fine furniture. Heavy construction. Restoration.

Staring with nothing but his hands and a good set of tools, he'd taken odd jobs, worked at building a reputation, saved every dime for future investment. And it had paid off. Twenty-four years later, Sierra owned four stores, an office building and eleven apartment buildings, including the old Victorian at 125 Forge Street. The Victorian had been one of his earlier projects, one of his best. Rescuing it from the wrecker's ball, he'd single-handedly gutted the place, then rebuilt it into three apartments. A few years ago, he'd transformed the basement into a fourth.

"Dear Mary," the letter he was composing began.

"It is with true sadness in my heart that I write this, but you give me no choice. Now you are four months behind on the rent. Many times, I call and write, and you say that you will pay but you do not. I understand that money has been tough for you and you have many bills but I have many bills too. Most landlords would not let one month go by without taking some necessary action. Four months I let pass and nothing from you.

"I will give you one more week and then you give me no other choice. I will have to go to the court and get an eviction notice. The pandemic emergency moratorium is over, and I will be able to. Please do not make me do this. Please pay me the back rent. At your monthly rate of $1,095, that's $4,380. If you pay half at least, maybe we can work out an agreement.

"Thank you,

"J. Sierra.

"President, Sierra Properties.

"cc: Neil Nolan, Esq."

Across Providence in an opulent suite in the Ocean State National Bank Building, two lawyers—a father and his recent-law-school-graduate son—were talking with a woman who'd spoken with an attorney before.

Mrs. Bartholomew was nervous and it showed.

But the lure of the law firm's TV news-hour ads had proved strong.

Got pain? Make THEM hurt! one of them trumpeted.

No fee until we win and we ALWAYS win! went another.

FREE consultation! went a third.

And the most recent: *Take THEM on a ride through The House of Horrors, where they pay YOU to go on!*

"My son still has nightmares," she was saying.

"Of course," said Rudolph Howe Sr. "It was a very traumatic thing to happen to a young boy. A very traumatic thing that didn't have to happen."

"Thank God, the doctor says there is no reason Robert shouldn't recover 100-percent," the woman said.

"Have you ever suspected that they could be telling you that just to make you feel better?" Howe Sr. said.

"Gosh, no," Mrs. Bartholomew said. "Dr. Butterworth is a very good doctor."

Howe Sr. chuckled—the sort of bemused chuckle that said: *Ah, but we on the front lines of the practice of law know better!*

"The truth is," Rudolph Howe Jr. said, "that no one, not even the most skilled cosmetic surgeon, can predict with complete certainty the extent of recovery from a bad burn. And your son suffered a very bad burn."

"The doctor says his scars will fade," Mrs. Bartholomew replied weakly.

"But what if he's wrong?" Howe Sr. said. "What if Robert's scars don't fade? What if, like another client of ours I have in mind, instead of fading they become more pronounced the first time he steps into the sun, say, on a beach? Does your son like the beach, Mrs. Bartholomew?"

"Yes."

"So did this client. But no doctor told him how easily ultraviolet light could undo the finest plastic surgery. This client today looks like... you hate to be cruel, but the word Frankenstein does pop to mind. Doesn't it, son?"

"You refer, I assume, to Mr. Langston?" Howe Jr. said.

"Yes."

"Frankenstein," the son, "would be a polite description. I would suggest more like Jason Voorhees, the character in *Friday the 13th*. Have you seen it, Mrs. Bartholomew?"

"Oh my God, yes," said Mrs. Bartholomew. "I still have nightmares."

"Let's hope it doesn't happen to your son," said Howe Sr. "But what if, God forbid, it should? And what if ten or twenty years down the road your precious Robert decides he wants to become a TV anchorman or get into movies? And he has everything—the smarts, the college degree, the ambition—everything but the *face*?"

Mrs. Bartholomew squirmed.

"I never thought of it like that," she said.

"In terms of career earning potential, those scars the doctor so confidently says will fade could mean a loss of hundreds of thousands, conceivably even millions, of dollars. Not to mention the dollar value that might be assigned to the pain and suffering you and your family already have incurred."

"Under the law," Howe Jr. said, "you are entitled to collect damages."

"Some would say it was not only your constitutional right, but your duty," said dad.

"Would I have to go to court?" Mrs. Bartholomew asked. "The thought of testifying in front of all those people... well, it terrifies me, is what it does."

"Ninety percent of these sorts of negligence actions are settled out of court," Howe Sr. said.

"Thank goodness."

Howe Sr. leafed through the folder he'd started the day when, smiling broadly, he'd read the newspaper story about the Ocean State fire.

Real-life horror in House of Horrors, the headline read.

Mrs. Bartholomew wasn't the only one to respond to the firm's ads. Howe, Stapleton & Steele already was representing two other victims.

"Would you like us to take your case, Mrs. Bartholomew?" Howe Sr. said.

"You're sure I won't have to pay anything?" the woman said.

"As our ad says, not a penny unless we're successful. Should we win—and we always do!—our fee will come right off the settlement. There is nothing you would pay up-front. Not one red cent. Boy, am I dating myself saying that!'

"Then I'd like you to take the case," Mrs. Bartholomew said.

"Splendid!" the older Howe said. "I'll put my son to work on it immediately. Rudy, we'll want to name the park as a defendant in our filing, of course. And the manufacturer of the ride—if they're still in business. And that woman... what's her name?"

"Mary McAllister."

"Right. The nut who started all this."

"But she hasn't been charged yet with anything," Howe Jr. said. "The investigation is ongoing."

"What *did* they teach you in law school?"

Howe Sr. laughed. His son had graduated only last year, and his inexperience had been a running joke since.

"Arson investigations, son," the father said, "are like airplane crash probes: notoriously slow. It could be months before she is charged. Even if she isn't, there's nothing preventing us from seeking civil damages. It's what makes America great! The right of every aggrieved citizen to seek redress under the law! Yes, we'll go after Mrs. McAllister, too."

"I have a friend who has a cousin who works with someone who knows her," Mrs. Bartholomew said.

This was Rhode Island, after all, the "I-know-a-guy" state where there was never more than three degrees of separation.

"And I don't think she has much money," the woman said.

"Well, we won't know unless we try, will we?" Howe Sr. said. "You'd be surprised what some of these people who 'don't have much money' really have. Hidden assets. A rich relative. We get a judge to garnish wages. Oh yes, you'd be surprised, Mrs. Bartholomew. Now I'm going to leave you with my son. He'll see to it that we get started on this immediately."

Chapter Sixteen: A fiery mess.
Wednesday, June 30

After doing the dishes—she was always doing dishes lately, sometimes the same dishes over and over—Mom had taken her purse and announced she was going to 7-Eleven for milk. She did not want Billy to run the errand for her, she said; she did not want him to accompany her, and that was an order.

Much as he might have wanted to go along, Billy knew better than to beg. He knew better than to ask for Fritos or Twinkies or gum or something that might prompt an indignant or angry response. Every dollar, he knew, was precious.

Because things had been smooth lately, with Billy on his very best behavior. To quote one of Uncle Jack's favorite sayings, lately he'd taken pains to dot every i and cross every t. He'd been taking out the trash without having to be asked. Stayed away from Death Alley. Home punctually for lunch and dinner. Gone to bed when Mom said it was time.

Oh, yes. Billy McAllister was being the best big boy.

As he waited for Mom to return, he wrote in his journal.

In their cage—their immaculate, cedar-scented cage—He-man and Wiggle were into their evening antics. No question about them being nocturnal. It was like they had little alarm clocks built into them. Every day, as soon as dusk had settled over the apartment, they got frisky. They chased each other, circles inside their wheel, nibbled at the fresh carrot Billy gave them every morning.

In the old days, Billy had read, people used to set their clocks by trains. You could do that with his hamsters and it probably would work.

Dear Jess, he wrote,

> *Sorry it's been so long. I've been very busy. School is over. We had graduation. I won the essay contest and got to read it at assembly. It was scary but I made it through OK. Now it's summer. I love summer, just like you. The weather's been nice lately. Andres and I go swimming lots. We shoot hoops and play touch football with some kids at the playground.*

> *I'm worried about Mom. She's been wicked weird lately. The worst thing was when we went to Ocean State. Something happened inside the House of Horrors. Mom flipped out. She attacked one of the fake monsters. There was a fire. A bunch of people got hurt. Mom got burned and had to go to the hospital. But she got out soon and they said she was lucky. She's got a wig now. She'll be OK but she can get in moods and be angry.*

> *So I'm trying extra hard to be good. That's what Uncle Jack told me is be as good as I can. Mom's always been sensitive, he said. Even when she was a little girl and he was the older brother. Like I'm your older brother. She was probably born that way is what he thinks. And things haven't always been easy for her.*

> *Maybe I wasn't as good as I should have been. Maybe I helped get Mom upset. Not by something big like doing drugs or stealing or hanging with the wrong kids. But little things can get grownups upset too. Not just the big stuff. You know that.*

> *Disobeying can bug them. Going where you're not supposed to, like I did in Death Alley that time chasing Angel. Getting your glasses broke in a fight. Sometimes it's hard to figure grownups out. Even close ones like Mom and Uncle Jack. It's best not to take chances. I don't. I try real hard to do all my chores and obey good*

and not ask for anything that costs a lot.

Well, that's about it. I keep my journal hid where nobody can find it. That's 'cause somebody might think it was strange. I don't think it's strange. You're my sister. You'll always be my sister, even if you aren't right here. Uncle Jack says when you're in heaven you can watch everything we do down here. He ought to know, he's a priest.

So I hope you're watching and taking care of us. Our own guardian angel! Uncle Jack says you could do that, too. Will you be that for me and especially Mom? Thanks, Jess.

Love,
Billy.

The ruckus suddenly from the hamster cage caught Billy's attention. Something had spooked hiss pets and now they were squealing. Squealing and hurling themselves against the glass walls of their home in a desperate bid to escape.

"What is it guys?" Billy said.

Their frenzy startled him.

Then Billy heard it—the sounds of Mom returning that he'd been waiting for: The close of the outside door, followed by familiar footsteps across the kitchen linoleum.

The footsteps stopped.

The hamsters, too.

Their frenzy had given way to paralysis.

"Mom?"

No response.

Just the slight whiff of something foul, like a backed-up sewer main.

"Mom? Is that you?"

Billy's eyes flitted toward the hall, then back to the clock he'd been watching since wrapping up his journal. Mary had gone out at 8:30 and it was almost 10:30 now. For the last hour, Billy had pondered how late she'd have to be before he picked up the phone and called...

He wasn't sure who he'd call. The store first, maybe. And then, if it got to be midnight, maybe Uncle Jack.

"Mom?"

The voice that answered wasn't his mother's.

It was more like a man's: timbered, almost hoarse.

It said: "*Mom?* Are we interested in playing you foolish games again?"

A chill crept down Billy's spine.

"Did you... get the milk?" the boy said.

"No games, Theus," the voice said. "The time for games is past."

Mary was in Billy's doorway now, blocking escape.

In the light, she seemed bigger than she really was, taller and heavier, as if she'd gone out for milk and come back bigger.

"But I'm not playing any games," Billy said.

"Oh, my," the Mom-thing sighed. "You are even stupider than I could imagine. But I—I am not stupid. Your true identity has been confirmed and your incursions into my thoughts have been recorded, as have your pitiful attempts to neutralize me. But I have outfoxed you, Theus. You and Ordo and the rest of your crew have come halfway across the universe, but still I continue to outmaneuver you."

Crazy laughter filled the apartment.

Billy wondered if they could hear it upstairs. He wondered if they would notice the sudden smell of electricity and think something was burning.

"I remember you from the war," the Mom-thing said, and now the hysteria in her voice was moving down a notch.

"You were a coward," it continued. "A coward and a fool. I look at you now, cringing like a child, and I am reminded that some things never change. I remember you being in Priscilla High Parliament the day Ordo personally handed my death sentence down. I remember the banner you waved, the way you whipped that crowd into frenzy."

"I was—"

"Shut up, Theus. This is my show now. Of course, you were not on hand when I escaped. Ah—the escape! Thinking of it even now brings pleasure. Such exquisite timing! The war seemingly ended after so many years, your entire nation giddy with victory, the partying and dancing across the land, Ordo, your so-called fearless leader, issuing proclamations and hoisting toasts and bestowing medals.

"And I, Z-DA—the 'notorious war criminal' as the news reports screamed—I, 'Killer of Thousands'—'Heinous Butcher'—'Last of the Lepros'—condemned to death. Yes! The rest of my people slain and only me standing between you and extinction of my race!

"And what should happen? Do you remember the unexpected little glitch that arose? Z-DA escaped, that's what! I, Z-DA, sentenced to die at sunrise the next day—gone with the wind! What embarrassment for the Security Secretariat! What shame!

"Me free—and free to propagate—free to begin my campaign to attempt to conquer anew! Panic sweeps the land! A national pall where only yesterday was great triumph! Celebration giving way to emergency cabinet meetings! Search teams dispatched throughout the galaxy—with the great President Ordo himself taking charge of the proceedings. This time, no prisoners to be taken. This time, the standing order is: Kill on first sight!"

"Mom, you need—"

"Shut up, you fool! Did I think that eventually you would find me? I have not survived so long by being naive. I knew that no matter how safe the haven—and this has been, until the arrival of your comic crew, a *very* safe haven—eventually the odds were that I would be discovered. Although, as I had hoped, it took a long time.

"Because why would the Security Forces look to this planet when so many others would make better sense—would offer safe and peaceful haven for my health to be restored, and then to embark upon the rebuilding of my race? This wretched planet called Earth is neither safe nor haven, but a cesspool of war and pollution that is endangering the survival of every species of life from amoeba to primate—and now this pandemic, a scourge upon the land.

"But for this very reason—the unlikelihood of Planet Earth affording me the necessary time to feel my strength return—I chose here. And on this earth, I chose a city, a neighborhood and a dwelling that would not top Ordo's list. Until, having exhausted all other possibilities, he did identify this place as a hiding spot for me."

The Mary-thing paused, allowing Billy to catch his breath.

When he did, it was with hope that his mother would return to her senses, might listen to a new tactic that had occurred to him: gentle reasoning. Amanda had encouraged him to be patient and empathetic.

"But you're Mary McAllister, Billy's mother," the boy said.

"What proof do you have?" the Mary-thing said. "And if I *am* Mary McAllister, am I her all the time? Or do two entities share the same body, alternating between hiding and appearing? First one, then the other, back and forth, back and forth. Just like you, Theus—first Priscilla, then human child, though I do say you seem to prefer the boy persona. Whatever, the charade is destined to end soon."

"But I am Billy," the boy said.

"Have we not been over this ad nauseum? Do you wish me to pay you a compliment, Theus, for what admittedly is a most clever disguise? Then I shall! Good work, Theus! Bravo!

"And now, the nitty-gritty. My hope was that I would have sufficient breather to propagate, to assemble the nucleus of a force that would be able to resume the resistance—and eventually, reclaim what is mine. And I have had that time. I feel stronger than ever and eager to resume the cause. But what should happen as I prepared to return?

"Lo and behold, the mighty Ordo, distinguished navigator, decorated warrior, leader of all the Priscillas—bringing his craft in for what should be a routine landing, something he should be able to do in his sleep, what should befall him? He crashes in a fiery mess! Craft destroyed! With it, all your weapons! All members of his crew but you instantly incinerated and he too disoriented to use the power he has—the power of Prana—to bring them back to life. The mighty Ordo is gravely wounded, no opportunity to send out a distress call!

"Let us pause here for a tear or two, Theus, for your beloved departed comrades."

A tear ran down the Mary-thing's cheek.

"That's mock crying," it said. "I hated every fucking one of them. Where were we? Ah, yes, the rest of the story. I learned, of course, very quickly of your circumstances. Not so quickly as to find you on the scene—you had taken Ordo and fled by the time I traced you to this planet—but quickly enough to discover the circumstances you operate under now. An analysis of the situation reveals that Ordo is recuperating in some safe place, whereabouts as yet unknown to me."

"But—"

"But since I was able to trace him to Earth, why cannot I not identify precisely where he is without your help? You know the answer to that, Theus: Because he has wrapped himself in a protective shield that blocks the wavelengths of my sensors. But not yours! You are in regular communication with him! You know where he is and what he is doing: hiding, regaining strength, awaiting the arrival of fresh forces. For distress call or no distress call, your loss and his has been noted and help will soon be dispatched.

"But by then, it shall be too late. By then, your stubbornness and resolve shall have melted in the face of your cowardice, and you shall have led me to Ordo, where I will drive the stake through his heart before help can arrive."

"But—"

"But why, knowing Ordo is not far, do I not just flee for my life? Is that the question on your lips? Simpleton! Because this time it is not Ordo backed by the might of his empire. This time, it is only him—a hapless version of his former self. This time, it will be him against me. And this time, I shall prevail. Ordo shall die! The Priscillas' will shall be broken! The Lepros—our race shall regenerate itself, I assure you, the way a starfish losing a leg regrows it—ah, the wonder of our species!—and we shall then begin our triumphal march to glory!"

Billy was listening, alternately spellbound by this tale Lucas might have spun and terrified that its teller was his mom. Terrified that she seemed to be living one of her science-fiction stories—and believing it as if the real world had ceased to exist.

Now, another emotion surfaced: an indefinable sadness because sooner or later, somebody was going to find out. Sooner or later, Mom was going to lose it like this in public, and there was going to be a big scene and it wouldn't be like at Ocean State, when no one but Billy had seen her—when no one, not even Billy, could really be sure of what had gone on. The police would come, and the doctors would be called in and Mom would be taken away and...

He started to cry.

"Coward!" the Mom-thing shrieked. "Think you that with

some clever emotional outburst I will be distracted? Nothing could be further from the truth! Ordo has been here in this city! Perhaps in this very apartment! Many times have I sensed his presence! Traces of him are strong still, particularly near you! Last time, I gave you your chance to be cooperative. I promised you your freedom—and in return I received nothing.

"I can no longer fiddle about. Time is fleeting. Who knows when reinforcements shall arrive? I have been very patient with you, but now my patience is wearing thin. I shall give you one day—one month, in earth time—to bring me to him and if you do not, then you shall die. For now, that is all."

Billy composed himself. The smell of electricity lingered and it was uncomfortably hot.

She needs a drink of water, Bill thought. *That will help her.*

The boy crossed the kitchen to the refrigerator, found a bottle of water, and poured a glassful.

He brought it to his mother and was handing it to her when he tripped.

The water splashed Mary's upper body and face.

She screamed.

"You idiot, what have you done!" she shouted.

She was writhing now.

Smoke rose from her head.

The smell of electricity was stronger than ever.

She ran past Billy into her room, slamming the door behind her.

Billy was crying and scared, for Mom was not quiet in her room this time.

Mom was talking to herself again and swearing and there was a static sound, like an old-fashioned AM radio between stations—even though she did not have a radio in her room.

The lights flickered and died.

There was a pale glow and then a second of darkness and then the lights came back on. It was like during the approach of a thunderstorm, when some distant circuit is interrupted, the current wavers, and then everything is normal again.

The reek of electricity, so strong before, was overpowering now.

It was nearing midnight.

Billy had a choice. He could take his chances in his room, next to hers or he could leave.

He left.

Chapter Seventeen: Stand by me.
Thursday, July 1

Billy walked. He walked to Andres's, but the lights were out. He walked to 7-Eleven, but it was closed. Too dazed for tears, his thoughts a tangle he couldn't unravel, he walked the landscape of urban America in the third decade of the twenty-first century: past a couple arguing in a car; past two dudes sharing a joint; past a hooker and her john; past a man wearing a winter coat and clutching a paper bag and sleeping, oblivious to all, on a bench in Armory Park.

Somewhere over on the fashionable East Side, where people with wine cellars and staffs dreamed more comfortable dreams, a church bell struck midnight. The final peal was still in Billy's ears when a police cruiser started up the street toward him. His first instinct was to flag them down, blurt everything out, ask them to call Uncle Jack, then go with them into his home to straighten everything out with his mom.

At first, the cops probably would be nice to Billy. They would tell him everything was going to be OK. Then they would take him to the station and call Child Welfare, which would put him a group home. Everybody knew about group homes. How some kids got sucked into that system... and never saw home or their mom or their favorite uncle or their pet hamsters again.

Billy ducked into a driveway, where he hid behind a garage until the cruiser had passed.

Another hour passed.

Billy, who'd never stayed up past midnight, was fading. All that energy Mom had scared up in him—it had mostly drained away, leaving numbness and the desire to sleep.

Billy emerged from shadows and crossed Forge Street into the entryway of their apartment building, this once-grand Victorian. He tried the door handle.

It was locked.

Billy crept around to the back of the house. Mom's window was shut, her shade drawn. There was no sound. If she was in, she was asleep.

Or waiting up for me.

Until now, that possibility hadn't occurred to Billy.

Walking, he'd spent most of his time trying to convince himself that Mom had been high—that she'd taken some powerful shit, angel dust maybe—and that the weirdness would pass as she slept.

He'd resisted being drawn down into his deeper fear: that Mom was crazy with the worst kind of illness, schizophrenia.

That sick as she was, she really did have it in for him.

That she's waiting.

Awake and waiting outside my door.

Maybe with a knife.

Suddenly, Billy was hyper-alert, every sense tuned to the night. He was at his bedroom window now. It was open, but with its bars, there was no way he could crawl through.

But he could look in. His room, like the rest of the apartment, was black, and he did not see that his bed had been stripped to its mattress. He could not see his dresser, every drawer open, his clothes spilled in a heap on the floor. He could not see Wiggle, paralyzed with terror in a far corner of their cage.

He could not see He-man, next to Wiggle, dead.

Dawn came on a palette of pinks and reds. A cold front was pushing down from Canada, bringing with it the threat of thunderstorms again. In the back seat of the car Grammy had bequeathed to them, there was movement.

Billy was awake.

He stretched, rubbed the sleep from his eyes, slicked back his hair, cleaned his glasses on his shirt, rolled the window down, looked around the yard—lingering a moment on the old wooden fence that shielded Death Alley—then turned his full attention to the house.

The three families who shared the old Victorian with the McAllisters were stirring.

From a TV on the top floor, Billy heard Al Roker prattling on about clouds over Wyoming and the jet stream continuing to bring high humidity and temperatures and the threat of soaking rain to the Northeast. Billy smelled bacon being fried in another apartment. A dog yipped and yapped. The back door opened and Frodo, the good-natured terrier owned by the folks on the second floor, came bounding down, intent on relieving its bladder.

Inside the McAllister residence: nothing.

Nothing Billy could see or hear, anyway: Mary's shades were still drawn, the window still closed and locked.

Billy got out of the car. Frodo had been doing his business by the front grille; spying Billy, he came trotting over, tail wagging. Billy shooed him away and slunk toward the house.

The door was still locked and he had forgotten to take his key.

He could knock—sooner or later, he *had* to knock—but not now. If Mom really was asleep, she wouldn't appreciate being disturbed. And if she wasn't asleep...

He couldn't deal with that just now. Maybe a little later on, when he wasn't groggy and hungry.

Slicking back his hair again, ashamed he hadn't brushed his teeth or changed his clothes or showered, he set off for Andres's.

"Hi, Billy," his friend said at the door. "Come in."

"Is your mom at work yet?"

"Hell, yeah," Andres said. "She's always out by six thirty. And my brother's still asleep, the lazy ass. Wanna play Nintendo?"

"Well... not really."

"Wanna shoot some hoops then?"

"Nah."

"You want some Lucky Charms? Like, are you hungry?"

"What I really wanted was to ask a question," Billy said. "Something that's gotta be only between blood brothers."

"You got it."

"You can't tell anyone what we talked about."

"Like you think I don't remember our vows?"

"You sure your mom's at work?"

"Yeah, man. What's the question?"

Andres stared at his friend.

What was wrong with this picture?

It wasn't the hour—Billy had been at his door lots of mornings by seven thirty, even seven once or twice. No, it was the fidgeting, the way his friend's foot was nervously tapping, how he couldn't look Andres straight in the eye. Billy's gaze was bouncing all over the kitchen, as if he still didn't believe Mrs. Washington was really at work or Andres's brother was really asleep.

"OK," Billy said, inhaling deeply, "what's it like when somebody loses his mind?"

"You mean goes crazy?"

"Yeah, like really crazy. Locked-up kind of crazy."

"You see things that aren't there. You think people are watching you when nobody's around. You talk to yourself—or to someone imaginary. Even to the TV, like in *Poltergeist*. Wacko stuff like that. Why?"

"Nothing. I was just curious, that's all."

"You're awful serious for just being curious," Andres said.

"Well that's all I am."

Andres didn't believe Billy, but his friend's comments had prompted a memory.

"My mom knew someone who lost her mind," Andres said. "Maggie Mercier. She lived down the other end of Foundry. In a back apartment right on Death Alley, just like yours. Did you know her?"

"I don't think so."

"Must've been before you moved in. Anyway, one night—a summer night, wicked hot and everything, everybody was outside, running through the hydrant—she came tear-assing down the street, screaming that Martians were after her."

"Crazy," Billy said.

"Totally," Andres said. "She said they'd kidnapped her kids and gone inside the TV with them, where they were being held prisoner."

"Holy shit."

"And that wasn't all. There she comes, running and screaming down the street, everybody watching—and she don't have any clothes on."

"Really?"

"Really. Somebody called 911 and the cops came and took her away. And that's the last anybody saw of Maggie Mercier."

"What about her kids?"

"She didn't have any kids. That was the point: she was crazy.

She'd made everything up, even the part about kids."

"When she came running down the street, was she talking in a different voice?" Billy asked.

"You mean like loud?"

"No, I mean… different. Like it was somebody else speaking, not her."

"No," Andres said, "it was her voice. But you remember Dickie Raymond, don't you? You gotta remember Dickie Raymond."

"He's the guy who killed those kids."

"Right."

More than a year had passed since the Dickie Raymond case, a real-life nightmare that had plunged a region into fear.

Three different and unrelated children, each strangled, a month apart.

It was another instance of Sick Americana: Serial killer on the loose, with attendant media hysteria, a concerned mayor throwing every available cop on the case, a no-nonsense governor offering the services of the National Guard, the FBI called in. And an entire state amazed—chagrinned?—when the killer turned out not to be a Ted Bundy or a John Wayne Gacy or a Jefferey Dahmer, but Dickie Raymond, a skinny, bespectacled 19-year-old who had been horribly neglected and abused since infancy, and who, in his most severely psychotic mode, envisioned himself the manservant of Satan.

Dickie Raymond, this pitiful young man whose only crime was having been born with an imbalance of chemicals deep in his brain, an imbalance exacerbated by a lifetime of trauma. A sad double-whammy of nature and nurture.

"On the news, they said Dickie Raymond had been hearing voices," Andres said. "The voice of the devil. And he was talking in different voices when they arrested him. Like the girl in the Exorcist. Remember we watched that? It was an old movie but still good."

"Can crazy people hurt people they like?" Billy asked.

"Of course they can," Andres said. "Look at Dickie Raymond. He killed three boys."

"But he didn't know them," Billy said.

"Oh yes, he did. They weren't relatives or anything, but they lived in his neighborhood. He used to see them on the playground. Used to buy them Popsicles. That's what my brother told me. And

he knew Dickie Raymond. Why are you so interested in crazy people all of a sudden?"

"Just something I saw on TV, that's all," Billy said.

"When?"

"This week."

"What show?"

"I forget the name. It was a TV movie."

"I didn't see anything like that," Andres said.

"OK, it's not someone on TV," Billy admitted.

"Who is it?"

"Promise not to tell?"

"Cross my heart and hope to die," Andres said.

It's time, Billy thought. *Time for me to tell someone. I can't keep
it to myself anymore.*

"It's my mom," Billy said.

"Holy shit."

"I think she's going crazy and I don't know what to do. You
gotta help me, Andres. You can't tell anyone, not even your mom,
but you gotta help."

It gushed out then—a long telling of the events of the past
month.

"This is way worse than she had to go away to that place in
Maine that you told me about," Andres said when Billy was done.

"Way worse," Billy said. "Those times, she was just really,
really sad 'cause of my sister and then my Grammy dying."

"Do you think it's drugs?" Andres said.

He was trying to be helpful but not sure he was. What Billy
had told him was so whacked-out, so beyond super-crazy that
only LSD or some drug like that could be responsible.

"Maybe," Billy said.

"She ever done acid?"

"I don't think so."

"Well, crack will stew your brain something wicked, too,"
Andres said. "Kind of like LSD, is what I've heard. You think she's
on crack?"

"I've never seen her do it," Billy said. "I think she did when she
was with Crimson Vanner, but that was a while ago."

"You gotta take it to her, Billy," Andres said. "Be up-front about
it. That's what they say in health class, when they're doing Just Say
No. Remember? You gotta ask."

"And then what?"

"And then," Andres said uneasily, "you gotta go to a grown-up. Somebody you trust. Somebody like your Uncle Jack."

This time, Mary was at the door to greet Billy.

"What time is it?" she said.

She was hazy, as if she'd just gotten up, and she looked a mess: uncombed hair, circles under her eyes. But there was no madness in her voice.

"It's nine thirty, Mom," Billy said.

"How come you left without waking me?"

"Don't you remember last night, Mom?"

She didn't.

Not accurately.

She did remember needing something at 7-Eleven. She did remember leaving, walking, getting dizzy, having to sit down... then being overcome by a comforting feeling, a womb-like feeling of darkness and warmth... and beyond that, anger and rage, the comfort giving way to something hostile and uncontrollable.

Next she remembered, it was morning.

This morning.

She was in her bed.

Wearing sunglasses.

Her hands were filthy.

The sofa was against Billy's door.

And when she'd moved it and walked in, Billy's room was a wreck. She'd managed to restore it to a state of normalcy before he'd seen it, but there was nothing she could do about He-man, cold and dead.

"What happened last night?" Mary said. "I wasn't drinking. I didn't even have a beer. Did I?"

"Not that I saw. But you were acting... strange."

"Tell me, Billy," she said. "Tell me everything."

"You told a very strange story," he said. "It had to do with aliens, and some kind of war on another planet and a spaceship coming to earth and crashing and a big fire. You said I was on board. You said my name was Theus. You used that word Ordo again. You said he was a leader and that I worked for him."

"I said all that?"

Billy nodded.

"And you called me a coward," the boy said.

"Oh, God, Billy, I'm sorry. You know I don't think you're a coward. You're the best boy a mother could have. But I don't remember saying that—or any of it. Honest I don't. Do you believe me when I tell you that?"

Billy closed the door and took another step into the kitchen.

But he did not sit down.

"I guess so," he said.

"It's the truth. I swear to God it's the truth."

"I have to ask you a question," Billy said. "And you have to answer it honestly."

"Ask me anything."

"Are you doing drugs?"

Mary looked at her son and saw the hurt and confusion.

"I'm not doing drugs," she said. "I almost wish I were. At least I'd have an explanation. Because I don't know what's happening to me, Billy. All I know is I'm scared. More scared than I've ever been in my life."

Tears were not far away now.

"Can I ask you a question?" she said.

"Sure."

"No matter what happens, you'll stand by me, won't you?"

"Of course, Mom."

"Even if things get really bad?"

"Of course."

"I love you, Billy. More than anything in the world."

"I love you, too, Mom."

"Will you give me a hug?"

They met in the middle of the kitchen. Crying, Mary hugged her son. Billy was crying, too.

"I have something really bad I have to tell you," Mary said when they were done. "He-man is dead."

The news saddened Billy but did not shock him.

Nothing did anymore.

"What happened?" Billy said.

"I don't know," said Mary. "When I went into your room to check on them, Wiggle was running around on the wheel. He-man was quiet in a corner. Sleeping, I thought at first, until he didn't move. I touched him and he was cold. I'm so sorry, Billy."

"He was a good hamster," Billy said.

"Yes, he was. And I promise we'll get another one to keep Wiggle company."

"Can I see He-man?" Billy said.

"That's not a good idea," Mary said.

"But I want to say goodbye."

"I've put him in a paper bag," Mary said, "to prepare him for burial. We can bury him in the corner lot, in the shade of those trees."

Carrying the bag containing the dead hamster, Mary led her son to the lot at the corner of Forge Street and Railroad Avenue. No one was there. In this desolate part of the city, that was the customary situation.

They found an area beneath an old oak and Billy began digging with the hand trowel his mother once used to plant flowers, back when they lived in a place with a garden.

"This deep enough?" the boy said when he'd dug down about a foot.

"Deeper," Mary said.

When he'd reached a depth of almost two feet, Mary told him to stop.

"That's deep enough," she said.

The mother placed the bag containing He-Man at the bottom of the grave.

"Let's say a prayer," Mary said. "The Our Father will do."

The mother and son began to pray.

Our Father, Who art in heaven, hallowed be Thy name;

Thy kingdom come; Thy will be done on earth as it is in heaven.

Give us this day our daily bread; and forgive us our trespasses as we forgive those who trespass against us; and lead us not into temptation but deliver us from evil.

Amen.

"You can throw the earth in now," Mary said.

Billy filled the trowel and stopped.

"Well?" Mary said.

"It's not right," Billy said, "that I can't see him one last time."

He reached into the grave and opened the bag.

It was He-man, all right.

He-Man with his head exploded, his fur singed.

Suddenly, the smell of electricity.

"I told you not to," Mary said. "I didn't want that to be the last image of your pet."

"What the heck happened, Mom?" Billy said.

The sight of He-Man had left him numb.

"I don't know," Mary said. "I was as horrified as you are now."

Mary, the woman who was Billy's mother, was speaking truthfully.

Chapter Eighteen: Grisly fate.
Saturday, July 3

Two days later, at six thirty p.m., after Billy had cleared the dinner dishes and Mary had retreated to her room with another migraine, Channel 12's evening news broadcast opened with a live shot. The location was The Culvert. A camera panned Mashpaug Pond and came up the Food Chain parking lot before stopping on a body bag being loaded into the medical examiner's wagon.

Next to it, a reporter said:

"At the top of the news: Two months after a young girl was found murdered inside a storm pipe here in Providence's Armory District, a fourteen-year-old boy has met a similarly grisly fate.

"Police say they received a call some two hours ago from neighborhood kids, who on a dare had gone inside this huge concrete culvert, which is dry except during rain. Several hundred feet in, they found the body. It is not known at this time if the boy died there or was brought there after his death. The medical examiner has ruled the death a homicide.

"Although police are not releasing his name, Channel 12 has learned that a relative called to the scene tentatively identified the boy as Paul Iannotti of the Armory District. Iannotti, whose nickname was Angel, was a school dropout.

"According to Det. William Tillinghast, there are as yet no persons of interest, but this remains an active investigation."

Channel 12 cut to a detective.

"It definitely was murder," Tillinghast said. "A real vicious kind of thing. The body was mutilated in a way you don't see every day. I am sorry I cannot say more at this time."

"As for motive," the reporter said, "police are not ruling out a link with drugs, despite the youth's age. They note that youths as young as 11 have been enlisted by dealers to be runners in certain areas of the city, like this."

Channel 12 went back to the studio, where the weekend anchor was poised with a question.

"Chelsea," she said, "is there any link between this case and that of Margaret Bucci, the seven-year-old girl who was found murdered in the same pipe?"

"Kait, that's clearly one of the pressing questions police will have to address," Chelsea said. "My sources tell me that the apparent manner of killing—mutilation—was similar in both. Beyond that—well, the police have their work cut out for them."

"No one was ever arrested for Margaret Bucci's murder, right?"

"Right, although authorities still label it an active case as they await possible new leads. With DNA science expanding almost daily, that is a distinct possibility. And this latest murder will only encourage a new look at the evidence."

"What's the mood in the neighborhood this evening, Jack?"

"What you would imagine, Kait: people are scared. We talked to one boy who was a friend of some of the kids who found the body and he said for months there have been rumors of some-one—or 'something,' as he put it—living in that storm drain, which apparently connects to a large network running under much of the city.

"A subterranean Phantom of the Opera kind of thing, as it were. But of course that may be nothing more than a child's active imagination. All we can say for sure is doors in the Armory District will be locked tight tonight."

The anchor said: "We understand that the police are ask-ing anyone with any information to please contact them, even anonymously."

"That is correct," the reporter said. "If you have any informa-tion that might help, please call the tip line or send an email. The number and address are on the bottom of your screen and also on wpri.com."

The possibility that his mother might have been involved was not Billy's first thought.

The fact that he and his friends had been skateboarding down there recently was.

We were so close... it could've been one of us.

Nor was Mom his next thought.

Angel was.

It must've been drugs, like the TV guy said. That's what happens when you're heavy into drugs, right? You wind up dead.

Mom was his third thought.

I heard that word there! Ordo! The word Mom uses!

But Mom's not involved. Mom couldn't be involved. She's never been down there. She's never done anything but... talk really weird.

So it couldn't have been her.

Just couldn't.

And for quite some time, almost to the end, Billy McAllister was able to believe that.

Billy went to Mary's door and heard snoring. He went back down the hall, double-checked the kitchen lock, then picked up the land line and dialed Andres. His friend answered.

"Did you see the news?" Billy asked.

"Yeah. Can you believe it?"

"Cops said he was murdered."

"Sliced is what I took from it," Andres said. "Man, we were just down there."

"I told you The Culvert wasn't cool," Billy said.

"You were right. I wonder if it was drugs. I bet it was. That's what happens when you hang with a scuzzy crowd, like Angel did."

"But murdered," Billy said. "I mean, he was an asshole and everything, but *murdered...* It's wicked scary."

"Sure is. My brother wants my mom to get a gun, but she says no. He's thinking of getting one anyway and keeping it in his drawer or someplace."

"You don't think the killer lives in there, do you?"

There was silence as Andres turned that over. The possibility hadn't occurred to him.

"You mean because The Culvert runs under Death Alley," he finally said. "Right behind our houses."

"Yeah."

"Nah," Andres said, unconvincingly. "No one lives in there."

"What if it's not a someone. What if it's a... *something.*"

"You mean like Beauty and the Beast?"

"Or Phantom of the Opera. Like they said on the news."

"That's silly," Andres said. "Those things don't exist. Except on TV and in the movies."

"Well what if they did?"

"Well they don't," Andres said. "'Sides, you heard the man. The cops are checking that culvert inside-out. If there's something there, they'll find it."

If it's not invisible, Billy almost said.

Instead, he raised another disturbing possibility.

"You don't think The Culvert is connected to the sewer, do you?"

"You mean like where the pipes come into our houses?" Andres said.

"Yeah."

"Get real, man," Andres said. "Even if The Culvert *was* connected, which it can't be or it'd smell a million times worse—not even the worst killer could tolerate it—nobody's small enough to crawl through a sewer pipe, not even a kid."

"Like you're not scared?" Billy said. "You're talking about getting a gun!"

"OK," Andres said, "I am scared, a little. I just don't think we should get too bent out of shape. You know Angel. It was over the drugs, man. It had to be. Why else would someone want to kill him?"

"It could've been a crazy person."

"Nah," Andres said. "You watch. When the cops get him, it's gonna be drugs. Angel burned the wrong dude and that wrong dude decided to teach a lesson. You just wait and see."

Chapter Nineteen: Comfortably numb.
Monday, July 5.

Channel 12 and all the other TV and radio stations, newspapers and web sites did follow-up stories on the murder of Angel Iannotti, but the only new information that had surfaced over the weekend was a sliver: the conclusion by the coroner's office that while the death was indeed a homicide, the manner and cause remained undetermined.

The results of toxicology tests, which could take weeks to come back, hopefully would provide some clues. In the meantime, the mayor announced at a press conference that featured more questions than answers that Armory District residents could take comfort knowing that he had tripled police patrols of their neighborhood.

Life continued on.

People went to work as usual.

The laughter of kids, including Billy and Andres, filled the summer air.

Mail was delivered, trash picked up.

The ice cream truck came along, music playing.

And at 3 p.m. on that Monday, Mary McAllister answered her buzzer.

"Mrs. McAllister?"

"Yes?"

"I'm Sheriff James Partington, Providence County. I'm here to serve notice of a civil lawsuit brought against you on behalf of Robert Bartholomew, whose address is..."

Mary stood in the kitchen, her fingers creasing and uncreasing the copy of the suit.

Her head was swimming. This was not what she needed now, or ever. Everything had become so tentative of late, but this...

This was a shock. A frightening and dangerous new shock she could not sustain without alcohol.

For more than a week, she'd been good—but now, she went to the cupboard, found a tall tumbler, filled it with ice, then poured to the top from the bottle of rum she'd hidden from Billy behind the cleaning powders arranged so neatly under the sink.

She drank.

In five minutes, she was ready for another.

She fixed one.

Drank again, long and hard and deep.

The alcohol was beginning to work, soothing her agitated neurons, seeping down into a place where memories had hidden.

The alcohol found Jess, and when it did, it stimulated a flashback of Jess's funeral so powerfully real and painful that Mary had to sit, teetering on the edge of consciousness as that day replayed in her mind.

That day, the staff of Portland Behavioral Health Center had assigned her a counselor and driven her three hours in the hospital van to a small Catholic church in Blue Hill, Maine.

They arrive when the service is underway, but there seems no harm in that.

No one says anything.

Billy gives her a frantic hug and a kiss, tears fall, and she sits down next to him, next to the casket of Jess.

The funeral proceeds.

It is nothing, really, that Mary, heavily sedated, cannot handle.

In fact, she is comfortably numb.

As unreal as everything is at Portland, this is surely a hallucination, some side-effect of the pills they feed her, or a dream, or a scene from one of those novels they've been letting her read in those endless hours between group and individual therapy sessions and AA.

Nothing, really, she can't take.

Until she spots her ex-husband, William McAllister, nearly hidden on the other side of Jess.

Until Billy faints and everyone in that packed, stuffy building rises to their feet uttering a collective gasp.

Until Billy is carried out by two undertakers.

Until her brother, the Rev. John Lambert S.J., moves quickly to end the service.

Accompanied by the altar boys, who have swapped candles for incense, Jack descends the altar and walks to the head of the casket. He sprinkles holy water again and intones:

"Our prayers now are ended, and we bid our last farewell to Jessica Mary. There is sadness in parting, but it should fill us with hope, for one day we shall see our sister again and enjoy her love. By God's mercy, we who leave this church today in sorrow will be reunited in the joy of God's kingdom.

"Let us comfort one another in the faith of Jesus Christ.

"Let us pray."

He bows his head. The mourners follow.

Suddenly, it's very real for Mary.

Jess is dead.

Never coming home.

It is that simple.

That cruel. If only Mary could trade places… she'd do anything.

Mary is entranced, her eyes not budging from her daughter's casket. A new thought has occurred to her—a thought more terrifying and bleaker than all the other terrifying and bleak thoughts throughout this ordeal.

Very soon—just a matter of minutes, really—that casket will be at the McKay mausoleum. More prayers will be said, more holy water sprinkled, and then everyone will leave.

When they are gone, workers who have never met Jess, never heard her laugh, never hugged or kissed her, are going to slide that coffin inside cold granite.

The granite is going to be sealed and no one is ever going to break that seal—not man, not angels, not God I am the Resurrection and the Life.

The seasons will change, the tides ebb and flow, the years pass.

Elsewhere, babies will be born. Schoolchildren will graduate. Sons and daughters will marry and bring grandchildren into the world, *but Jess, my precious little Jess, will be forever in that crypt. Forever and ever, without end.*

As Jack continues, a new course of action is revealing itself. Something that will…

take Jess away from all this.

"May the angels lead you into Paradise..."

Yes, she can do it.

Because what are Mommies for if not to help their little girls in their darkest hour of need?

"...may the martyrs come to welcome you..."

Not just can do it. Must do it.

"...and take you to the holy city, the new and eternal Jerusalem."

Jack takes the thurible from the altar boy and circles the bier, incense following him in a cloud. The smell reminds Mary of her youth, of Easter Week and stations of the cross and their father, a devout Catholic, holding her hand.

"May the choir of angels welcome you, Jessica Mary..."

Sorry Jack, Mary thinks, *I can't allow it.*

"...where Lazarus is poor no longer..."

Can't allow anyone, not even God, to have my baby.

"...may you have eternal rest. Amen."

"Amen," the congregation responds.

Jack nods toward the rear, where pallbearers are waiting. They approach.

Mary is mesmerized, her eyes locked onto the coffin, so close she could touch its shiny metal surface.

The pallbearers are halfway to her daughter when she stands, steps from the pew into the aisle, and gently nudges her brother away from the casket.

She places her hands at its head and announces in a voice that carries to the last pew:

"I'm taking her, Jack."

The hospital counselor slides to the end of the pew.

"Mary," the counselor whispers, "please come back."

"It's not her time yet," Mary says.

"Mary Lambert McAllister, get back into this pew this instant!" Grammy barks.

"I'm sorry, Mother," she says, "but I can't."

Before anyone can say more, she is moving down the aisle, pushing Jess ahead of her.

"It's all right, honey," she says. "We're going home now. Everything's going to be all right, I promise. No more hospitals or any of this funeral stuff. We're going home and I'm going to tuck you into bed with your Baby Bear and read you a bedtime story."

The congregation is paralyzed.

Even Mr. Hawthorne, who has conducted thousands of funerals, has never seen anything like this—and Mr. Hawthorne was sure that he's seen it all. Until now.

He's seen distraught mourners fling themselves onto the caskets of their loved ones. He's heard wailing and shrieking in many languages. He's witnessed enough tears to fill a pond and he's seen people that had to be led out of funerals and wakes in three-point restraint—but this, this is one they'll be talking about in Blue Hill for years.

It occurs to him that everyone is looking to him to do something.

"Mrs. McAllister?" he calls. "Mrs. McAllister?"

Mary is three-quarters of the way down the aisle. She does not turn around. Those closest to her will later swear she was smiling... a smile that raised goose pimples.

"Jesus, help us," an elderly woman croaks.

Mary is surprised by how easily the bier and its precious cargo move. It will be no problem at all to get them out of the church, into the back of the hospital van, and onto the Maine Turnpike for the ride home to Rhode Island. One of the neighbors can help her bring Jess up into her bedroom, where she will need to stay until she is back on her feet.

But weight is one thing; maneuvering another.

As light as it seems, the casket sways like a speeding car on wet pavement.

She is almost to the door when she loses control.

The casket careens into the last pew and falls to the floor. There is the sharp retort of metal on wood, then another, softer sound: the thud of a small body inside settling into a new position.

And then, for Mary, darkness.

What followed was a prolonged stay at Portland Behavioral Health. A planned one-week admission for what staff had hoped would be "a tune-up" lasted more than a month as the professionals tried to confirm a diagnosis and decide the course of action.

One psychiatrist was confident Mary McAllister was experiencing late onset of bipolar disorder 1; his recommended regimen, once the immediate crisis had passed, was lithium maintenance. Another doctor suggested Mary McAllister suffered from a form of post-traumatic stress disorder, and he doubted that a lifelong program would be necessary—only management of flashbacks, nightmares and situation avoidance. Both doctors agreed that her condition, by whatever name, was aggravated by substance abuse: in her case, alcohol.

And both agreed chemicals would be Mary McAllister's salvation. Lacking her informed consent, they obtained a court order giving them carte blanche to prescribe from that pharmaceutical horn of plenty, the sacred PDR.

Even so, the case of Mary McAllister puzzled the Portland professionals as few had in their long collective experience. Their bafflement was evident during the final case conference before Mary was discharged.

Mary happened to overhear it.

Stabilized finally, she had been granted free time and library privileges. The center's library offered a selection of fiction and non-fiction, including three shelves of science-fiction titles by some of her favorite writers. Clarke. Asimov. Le Guin. Bradbury. McCarthy. King.

Yes, the library had become a sort of salvation in itself.

She was on her way there on the day of the last case conference when she passed the meeting room and heard the voices of her two doctors.

No one was in the hall. She put her ear to the door.

"We've only ever had a case like this before," one doctor said. "Years ago."

"I remember," the second doctor sad. "Very sad. We tried everything, but in the end, we lost that person to death by suicide."

"There are limits to what even the best psychiatry can do," said the first doctor. "But we haven't reached those limits yet with Mary. I suggest we revisit the possible diagnoses again. We'll need the DSM. Let me get my copy."

He referred to the Diagnostic and Statistical Manual of Mental Disorders, the diagnostic and taxonomic tool published by the American Psychiatric Association, the bible, as it were, of the profession.

"OK," the first doctor said when he'd pulled the manual from a bookshelf. One strong possibility is dissociative identity disorder, abbreviation "DID"—what in years past was called multiple personality disorder. It's a sickness in which two different personalities co-exist, typically with the one not knowing there is another.

"A distinctive feature of DID is gaps in memory that cannot be explained by run-of-the-mill forgetfulness. Other conditions that may also occur include sleep difficulties, amnesia, anxiety and substance use disorders, depression, recurrent headaches, suicidal ideation, and post-traumatic stress disorder."

"So far, that's Mary to a T," the second doctor said. "Let me pick up from there. Patient history often includes earlier diagnoses of a multitude of disorders and failure of treatments, especially over the long-term. In other words, intractable. Furthermore, a history of bipolar disorder and borderline personality disorder is seen in some patients with a DID diagnosis. And this is also deeply concerning: there is mounting evidence that DID patients exhibit psychotic symptoms similar to people diagnosed with schizophrenia."

"Sounds like a textbook Sybil," the first doctor said.

"Sybil, as it turns out, was fake," the second doctor said. "Mary McAllister is not. Whether or not she has DID is debatable, but her trauma history is not. She's experienced some of the worst traumas imaginable: the gruesome death of her father, the equally horrible death of her mother, and now, the death of her daughter. As for psychotic symptoms, look no further than what she has revealed about what she describes as alien voices."

"Commanding her to demand that her son take her to this character named Ordo," said the first doctor.

"With an elaborate back story that, were it a novel, would make sense," said the second.

"But in real life, is frightening to those around her. I'm thinking, of course, or her son. Thank goodness she has a brother who can care for the boy during her hospitalizations."

"Whatever the diagnosis," the second doctor said, "I think we can agree on this: All that's left are traces of Mary."

"What are the chances we can bring the rest of her back?"

"Slim. But we are in this for the long haul. We owe her that. Let's not forget the goodness we have found, along with the pathology."

Devastated, Mary stopped listening and completed her trip to the library, where she could not so much as open a book. Pink Floyd's song "Comfortably Numb" was playing in her head, drowning everything else out, and she couldn't stop it. She felt like she was receding again.

The last month, the past two weeks especially, reminded Mary of that stay at Portland Behavioral Health Center.

But only reminded.

Things were not the same this time.

They were worse.

Mary looked in an online directory for a number, found it and dialed.

"Psychiatric Associates," said the voice on the other end of the line.

"Doctor Kim please."

"Doctor Kim is with a patient. May I help you?"

"This is Mary McAllister. I have an, ah, appointment for tomorrow and I, ah… something has come up. I'll have to reschedule. I'm sorry."

"Is this an urgent matter?"

"Oh, no," Mary insisted.

"When would you like to reschedule, then? I'm afraid Doctor Kim is booked through the rest of this week and then is on vacation for the rest of July. Would early August be all right?"

Mary made an appointment for the first week of that month, one she would not keep.

Chapter Twenty: A ticking clock.
Wednesday, July 7

For Billy McAllister and his mother, all but the final half hour of this day was charmed: a classic sun-drenched day that included hot dogs, pizza, Cokes, and an outdoor concert at Roger Williams Park that ended in torch-lit darkness.

They returned home at 10:30 p.m. Grammy's old Toyota Corolla had finally died, and the McAllisters relied on mass transit now. And bus connections take time.

"Half an hour TV, then bed," Mary said.

"Can't I have an hour? *Please?*"

"One hour and then in without a whimper. Promise?"

"Promise!"

Until the end of the 11 o'clock news, from which the Angel Iannotti story had finally exited, Billy paid no attention to his mother. He heard dishes being washed, a vacuum, water running in the bathroom.

Then there was silence.

"Ma?" he called out softly on his way to his room. "You asleep, Ma?"

The kitchen was sparkling clean but deserted.

The bathroom was empty.

Her bedroom was empty.

She's gone again, was his first thought, one that chilled him. *God, it's happening again.*

But she couldn't have left, Billy concluded after a brief investigation. The kitchen door was locked—the slide bolt and safety chain engaged. Every window was closed. Since Angel, that had been status quo.

"Mom?" Billy called again, more urgently. "Mom? Where are you? Are you alright?"

"I'm here."

She sounded distant but calm, none of that craziness in her voice.

"Where?"

"In here."

The voice was coming from inside her room—from *really* inside her room, as if she were in the walls or ceiling or something. Billy stood in her doorway, scrutinizing more intently this time. He did not find her. Her bed was untouched.

"Ma?"

"I'm here."

Muffled, as if she were under the bed.

Could she be under the bed?

Doing what?

Why?

Billy swallowed; his throat was suddenly scratchy and dry. Among Mary's favorite authors was a guy named Richard Matheson and he'd done a bunch of original episodes for *Twilight Zone*, which Billy caught now and then on Andres's cable TV. One of Matheson's stories was about a little girl who had crawled under a sleeper-couch and been sucked into another dimension. Billy had seen that one.

No monsters, no psychos, not even any blood... and it had been one of the scariest shows he'd ever seen.

Billy dropped to his knees and lifted the spread.

He saw no dust kitties or a stray slipper or shoe.

"Ma? Ma?"

"I'm in here!" she said, and this time her voice was carrying irritation.

Now he got it. Now he did!

At the back of Mary's closet was a small door; it provided access to the burners, electrical boards and sewer and water hook-ups for all four apartments, plus limited space for storage.

No self-respecting architect would ever have designed a building from scratch like this, but in rehabbing the old Victorian, this had been the only way Mr. Sierra could get the basement apartment he needed to make his purchase profitable. With such infrequent need to get into the utilities area, Billy sometimes forgot the cubicle was there.

Billy squeezed past slacks and blouses and went through the second door. A single bulb burned in an overhead fixture.

Mary was stooped over a cardboard box, one of several piled next to the McAllisters' only trunk, an old-fashioned steamer Grammy had passed along to them.

"What are you doing, Mom?"

"What does it look like?" she said. "I'm going through these."

Quite carefully, it appeared.

Several of the boxes that had been stored in the trunk were empty, their contents stacked next to them in neat piles. There were books: a few old hardcovers from Grammy and a larger number of paperbacks, mostly the science-fiction titles Mary preferred. There were clothes. Old shoes. Plates. A lamp. Mary's high school notebooks, including several short stories from her creative phase.

"Very interesting stuff," Mary remarked, and the tone in her voice, the hint of intrigue, made it seem she'd never set eyes on any of this stuff before. "*Very* interesting."

She was rummaging inside the final box now.

"You know what this is, of course," she said. "It's the telescope your father gave to you when you were little."

"You used to tell me how he was into stars and planets," Billy said. "Uncle Jack says if his eyes had been better, he might've been an astronaut. Uncle Jack said he guesses I got his eyes."

A long pause.

"As primitive as it is, you'd be able to see the galaxies with this, wouldn't you?" Mary said.

"Sure, Mom. Some of them, anyway."

"Very interesting."

Setting the telescope aside, Mary moved on to another trunk.

Jess's trunk, packed by Uncle Jack during the time Mary had been hospitalized.

"As interesting as all *that* was, I think *this* will be even more interesting, don't you?" Billy's mother said.

She undid the hasp.

She's never opened it, Billy thought. *I've heard her tell Uncle Jack she could handle a lot of things, but not that.*

Billy remembered the day they'd moved into this apartment—remembered the van Uncle Jack had rented, remembered Uncle Jack and Mary and this new friend Andres Washington all helping to carry boxes and chairs and tables.

Most vividly, he remembered how Mom had cried when it had come time to bring in the trunk—and how, through her tears, she'd said she didn't believe she could ever look inside there, just as she could never throw any of it away.

"I don't think you want to go through that, Mom."

"Oh, but I do," Mary said. "I think this will be an *event*. Aren't you interested what's inside?"

"I know what's inside."

"I bet you do," Mary said, and a tiny smile danced across her lips.

Mary lifted the lid.

Billy saw Jess.

She was lying on her back, fingers entwined around rosary beads, hands folded across her belly, exactly as she'd been inside her casket.

Except she'd rotted.

Her fingers and arms were skeletal and the flesh had peeled away from her face, exposing bone. Her eyes were sockets filled with maggots. Blindly, they were exploring what once had been pink cheek. The odor was nauseating.

And then Jess sat up, just like at her funeral.

Sat up and slowly waved at her big brother, begged him in her sweetest Jess voice to let her out, to *please help me, to please oh please not let them do this, the mission is not complete.*

Billy gagged.

Jess disappeared.

But of course no one really was inside the trunk.

No rotted smell.

No skeletal wave.

No whispered plea.

Only stale air and a collection of tissue-wrapped memorabilia that had further stoked Billy's overheated imagination.

Methodically, mechanically, Mary began to unwrap everything.

A grocery bag of get-well cards from all over the country.

The pink polka-dot dress Jess had worn coming home from the hospital the first time.

A manila envelope of magazine and newspaper articles Grammy had clipped.

The basketball that Celtics All-Star Isaiah Thomas had presented Jess.

Three stuffed lions and six stuffed bears.

A stuffed kitty.

Barbie dolls.

Cabbage Patch dolls.

A dried bouquet of carnations in a Ziploc plastic freezer bag.

One Morning in Maine, Jess's favorite book, signed by the author, Robert McCloskey.

The trunk also contained several letters.

Mary thumbed through them and chose one to read aloud.

March 26, 2016

The Rev. John Lambert, S.J.
Dean Street Shelter
144 Dean St.
Boston, Mass., 02105

My Dear Mary:

> *Sometimes it's easier to put words on paper. Sometimes, it's better even than sending them by Facebook or in an email. We can collect our thoughts. And we can say things we might not say in person, for a host of silly reasons.*
>
> *I want to say I love you, Mary. Not just as your brother—that goes without saying. I love you as a member of Christ's family. I love you as a person. I love you as a woman who has been through an unimaginable ordeal, for reasons that He understands, whether or not we do.*
>
> *You know what I think of Jess. Has ever a more precious child lived? Has one ever possessed greater courage?*

I look at her, as do you and Mom and the entire hospital staff, and often have to stifle tears… but just as often am in complete awe of her. Her good humor, her fortitude in the face of an experience no child should have to go through, are lessons to us all.

A word about Mom. Jess's sickness has gotten to her, as it has to all of us. She is as upset as anyone, and even if she cannot show it the way others might—even if her anguish takes the form of carping, demanding, sticking her nose where it doesn't rightfully belong, driving Billy up the wall—please try to understand. Mom has always been her own person, as I need not remind you, and now is no different. In her own unique way, she loves you—all of us—very much.

As for you, my dear Mary… I know how hard this is. I know how cruel it seems. I know there are days when you feel you can't take any more, you just feel like collapsing. Every night, I pray to God to give you the strength you need to carry on. Place your faith in Him, Mary. He will be there for you.

Whatever happens to Jess—her fate is in God's hands—I want you to know I'll always be by your side.

Love,
Jack.

P.S. Quite a "heavy" letter, even for old Father Jack! But I think there's a kernel or two of truth in it. See you this weekend. I'll call when I get information on my flight.

P.P.S. Say hello to Doctor Cooke. Where would we be without him?

The next item was a newspaper clipping from Page One of *The Providence Journal* dated April 8, 2016. The headline read:

JESS DIES AFTER THIRD TRANSPLANT EFFORT FAILS

Governor hails terminally ill girl's courage
by Thomas G. Martin
Staff Writer

PITTSBURGH—Jessica Mary McAllister, the pigtailed, smiling girl whose lifelong struggle against a terminal liver disease captivated an entire region and drew national sympathy, died yesterday afternoon with her mother at her side.

McAllister, five years old, underwent her third liver transplant a week ago at UPMC Children's Hospital of Pittsburgh. Jess, as everyone called her, did not regain consciousness after the eight-hour procedure, which doctors had given only a 25-percent chance of success.

Asked the night before her final operation what she wanted to tell the tens of thousands of people who have so closely followed her, Jessica said: "I love Mommy, Billy, Grammy and Uncle Jack! And I hope the Celtics win it all!"

Jess, a devout basketball fan despite her youth, was visited last month in the hospital by Isaiah Thomas, the All-Star point guard for the Boston Celtics. Thomas presented her with a basketball signed by every member of this year's Celtics team.

"She was a great kid," Thomas said from his home outside of Boston.

"Our state—indeed, the world—has lost a brave, beautiful young girl," Rhode Island Governor Gina Raimondo said in a statement issued from the State House last night. "In her beautiful way, Jess McAllister reminded us of an important lesson: namely life, no matter how tragically brief, should be lived to the fullest. That is what Jess, with her sense of humor and that sparkle in her eyes, did every day."

"I just feel empty," said a tearful and tired Alice McKay Lambert, Jess's grandmother, who flew to Pittsburgh when it was apparent the end was near. "This has taken such a toll on us. I don't know how we can ever be the same, any of us."

Mary McAllister, who candidly admits her daughter's illness has taken a heavy emotional toll, was not available for comment. Shortly after Jess was pronounced dead, she left Children's Hospital in the company of an unidentified person, apparently a nurse.

Jess's funeral and burial will be in Blue Hill, Maine, where Mrs. McAllister was born and raised and where Mrs. Lambert still lives. Arrangements are not yet complete.

In addition to her grandmother and mother, Jess is survived by a brother, Billy, 6, and an uncle, the Rev. John Lambert, a Catholic priest who runs a soup kitchen and shelter in Boston.

Since Jess re-entered the hospital in early March, Billy has been living with Mrs. Lambert at her Maine residence. Mrs. McAllister has been staying at the Ronald McDonald House in Pittsburgh, which provides quarters for terminally ill children and their families at minimal cost.

Jess was born with biliary atresia, a rare liver disorder that eventually leads to death if not corrected. Complicating her condition was an associated vascular disorder. Jessica had an initial operation when she was two, but when that failed, only transplantation held any hope.

Her first transplant came almost exactly a year ago.

Her recovery was remarkably quick, and by Memorial Day, she was well enough to leave UPMC Children's Hospital for her grandmother's house in Blue Hill, where it was thought she and her family would do best. The McAllisters ordinarily are residents of Providence's Armory District.

After what her physician, Dr. Arthur Cooke, described as an "encouraging" summer, Jess's body began showing signs of rejecting her new liver in September. Rejection—the body's own immune system working to "defeat" what it views as "foreign" tissue—is a risk with any transplant, despite advances in drugs which suppress the immune response.

In early October, when it became clear Jess's new liver was not going to be accepted, a second transplant was scheduled. Once again, Jess's initial recovery was smooth. She was home in time for Thanksgiving, and spent a happy Christmas in Blue Hill, surrounded by her family.

A picture of Jess holding the basketball that Isaiah Thomas gave her and "the Teddy Santa brought," a Teddy bear she had named Baby Bear, was published in *The Journal* and also appeared in the current issue of *O, The Oprah Magazine*, which published a photo-feature on the girl with a heartfelt message from Oprah Winfrey herself.

The photo of Jess with "Baby Bear" prompted a flood of Teddy bears to the hospital.

By late February, it was apparent that Jess's second transplanted liver was being rejected, too. After a conference, doctors decided to try a third time, a relatively rare event. Once again, the frantic search for a donor was on.

On March 31, an anonymous donor—reportedly a four-year-old boy left brain dead in a Los Angeles car crash—was found. The organ was flown to Pittsburgh and Jess's third operation began at 8 a.m. on April 1.

By one estimate, Jessica's medical bills have topped $750,000. State and federal insurance programs have covered some of that, but a large debt remains. A GoFundMe campaign has been started

to help cover that. As of this writing, $33,565 of the
$100,000 goal has been raised.

On Mary went through the trunk until she found a box filled with
photos. They had been printed from her cell phone at a CVS store.

With Billy looking over her shoulder, Mary went through those
even more carefully, holding each to the light, like a radiologist
scrutinizing films. Billy was in most of the photographs or could
remember when they'd been taken.

There was Jess in her baptism dress. Jess on her trike. Billy on
his. Jess with the TV reporter who'd first reported on her disease.
Jess getting out of the hospital the first time. Jess and Billy and
Uncle Jack at Ocean State Park. Jess with Isaiah Thomas. Jess with
Governor Raimondo. Jess on Grammy's lap. Jess and her brother,
mother, grandmother, and uncle near the ocean in Blue Hill, not far
from the mausoleum where she would eventually be entombed.

Mary said nothing—until she'd reached the final shot, which
showed Jess at Christmas holding her new Teddy bear, Baby Bear.
Billy was near the tree and in back of his sister, smiling.

Mary had bought that stuffed animal a bric-a-brac shop on
Black Friday, the day after Thanksgiving of last year, the last
Thanksgiving Jess would have. With an excuse about "going on
special errands," she'd left her daughter and son in the care of her
brother so she could begin her Christmas shopping. Jack had recommended the shop: it had plenty of porcelain dolls and clean, if
used, stuffed animals—all at reasonable prices.

Baby Bear had projected unusual appeal—a Teddy that seemed
to have Jess's name written all over it. It would be a prized addition
to her collection.

And indeed it had been her favorite gift from Santa that year.

But as she looked at the photo, Mary's mind was blank on all
of that.

It was as if the memory had been erased from her mind.

Billy smelled it now: electricity.

Oh, no, he thought.

"See?" Mary said, her voice not manic, but no longer hers,
either.

"Here is proof, Theus! Ordo with you and that girl!"

"That's Jess, Mom," Billy said.

"That is Ordo," Mary said

She pointed to Baby Bear, the stuffed animal in the photo.

"Not the girl," Mary said. "Ordo. Do you not recognize your leader? Or is this another area where your memory conveniently fails you?"

"Ma, you're doing it again," Billy said, and now the utility room seemed hot and small.

Pocketing the Baby Bear photograph, Mary began to repack the rest.

"I will only remind you of your deadline," she said. "Don't forget: the clock is ticking."

Chapter Twenty-One: Kisses.
Wednesday, July 7.

Billy cannot sleep. He is caught in a memory, one he's had many times before.

He is in Pittsburgh. He has travelled here with his grandmother on a jet from Maine because yesterday, after a phone conversation with Uncle Jack, Grammy tearfully announced that Jess was "near the end." Her third transplant was not taking and now, five days later, she was still in a coma and "fading fast," according to Grammy.

Billy, six years old and scared, holds Grammy's hand as they ascend the front steps of the hospital. Across the lobby. Up the elevator. More tears with Mom and Uncle Jack in that waiting room, the one with the same old magazines, outside UPMC Children's Hospital's intensive care unit.

"She's very, very sick, hon," Mary says as she hugs her son.

There is no strength in that hug, no firmness. Mom seems far away.

"Is she going to die?"

"She's going to be with Jesus," Uncle Jack says.

"Right next to him?"

"Right next to him. Jesus will wrap her in his arms and make all her suffering go away."

"And then will she be able to come home?"

Silence follows.

Silence punctuated only when Uncle Jack says: "Her home will be heaven, Billy. Just as someday you and Grammy and me and your Mom—all together, with Jesus. This is what the Son of God promises those who have been baptized in his name."

They enter Jess's room, which has no door and is directly

across from the nurses' station. Jess is its only occupant. The curtains aren't drawn. A machine with tubes and cords and gauges and a bellows is doing what her lungs no longer can. On a screen, a succession of rising and falling green pyramids tells the story of her failing heart. Clear liquid drips from a bottle into a long plastic tube connected to her arm. Yellow liquid has collected in a plastic bag that is attached to the side of the bed.

Billy has seen everything before, knows what everything's for.

He's seen Jess like this before, too, after her first and second operations. Seen the yellow skin, the closed eyes, the cracked lips, the matted hair.

Her home will be heaven.

Billy starts to cry.

As he does, he notices Baby Bear.

Jess's free arm is wrapped around the stuffed animal, snuggly and cute. The nurses must have arranged it like that. The nurses must have remembered how special Baby Bear was to Jess.

Maybe, Billy thinks, even in her coma Jess knows Baby Bear's there. He hopes so. How she loved her Baby Bear. It was one of the last gifts she unwrapped under the Christmas tree, one of the smallest Santa brought, but from the instant she saw it was Jess's all-time favorite toy. Baby Alive, her Cabbage Patch doll, her American Girl collection, the dozens of stuffed animals sent by people who'd seen Jess on the news—those were great, but from the moment Baby Bear emerged from the box, they took second place.

Billy looks at Baby Bear, perched in the crook of Jess's arm.

What was it about that thing?

Billy felt it too, at least some of it: the attachment Jess had for that toy, the security it gave her. It wasn't the way Baby Bear looked, a bit tattered and old and chipmunk-like, like many of her Teddy bears. No, there was a certain… *warmth* whenever you touched it. Its glass eyes were dark and deep—and friendly and kind. Peering into them was like looking down Grammy's well and seeing your own face, smiling in the distance.

Sniffling, Billy goes to his sister's side.

"I love you, Jess," he whispers into her ear. "You're going to be with Jesus soon in heaven. You'll like it there, I promise. Heaven's got all the ice cream you can eat and nothing hurts. Uncle Jack told me and he knows 'cause he's a priest."

Billy wishes she could answer.

He wants her to open her eyes and sit up with Baby Bear and give him a high-five with her free hand, but of course she does none of that.

It is the last time Billy sees Jess alive.

Two hours later, a red light starts flashing and an alarm sounds. A nurse stills the alarm and watches as the green peaks turn into curves, which become a straight line. The instructions of the family, none of whom is in the room at the moment, is for no heroic measures.

The memory shifts to Blue Hill. It is the morning of Jess's funeral. They are at the funeral home and Uncle Jack has conducted a short service with Hail Marys and an Our Father and other prayers Billy has never heard. Now, almost everyone has left, bound for the limos and cars that are lined up in a caravan that stretches all the way around the block.

"Do you wish to pay last respects?" Mr. Hawthorne says.

"Oh, yes," Grammy says.

Grammy clasps Billy's hand and leads him toward the Batesville Promethean Bronze casket.

After yesterday's wakes—there were two, afternoon and evening—the horror of seeing Jess dead has subsided to the point where he can almost look at her without turning away. Her skin's not the right texture, her eyes and mouth are shut in peculiar positions, but she looks, well... if not alive, then better than the last time he saw her in the hospital. That yellow color is gone. Her arms, which had withered, don't look quite so skinny. And those needle marks—tiny and red, like the aftermath of a mosquito swarm—those are gone.

"Do you want that stuffed animal to go with her?" Mr. Hawthorne says.

"Oh, yes," Grammy says. "That's her precious Baby Bear."

"And the rosary beads?"

Uncle Jack nods his assent.

"Those were John's," Grammy explains, "when he was about her age. I honestly believe it was those very beads that set him on the road to the priesthood."

Silence.

Everyone staring at Jess, at the wall of flowers that surround her, at the candles, at the casket. Mr. Hawthorne adjusts his gloves again and lifts his sleeve to glimpse at this watch.

"I fear we must be going," he says. "It's almost ten."

Grammy kneels.

So does Billy.

Grammy closes her eyes and makes the sign of the cross.

Billy watches her lips move.

"Tell Jess goodbye," she says when she's done.

Now the tears are here.

"'Bye, Jess," Billy manages. "I'll love you forever and ever, Jess."

"Very good, Billy," Grammy says. "All that's left is kissing her."

Billy can't believe it.

He can't have heard right.

Grammy can't really intend to *kiss* Jess.

But she does.

She bends over.

Billy hears a pucker, at once impossibly tiny and unbelievably loud in this suffocating room with the thick curtains and funny-looking lamps and cloth wallpaper.

"Go ahead, Billy," she says.

"Mother..." Uncle Jack interrupts, but there's no fight in him any longer.

"John, let's not have a scene," Grammy says. "Not in front of Jess. Now, Billy? Mr. Hawthorne is waiting. Please kiss your sister."

Billy gets to his feet, stands on the kneeler, is looking down on her, his face close. He becomes aware of a smell, a subtle scent that's been masked by all these flowers. It is something of a soapy smell, but more complex than just Ivory or Dial.

A smell almost of burning.

Of weak electricity.

He closes his eyes again, afraid his tears will fall on her. He wants this over fast. His fingers contact casket. His mouth brushes his sister's cheek.

He recoils.

There is a taste on his lips—the taste of talc.

But that is not what will stick with Billy through the years. It is the temperature of Jess's skin. She is not cold, which is what he knows dead people are supposed to be.

She is warm, as warm as being under a wool blanket on a winter's night.

Didn't anyone else notice? he will wonder in the days and weeks to come.

He will never ask, never mention it to anyone.

But when what is to come comes, he will recall as another clue.

Chapter Twenty-Two: Evicted.

Thursday, July 8.

At 10 the next morning, after a night of little sleep, Billy was cleaning his hamster cage and Mary was in her room when there was a knock at the door. Billy answered it.

A sheriff was there. He had an eviction order, which he demanded to show Billy's mother. The premises were to be vacated by the end of the business day, the order said.

Mary was preternaturally calm.

Yes, she knew how far she was behind on the rent.

No, officer, she could not make arrears.

Yes, she knew Mr. Sierra had initiated eviction proceedings against her.

No, she did not want to exercise her right of appeal, did not want a public defender. What use would it be when the bottom line after all was said and done was this: she had no way of paying and pride prevented her from going to her brother again? All she wanted was time to find a moving company that would put their belongings in temporary storage: a company that would accept $125 in down payment, virtually all the cash she had.

"Mom, what are we going to do?" Billy said.

He was on the verge of tears. Only the presence of the sheriff—and his mother—stopped him. Mary was speaking in that distant, emotionless voice again. Billy heard echoes of last night.

"Nothing we can do," Mary said. "We've been evicted."

"They said we can get a lawyer."

"By the time we got before a judge this place would be rented again," Mary said. "That's the way it is."

Billy wasn't going to let it go so easily.

His mother was still floating somewhere between earth and

Planet X with Ordo and Theus and ZD-A. But when she returned from outer space, she'd see what a big mistake this had been, to just roll over. She'd praise him for fighting, once she was in command of her senses.

Yes, she would.

"We can go to Mr. Sierra," Billy said. "He's a good guy. He'd listen, Mom, if you were nice. He'd change his mind. I know he would. If he didn't, we could call Uncle Jack. Or Amanda. She'd help. She knows everyone. I bet she even knows a judge."

"Shh," Mary said, pursing her lips. "These things all have a way of working out for the best."

"But we won't have a home! We're going to be homeless!"

Mary shot a glance at the sheriff, still standing at the door.

His arms were folded but the way he was nervously tapping his fingers gave his feelings away. He hated evictions. Always women and kids—fuckups and low-lifes, maybe, but basically harmless.

"You know what he'll do if you keep on like this, don't you?" Mary whispered to her son.

Billy shook his head.

"Lock you up. That's why he's standing like that, waiting for you to make one wrong move. See those handcuffs? That gun? If I were you, I'd shut my mouth and do what I was told."

Would a sheriff do a thing like that? Billy wondered. *Not to a white boy. A Black kid would be a different matter. If it were Andres, they'd probably taser him.*

But what if he wasn't your everyday officer?

What if he was the meanest son of a bitch on the force? What if he hated kids? And welfare moms? What if he got ticked off something bad, and that boomeranged to Mom, and she got all worked up and started on her whole alien trip in front of him...

Billy looked from his mother to the sheriff and back to Mary.

A part of him was apprehensive, even afraid, but it wasn't the biggest part. He was suddenly angry—tight, like cable stretched past the breaking point.

Why couldn't he have a normal mother, like Andres?

Why didn't Mary share those qualities that made Uncle Jack so special: the calm, orderly way he went about everything, never getting ruffled or into jams.

Now Mary had them into another jam—in a lifetime of jams, maybe the biggest of all.

"I have to get some stuff in my room," Billy announced.

"I don't know if that's allowed," his mother said. "You'll have to ask the officer."

Billy turned toward the sheriff.

"Can I?" he asked.

"Sure, kid," the sheriff said uneasily.

Billy walked into his room and closed the door. His backpack was hanging on the hook, where it had been undisturbed since the last day of school. He took it down and went to his dresser. Socks. Undershorts. A tee shirt and a pair of jeans. He packed them.

As he looked around his room—at the wall posters, the dresser picture of Jess, his hamsters, his tape deck—the pressure inside of him started to ease. He could almost see it escaping, a release of emotions too volatile to be contained anymore. This was his room, dammit. *His* room—the one place he could call his own—the place that had provided refuge even against Mary at her craziest—his room, soon to be someone else's.

He knew that then, with a conviction that was as strong as his anger had been.

Once he left here today, he'd never be back.

Never, ever.

He took down his favorite Guns N' Roses poster, rolled it and tucked it into his backpack. The picture of Jess. His journal. His down-filled pillow, which he'd had as long as he could remember. With his penknife, he made an inch-long slit in the pack's pocket. It was long enough to let air in, short enough to keep Wiggle, his surviving hamster, from getting out.

He stuffed a handful of food into the pocket and dropped the water bottle in, too.

"There you go, little guy," he said as he removed the pet from its cage. "We're going on a little trip. But everything's gonna be OK. I promise it is. You just gotta be quiet. Go to sleep now. Thattaboy."

Billy slung the backpack over his shoulder, opened the door and started down the hall.

Chapter Twenty-Three: Medical miracle.
Thursday, July 8.

Zachary Pearlman, proprietor of Zack's Bric-a-Brac boutique, drove through the afternoon heat with the windows down to take in the salt air and flush out the odor emanating from the cardboard carton on the back seat.

For two days, Fluffy had been dead; for two days Pearlman, 83, had put off the inevitable. By this morning, third day of a heat wave, there no longer was any choice. After wrapping the dog in a blanket and placing the bundle in the box, Pearlman had left his Boston apartment bound for his summer home on Cape Cod.

Seventeen years ago on Cape Cod, his wife had come home with Fluffy.

Sixteen years ago in the same Cape home, Zachary Pearlman's wife had died in his arms.

Sixteen years—can it possibly be that long since Elizabeth's passed on? Pearlman thought. *Can it be that Fluffy lived to seventeen—an age of Methuselah proportions for a dog?*

As he crossed the Bourne Bridge and turned onto King's Highway, which ran along the shore, the memories cascaded over him.

Sixteen years, and not once had he been able to head down this last leg of the trip to the summer home without thinking of Elizabeth. He supposed he never would, no matter how long he lived. How she'd loved that little dog—loved it like the child they'd never had. When her cancer was diagnosed that spring day, and she'd come back from the doctor's having been given until no later than Christmas, her first concern had been Zachary.

Her second had been her precious Fluffy.

"Promise me you'll take care of her," she'd said, and he had.

Ten years went by, and then a dozen, and in doggie time Fluffy had become an octogenarian, doddering and prone to lameness and accidents on the rug.

One morning four years ago, with Thanksgiving just around the corner, Fluffy refused to budge from her blanket, wouldn't be enticed onto her feet even with her favorite biscuit or can of dog food. Zachary could almost hear Elizabeth speaking to him as he scooped the dog into his arms and took her in a cab to her veterinarian, across Boston in Jamaica Plain.

Two hundred dollars in tests were run, and an entire day was spent, and finally the vet diagnosed a terminal form of canine leukemia.

"The best you can do is make her comfortable," he'd said, "unless you'd like me to take care of things for you."

Zachary took her home and made her comfortable.

A week passed—a week when Fluffy barely ate, barely opened her eyes, barely wagged her tail when Zachary called her name.

Suddenly, a change.

In the span of a single day, energy pushed languor away. Fluffy left her blanket, returned to her regular rounds inside the bric-a-brac shop, began trotting outside again. The accidents ended. Appetite returned with a fury and Zachary couldn't keep her bowl full.

Such a day!

Possible for an old fart like him to believe in miracles again!

Seared into his memory not only for the resurrection of Fluffy, but because of a haunting coincidence Zachary had never been able to purge from his mind.

Only the night before, a young girl and her mother had been badly burned in a terrible fire a few doors down from Zachary's building, where he lived and ran Pearlman's Curios. A girl and her mother—two innocents—how awful it had been—how haunting the photos that had run in *The Globe*, including one of burnt stuffed animals in the charred remains of the building.

Zachary still had the clip, tucked into a drawer with photos of Elizabeth and the Pearlman's Curios storefront, back when they opened their shop decades ago:

Four-alarm blaze badly burns mother and daughter
Reports of gas explosion being probed

And he still had a second clip, also from *The Boston Globe* five days after the fire:

"Miracle" recovery of mother and daughter burned in blaze
Both discharged less than week after admission to Mass. General

BOSTON—The mother and daughter who were badly burned in last week's horrific Back Bay fire left Massachusetts General Hospital today showing no evidence of the extensive injuries doctors initially said would require months of rehabilitation if either was to have a life approaching normal again.

"This is unlike anything we have ever seen, and a review of the scientific literature finds nothing similar, either," Dr. Katherine Chan, chief of the hospital's Sumner M. Redstone Burn Center, said during a hastily arranged press conference. "I've never used this word before regarding medicine, but here I must. This was a miracle."

Tanya Audette, 11, and her mother, Sophie Audette, 34, attended the press conference, which was moments before their discharge. They bore no sign of burns or trauma, and both spoke happily of their experience—and delight to be leaving the hospital so soon.

"I can't believe it!" said Tanya. "We have been wicked lucky!"

"Lucky for sure," said the girl's mother. "But our Christian faith played a role here, I have no doubt. God took us under his wing and as Dr. Chan said, performed a miracle."

The Audettes will be staying at a hotel provided by the American Red Cross until a permanent new home is found. A GoFundMe campaign has been started to help the family, according to Francis Audette, Sophie's brother-in-law. Sophie's husband and Tanya's father, Marine Capt. Kevin Audette, died in a firefight in Afghanistan when his daughter was a baby.

Sophie and Tanya said they have no memory of their stay in the hospital until yesterday, when doctors brought them out of medically induced comas and told them what had happened. Sophie and Tanya said their last memory was watching a meteor shower, and then going to bed.

Neither knew about the fire until a social worker disclosed it during a pre-discharge counseling session.

Both Sophie and Tanya thanked their doctors and the hospital staff.

"They were a part of this miracle," said the mother.

"Sort of like our guardian angels," said the daughter.

Before the Audettes left to be transported by limousine to their new temporary quarters, Chan briefly recapped what staff had witnessed.

"We were set to begin skin grafts when the healing spontaneously began," Chan said. "Within hours, normal tissue had regrown over their entire bodies. The same was true of Tanya's and Sophie's hair—it returned rapidly and was soon what it had been before the fire."

Chan said the process was documented with still and video imagery, and with the Audettes' permission, they will be included as part of the paper they plan to submit to *Burns*, official publication of the International Society for Burn Injuries, and the *New England Journal of Medicine*.

Also present at the press conference was Sebastian Hernandez, owner of First Street Media, the advertising agency where Sophie Audette is head of marketing. Hernandez assured her that he will hold her job until she is ready to return and will pay her salary and continue her healthcare and other benefits during her leave.

Hernandez also presented the family with a $10,000 check, saying "use it for anything you want. If that means a trip to Disney World, book it!"

Sophie Audette broke into tears accepting the check, and her daughter gave Hernandez a hug.

Zach was at his summer place now. He turned into the drive. He was crying.

Chapter Twenty-Four: A fine line.
Thursday, July 8.

"I got back from vacation this morning," Amanda was saying over the phone to Father Jack. "I kept calling but there was no answer. So I decided to go over. A moving truck was taking their stuff out and delivering it to storage. The movers had no idea where they'd gone."

"Shit," Father Jack said. "Last time I talked to her—it must have been sometime over the weekend—she said everything was OK. I even asked how she was doing financially. I help her out whenever I can, you know. She said she was doing fine. I believed her."

"I checked with the landlord. She was four months behind on the rent."

"I had no idea."

"Neither did I," Amanda said. "I'm worried about what she might do next, Father Jack. Ever since Ocean State—since before, even—she's been walking a fine line. More stress is the last thing she can handle right now."

"Have you checked the shelters?"

"Not yet, but I will. I'm going to check the hospitals, too, just in case. Do you think she might be heading up to you?"

"There's a chance, but I don't know how much of one. There's been a distance between us the last couple of months. I don't know what's caused it, but it's been there."

"That's a bad sign," Amanda said. "She doesn't really have any close friends."

"I know."

"That's been part of her problem ever since I've had her case. No support network."

"I'll be here all day in the event she shows up," Father Jack said.

"What about calling the police?" Amanda said.

"If there's no word by tomorrow, maybe we should. But I'd hate to bring law enforcement in just yet, given their record of dealing with people with mental-health issues."

"Before I go," Amanda said, "there's one more thing I should tell you. She's cancelled her neurological workup. I called over there to check and they said Mary cancelled last week. She didn't reschedule, Father Jack."

"Shit," the priest said.

Chapter Twenty-Five: A spring in her step.
Thursday, July 8.

The wind stirred the curtains of the Cape house, chasing the heat and humidity away. Zachary sat in his favorite chair, the leather one to the left of the fireplace. The shadows were thick, but he did not want any light. He was sipping an Amaretto, Elizabeth's favorite aperitif.

He was wondering what he had to live for now that his duty was done.

It's over so quickly, isn't it? he thought, but he was not being morbid, only an 83-year-old stating a fact. *You're born, you make your way in the world, and then, after your allotted time, you're gone. Measured against the clock of the universe, gone in a flash.*

He'd buried Fluffy in the shade of the climbing rose Elizabeth had planted in the last summer of her life, the summer when the cancer ate her insides. Like his attention to her dog, Zachary had nurtured Elizabeth's rose, carefully pruning it every fall, carefully fertilizing it every spring, carefully spraying and watering it every summer.

Sixteen years, and now the rose covered one whole side of the house.

Natural cycles, he thought. *The turn of the seasons.*

Burying Fluffy, he'd thought again of getting another dog.

As Fluffy's health had failed over the last few weeks and the possibility of another miracle dimmed, Zachary had gone so far as peruse the pet-adoption sites.

But his heart wasn't in it. His heart wasn't in anything any longer. He was an old man, and his wife was dead, his dog now, too, and he had no children, only a place on the Cape and a shop he'd run for over 50 years. Neither meant much anymore.

Sitting here, he realized neither ever could again, not even if, God forbid, he lived to 100.

The memories swirled.

For what did an old man have, if not memories?

He remembered his wedding day, their honeymoon at Niagara Falls, the day he and his young bride bought that building just outside Kenmore Square, the morning they hung their bronze sign over the door to their shop. He remembered the tone they had set for their shop from the beginning: a tone of elegance and value, no garage- or tag-sale items in Pearlman's Curios.

He remembered the shop expanding into the second floor and moving their living quarters to the third. He remembered Elizabeth opening her porcelain doll display and, not a year later, the Famous Teddy Bear collection that was such a hit with their clientele.

He remembered, yet again, that disastrous day four years ago.

As Fluffy's infirmities had grown, climbing stairs had become difficult for the dog and Zachary had moved her bed down to a storage room behind the first floor of his shop.

The morning after that horrible fire—a fire that, given different wind direction or bungled Fire Department response, conceivably could have claimed Pearlman's Curios—Fluffy had been gone when he came downstairs.

Zachary was instantly alarmed.

There was no sign of her outside, either.

"Fluffy?" he'd called, a sinking feeling in the pit of his stomach. "Fluffy? Where are you, Fluffy?"

His search was interrupted by the newspaper, lying on the front mat. The entire front page was about this horrible fire.

Good heavens, it's just down the street, he thought as he got deeper into the story.

Mercifully, before he could put two and two together—fire, missing dog—Fluffy came trotting up the street.

Fluffy was all right.

More than all right: The dog had a spring in her step he hadn't seen in months.

And Fluffy had something in her mouth.

"There you are!" Zachary said. "I was so worried! What's that you've got? Where'd you get that?"

It was a stuffed animal: some sort of Teddy bear, with dark fur and bright blue eyes.

Zachary reached for it.

"Let me have that," he said.

But Fluffy would not let go.

"OK," the old man said. "Have it your way. Now come on inside here. It's time for breakfast. I was so worried!"

It wasn't until after Zachary had opened his shop, served his first customer, had another cup of coffee, read more about the fire, and seen the photograph of burnt stuffed animals that Zachary knew.

"You got that from the scene of the fire!" he said to the dog.

This close, Zachary could smell smoke on the dog and Teddy bear.

"We have to throw that away," he said.

And then he thought: *But why? It's cute, in its way. I'll have it dry-cleaned and put it in Elizabeth's case. I won't say a word about where it came from or whose it was, but I'll give it away free to the first person who has a little boy or a girl who would really appreciate it.*

The first person was Father Jack's sister, who came in the following week doing Christmas shopping for her daughter and son.

Chapter Twenty-Six: Underground.
Thursday, July 8.

Midnight neared. The darkness was palpable. Billy had no clue what would come next.

"He was just like you," Mary said to the boy. "A liar and a fool. He pretended not to know Ordo, or anyone named Z-DA, or a people called the Priscillas, or anything about a war, or a certain death sentence, or a highly notorious escape, or an ill-fated mission that stranded him and the mighty First Lieutenant Theus and their so-called leader on a planet—not unlike their own—halfway across the galaxy. Pretended ignorance, as if I were an idiot, incapable of seeing through such a flimsy charade!"

Mary knew where they were: in the old East Side trolley tunnel, built during the trolley age and unused since passenger train service from Providence to Newport had been discontinued, many years before.

The only sounds were dripping water and an occasional rat, the only smells rodent droppings and mildew and a deeper, darker odor, of cool damp earth that's never been exposed to fresh air or sun. Billy could see nothing; over an hour ago, the pinprick of light that was the tunnel's entrance had receded and finally disappeared. He had no idea how far in they were, or even if they were still in the main tunnel and not some spur abandoned when the motorcar had made museum pieces out of Providence's trolleys.

Mary didn't care.

Mary seemed to know where she was and where she was headed.

She wasn't stumbling over the rocks and old ties and other junk that were tripping Billy.

That was most alarming now to Billy.

Not the yarn his mother was spinning again—a yarn almost silly it had grown so bizarre—but the fact that she could navigate in pitch black. The fact that she was so familiar with in here. The fact that she quite obviously had been in here before.

Must have been here when I was at school or when I was asleep, Billy thought. *And not just once. Probably lots and lots of times.*

But why?

Mary went on. The deeper they had penetrated the darkness, the more agitated she had become. If Billy hadn't been with her to know better, he would have guessed she'd been drinking.

"What do you suppose his intention was?" Mary said. "You're of his race—you tell me. Did he think he could protect himself with such a transparent and flimsy excuse? Did he think he could conceal his identity, as you've so pitifully attempted to do? Did he really believe I would give up and go away? 'I don't know what you're talking about,' he said when first I confronted him. 'It's me—Angel! You know me! I'm a friend of Billy's!'

"What a pathetic sight, dirty clothes and face and hair all amuss. And that squawking. My, but he could squawk. 'I didn't mean to break his glasses,' he kept saying, 'honest, Mrs. McAllister, I didn't. I'll get him a new pair. I promise I will.' Such garbage, spewing from his mouth. I should have silenced him then, the second I found him.

"Because I remembered the so-called Angel—at least *he* did not attempt to lie about his name, as you have done—from Ordonia. He was nothing but an enlisted man, a coward and a loser. Were it not for his father, a High Justice and dear friend of Ordo, he never would have been a part of your crew. I should have known better. Should have known that he could not help, that such privileged information as Ordo's whereabouts could not possibly have been entrusted to him. That would be the responsibility of a captain or mighty first lieutenant, wouldn't it, Lt. Theus? Stupid as it was, I gave him his chance, just as I've given you yours. True to form, he fucked with me.

"On the second night we met, we had ourselves a little chat. We talked about his deadline. We talked about the urgency of finding Ordo. We talked of darkness, of how coincidental it was that he favored the place called The Culvert—a place so reminiscent of the underground world of Ordonia. We talked about his great friendship with you, a friendship you attempted to disguise with your phony feelings of ill will. We talked about your former place of refuge, Theus—how, naturally, it was situated in a basement, one so close to The Culvert.

"'How can you explain such coincidences?' I said to him.

"'But I told you: I don't know what you're talking about,' he said.

"'I'm talking about the whereabouts of Ordo,' I said.

"'I don't know any Ordo. Please. You have to believe me.'

"I had a grip on his arm, much as I've had on yours as we've moved through this tunnel. 'Perhaps you need a reminder,' I said. 'Perhaps this will help refresh your memory.'

"So I gave Angel a jolt. Tased him, as they might say down here. Hardly life-threatening—but how delightful to see him writhe in pain! What an exquisite experience!

"'There, now,' I said when he'd had a moment to collect his thoughts. 'Let us walk through this again. You are the so-called Angel: a member of Ordo's crew. A lowly member, but a member, nonetheless. Is that not true?'

"'Yes,' he said. It was the first honest thing he'd said to me.

"'Very good, Angel. And do you acknowledge what your mission was? To find and destroy me? Is that not correct?'

"'Yes.'

"'And your first lieutenant was Theus. He also has taken refuge in this city. You have been in contact with him.'

"'Yes.'

"'And there are others. One masquerades as a priest. One is a female with ties to the authorities here on earth. One is young and Black. One, a particularly offensive one, wears gold chains and has taken cover in the basement of an opulent house. All your allies. All dedicated to serving Ordo.'

"'Yes,' Angel said.

"'And were it not Ordo's express wish that he and he alone terminate Z-DA—such ego, needing another stripe to wear on his uniform!—otherwise any or all of you already would have attempted to do so? Is that not the truth?'

"'Yes.'

"'But Ordo, wounded in the crash, does not have sufficient strength yet. Meanwhile, as he recovers in his protected place, you desperately try to figure some way to summon help—because even when he is well again, not even the mighty Ordo can alone return himself and his merry men to home. That's it in a nutshell, isn't it, Angel?'

"'Yes,' he whined—and it was with that fresh whining that I saw I would get nowhere, no matter how long I tried. Once a coward and a fool, always a coward and a fool.

"'What is it that you want?' he said. 'Just tell me what you want. I'll do anything you say. Anything. Just please don't hurt me again. Please. *Please*, Mrs. McAllister.'

"'You mean Z-DA,' I said, losing patience with being called by that name.

"'Z-DA,' he said.

"'That's better. I want Ordo,' I repeated.

"'I can get Ordo,' he said, 'I just need time. If you let me go, I'll meet you back here tomorrow with him.'

"You can see where it went from there. What a pitiful ploy."

She killed Angel, Billy thought, but he would not give voice to it, would not allow himself to believe it, could not, not now.

She only saw the news, like everybody else, he desperately reasoned. *Saw the news and brought Angel into the make-believe world she's got inside her head.*

Billy reached into his backpack and gave Wiggle a squeeze.

We're gonna be OK, he thought, convictionlessly. *Everything's gonna work out.*

"I want to help you, Mom," Billy said.

"That tired old chestnut again?" Mary said.

"We could get lost and die in here."

"You don't let up with your foolishness, do you?" Mary said. "Is this what Ordo teaches his lieutenants, to persist to the bitter end? Listen to this: 'Lost and die in here,' as if you were uncomfortable in the dark. This is your territory, Theus! This must bring back fond remembrances of home! I have been here long enough to explore. I have seen the utility tunnels, the culverts, the drains and pipes and sluices and crawlspaces. This is your natural habitat, Theus—and Ordo's, so dark and so cool. But for its position in the galaxy, this could be Ordonia."

"I want to get out of here," Billy said.

All day, they had wandered the streets, riding buses, sitting on benches, at one point taking an Uber to Crimson Vanner's

East Side mansion, where a man in a guardhouse shooed them away. For dinner, they ate at Burger King, then walked up toward College Hill, toward Brown University. They were deep inside the tunnel before Billy realized she hadn't brought them there to sleep, but to walk... and walk.

Somehow, he'd managed to contain his fear.

Having Wiggle had helped.

So had his new resolution: as soon as they got out of here, he was going for help.

He was going to call Uncle Jack or Amanda—would even go to the police, if he had to. Since the eviction, Mary had filled him with talk of what happened to wayward little boys when the authorities got them, but anything was better than in here.

Anything.

We could die in here, Billy thought.

"I want to get out of here," he said.

Mary let loose a laugh—a wicked and cackling thing that echoed off the tunnel walls and sent the rats scurrying.

"You sound like Angel did," she said. "I should think that would be beneath a mighty First Lieutenant like you, Theus. I should think that might even be grounds for a formal reprimand— or worse—were Ordo to get wind of it!"

"Please," Billy begged. "No further."

"And who holds the key here? Not me, Theus, but *you!* Your fate depends on when, and whether, you lead me to Ordo. I had hoped that tonight would be the night when you would see reason. I had hoped that the story I have just related might serve as motivation. But there are other motivators, you know."

Suddenly, the smell of electricity was strong.

Stronger than at any time since Ocean State Park.

"I had hoped it wouldn't have come to this," Mary said, "but it has. Consider this but a preview of what it shall be like when your deadline is up. You do remember your deadline, do you not, Theus? Two nights from tonight?"

The sensation was, at first, like a bee sting on his little finger.

Billy's hand jerked, but she had a dead grip he could not break.

The sting intensified, began to move up his arm, began to multiply, a dozen bee stings, a hundred, ten hundred thousand, roaring through his body, stifling the scream inside his lungs, stifling his breath, claiming consciousness.

Chapter Twenty-Seven: The mist.
Friday, July 9.

A light, way up high above him. *A yellow-orange light, shadowy and weak, but a light, definitely a light, Billy thought. Looks like a streetlight shining down through… through what? A screen? A grate? Yes, a grate. Like what goes over a storm drain.*

Billy blinked, trying for better definition.

Am I in The Culvert?

How long was I asleep?

How do I know I'm awake?

Why's it summer and I'm so cold?

Where's Mom?

Then he saw her, just outside the grid pattern cast by the streetlight.

She seemed to be asleep. At least she wasn't going crazy any-more—she was only curled into a ball, turned into herself, like a kitten near a stove. Her sunglasses had slid down her nose and Billy, squinting, could tell that her eyes were closed.

She was still clutching the photograph she hadn't let out of her sight since she'd found it in the trunk: that photo of Jessica and her Baby Bear.

Slowly, Billy remembered.

It was like emerging from fog, the world taking on recogniz-able shapes again.

The eviction.

Walking all over Providence.

Mary watching him every second.

That bus ride to the zoo.

That other bus ride to Ocean State Park, which they didn't visit.

That Uber ride which took them around the city, including past Crimson Vanner's new house, where they had stopped and Mary had stared blankly for the longest time, as if trying unsuccessfully to recall something that wouldn't come.

The setting sun.

Going into the old trolley tunnel, thinking that's where they would sleep.

Mary's craziness getting crazier.

Moving.

Maybe still in the tunnel, maybe moved to a culvert or storm drain... so many underground places in a city... a city under a city...

The way she'd grabbed his hand... the feeling like bee stings, like... like...

Some parts Billy didn't want to remember, couldn't believe were real.

Nothing since the eviction—since long before the eviction, actually—had anything seemed real. All one unending *Twilight Zone* episode, all of them trapped inside.

Billy tried moving, but his arms and legs were frozen.

He concentrated, grit his teeth and struggled, but it was like one of those dreams when the monster's bearing down on you and you're paralyzed.

Only a feeling like pins and needles.

He was starting to be afraid again.

I can yell.

If there's a streetlight we must be under a street and if we're under a street there must be people.

But his mouth wouldn't move. Save for heart and lungs, all of his muscles were paralyzed.

He was considering his next move—was panicked with the thought that maybe, this time, there *wasn't* a next move—when he saw the mist.

He was sure it was a mist, vaporous, rising from his mother.

And that smell of electricity, stronger than ever.

When it was a few inches above Mary, the mist stopped, like a tiny white cloud, motionless against a night sky.

The mist rose again and disappeared.

Mary was moving now.

She was clenching and unclenching her fists, and her legs and arms were spasming, as if she were about to have a seizure. Her lips quivered but formed no words. She was sweating. Her nostrils twitched. The smell of electricity was fading. Tears formed but her eyes did not open.

She was crying in her sleep.

Mom's really possessed, Billy thought, and the weight of that settled around him like concrete.

Billy could feel his heart pounding in his chest. He waited, sure the mist would return, but it did not. Whatever it was had taken leave of her, at least for now.

That would explain everything, Billy thought. *Why when she's like that she doesn't remember Baby Bear or Jess or me—who I really am. It takes over her body and blots out her brain, just like Invasion of the Body Snatchers. Her brain doesn't know what's happened. It must go into some kind of numb state.*

Possessed by what?

That was the next logical question, a deeply disturbing one.

A ghost, like in one of those magazines she brings home sometimes from the grocery store? An alien, like she... it... claims?

Why her?

Why not Uncle Jack or Amanda or Andres?

The next thought hit hard:

Maybe it already has. Maybe they're in on it, too.

Billy was panicked that *it* would return.

He knew it would.

It always returns. It's been returning now for weeks and weeks.

That truth was inescapable.

I have to get help.

Mom's in real bad trouble.

There was some feeling in his fingers and hands now. It seemed to be moving up his arms, like a tide slowly coming in. Close behind was movement. He could flex his fingers. He could bend his wrists.

Come on, fingers.

Come on, hands.

Billy said a prayer. Feeling was returning to his shoulders now, and to his ankles and feet. He massaged his arms, the way a pitcher does after a game.

"Here we go, Wiggle," he said, reaching into his backpack for his pet. "Told you we'd be out of here soon."

Billy was looking up the shaft now, measuring it in his mind. It was nearly as high as he'd first thought: Barely over his head, in fact, and lined with plenty of rocks. He could climb it easy. Getting the grate off might be beyond him, but if it was, he could poke a hand up, shout and wave. Someone would come. Someone had to.

Billy could stand now.

He was wobbly, but he could manage.

There was the grate, just out of reach.

"You gotta stay here a minute," he said to his hamster. He zipped the backpack compartment. "I'll be right back."

Billy put one foot up the side of the culvert. He put his other foot up. This was a piece of cake. This was no harder than climbing a tree.

Almost near the top now.

His hand through the grate.

He did not see the mist returning.

Did not see Mary rise.

He felt the hand clamp around his ankle.

"Where do you think you're going?"

Billy screamed as the current zapped through his body.

The boy flopped unconscious back into the culvert.

Chapter Twenty-Eight: The police detective.
Friday, July 9.

Lieutenant Perry Callahan, the police detective, asked the Hasbro Children's Hospital emergency department secretary for a room where he could be alone with Amanda.

Billy was with a doctor, being examined. The staff had put the hamster they'd found in a cage, for return to the boy at the appropriate time.

"He's a good kid," the detective said when he'd closed the door.

"I know," said Amanda. "And Mary McAllister's a sick woman, Lieutenant. I guess I didn't realize just how sick until all this."

"Kid was lucky," the cop said. "Guy who found him was on his way to work. You should see the shortcut he takes: down this alley, across an empty lot, then along near an old warehouse where that sewer is. I bet there aren't five people in the course of a day who walk down there. And I can guarantee you there isn't another guy on earth down there that early. This is one of those go-getters who's into the office by 5:30. Yuppie sort; stockbroker or something. Who's to say what would have happened to the kid if he'd gone undiscovered any longer? His mother was doing double loops by then."

"Did she put up any resistance?"

"One of my men's got claw marks up and down his arms. I told him he was lucky he didn't get bit. And after what she did to that poor kid's hamster…"

"What happened to the hamster?"

"Near's we can figure, she tried to eat it."

"Oh, Jesus."

Amanda was suddenly nauseous.

"Definitely one for the ages," Callahan said.

"I take it you know her history," Amanda said.

"Not as much as my captain's going to want to know. We pink-slipped her off to the funny farm without getting much more than her name—which, of course, rang some buzzers 'cause of that Ocean State Park thing last month. *That* history we know, but not much more."

"Officer, I think you could be more professional," Amanda said. "'Funny farm.' This is 2021."

"Sorry," the cop said. "Mental-health training and all, old habits die hard."

"I assume you sent her to Butler Hospital," Amanda said.

"That's right," the cop said. "An emergency admission. Anyway, we tried asking the kid what happened, but he was too shook up, as you've seen. Apparently, he'd been in there long enough that he was starting to pick up on her whacky business himself.

"'Aliens,' he kept saying. 'They're taking her over.' Jesus. I feel sorry for the kid, having to grow up with a basket case like that."

"Officer?"

"Someone living with mental illness, I meant to say. Now let's get some background, Miss Sierra."

"*Ms.* Ms. Sierra."

"Ms. Sierra. You could start by telling me about when you got involved with the McAllisters, and why."

Hasbro Children's Hospital released Billy into Amanda's custody at quarter past one in the afternoon, seven and a half hours after he and his floridly psychotic mother were extracted from a sewer by a rescue squad and four police officers wearing rubber gloves and face shields.

Billy was to get plenty of rest, to be kept from stress and to be watched carefully by a responsible adult. In a week, the ED doctor wanted Billy's pediatrician to see him in his office.

"He's all right mentally?" Amanda said when the attendant had wheeled Billy around a corner.

"I'd keep an eye on him just to be safe, but, yes, I think he's all right mentally," the doctor said. "For the moment, that is. He's had a terrible trauma, being down there. I'm sure you will be arranging proper care going forward. Trauma sometimes can take a while to surface, and when it does, it can be debilitating. But given your work and your long history with this family, I'm sure you know that."

Amanda did.

"I want to see Mom," Billy said after the attendant had bid good-bye at the door.

They were walking to Amanda's car. Billy had a fistful of lollipops and his backpack. He'd insisted on keeping it, even with the fresh brown stain along the front of the pocket. The policeman had agreed.

"You can't see her yet, Billy," Amanda said. "Your mother needs to concentrate on getting better. She's a very sick person right now."

"But she's not!" Billy protested. "That's what I keep telling everyone! She's not crazy! Something's taken over her body and it isn't her anymore! Please, Amanda. I've got to see her. I've got to tell them what's going on. Please."

Amanda thought she'd seen everything—the stories and injustices and demands that are a social worker's business—but no master's degree class had prepared her for dealing with a kid who was convinced his mother had been possessed by an extraterrestrial.

"You've had a very rough time, Billy," she said. "I don't for a minute doubt that you believe your mother—"

"But I can prove it!" he said. "See—she found this picture of Jess holding Baby Bear. When she looks at it—she thinks it's Ordo, her enemy. I bet the picture's still back there in the sewer. We could get it, and show it to her, and then you'd see the mist coming over her, and... and..."

Billy was in tears.

Amanda hugged him.

"I promise we'll see your mom as soon as we can," she said. "Maybe in a couple of days. As soon as we can."

"You're not taking me to a group home, are you?" Billy managed through his tears.

Official department policy mandated that—placement of state wards only in state-approved facilities—and anyone caught violating official department was subject to immediate disciplinary proceedings.

But fuck policy. Amanda would take her chances.

"You're coming to my house," she said.

"When will Uncle Jack come?"

"Tonight, if he gets back in time. First thing tomorrow morning if he doesn't."

Billy squeezed Amanda's hand.

"Do you think I could write her a letter?" he said. "Do you think that'd be OK?"

"You can write her a letter."

"Will they let her read it?"

"We can only try."

"Thanks, Amanda," Billy said. "You're awful nice."

Chapter Twenty-Nine: Parasites.
Friday, July 9.

Amanda lived with her mother on the North Shore of Boston. In many ways, it reminded Billy of Blue Hill: the size of the house, the trees outside, the proximity to the ocean, the big bed in the room at the head of the stairs. Even the hushed voices of Amanda and her mother somewhere downstairs brought back bittersweet memories of Grammy's place.

Billy was at the desk in the room at the head of the stairs. His room, for now.

He'd emptied his backpack, putting his socks and underwear away in the drawer Amanda had said would be his. He'd thumbtacked his Red Sox banner to the wall in the place Amanda told him he could. He'd set up the picture of him and Mom and Jess and Uncle Jack at Ocean State.

And he'd written a letter to Mom and addressed the envelope: "Mary McAllister, Butler Hospital, Blackstone Blvd., Providence, Rhode Island."

Amanda had promised to hand-deliver it tomorrow.

Dear Jess, Billy wrote into his journal.

> *I'm staying with Amanda. You never met her, but I told you about her before. She's our social worker. She's nice. Her mom's nice too. They live in a big house like Grammy's. There's woods and everything all around and if it's quiet you can hear waves. Mom and I came here once for dinner so I knew I would like it when Amanda said I was gonna stay here.*

Mom's in worse trouble than ever, Jess.

It sounds wicked crazy, but something takes over her body sometimes. She's OK one day and then another day she's not. Even in a couple of hours she changes sometimes. It seemed at first like it was drinking. She was drinking again a lot. Uncle Jack was real worried. Then she wasn't drinking but she was still weird. Maybe weirder even. I waited and then I talked to Andres about it. He said it was in her head. For a while I figured that's what it was, too. Funny stuff in her head, like before when she had to go to the hospital and take special drugs.

But I know different because yesterday we got evicted. That means we got kicked out because we didn't have money for rent. I took Wiggle and some stuff, and we walked and rode the bus and took an Uber all over the city. When it got dark, we went into an old trolley tunnel. I thought we were going to sleep there. Homeless people do that and some of them, the junkies, can be dangerous. I was scared even before everything started happening.

In the tunnel, Mom changed like she does. Here's what happens.

Her voice gets different and her face too and she gets real angry. She wears sunglasses even in the dark. She calls me names. She says I'm her enemy. She says I'm not me even though I am me, doh. She looks at a picture of you and doesn't know who it is. She thinks Baby Bear's name is really Ordo and that I work for Ordo and Ordo is really from another planet.

She says she has to kill Ordo because Ordo was sent to kill her. It's like one of those galaxy feuds you see in a Star Wars movie or TV show. She says I know where Ordo is cause I helped hide him and I'll die if I don't tell her where he is. She said Angel was in on it and she had to kill him.

When it first started, I thought it was just more stuff in her head. Until she touched me and it was like putting your fingers in a plug. It hurt wicked and knocked me out. Nothing like that could happen if it was only craziness in her head.

When I woke up I saw a mist like fog on the ocean. It rose out of her body. I saw it real clear. When it was gone she seemed like Mom again, only tired and hurt. Then it must've come back cause she started attacking me again. Wiggle was gone and I didn't find him. A guy saved me by calling the police. I went to the hospital and everything, but I wasn't hurt too bad. They took Mom to a psychiatric hospital, not the one in Maine but the one in Providence. I wrote her a letter and Amanda's gonna bring it there and I hope the staff really gives it to her and not throw it away cause they think it will disturb her or something.

I told Amanda about everything even the part about her being in on it and Angel being killed but you can tell she doesn't believe me. She says it's all those science-fiction books Mom reads mixed up with her mental illness and alcohol. Uncle Jack probably won't believe me too cause he's already worried about her drinking and stuff but I'm still gonna tell him when I see him.

Do you believe me, Jess? Do you think an alien (or maybe a weird ghost) could take over her body? There's been scary movies about that. I saw a story once on the cover of a magazine near the register at Food Chain.

I wish you could help, Jess. You're in heaven and maybe you can ask God to help. Mom needs help real bad. I could use some too cause I'm real scared.

In Billy's dream tonight, ideas and sensations cascade through the darkness, like blinking saucer shapes across a moonless sky.

In the dream, he cannot see Jess.

He can only hear her voice, very close.

"Time goes different here," she is letting him know. "Much, much slower, Billy."

What do you mean? the dreaming Billy wonders.

"You can see the seconds float by," Jess says.

But you've been dead four years.

"Oh, no, Billy. I'm not dead. How could I talk to you if I was dead?"

Then what are you?

"Alive, Billy. Alive!"

So you're in heaven, like Uncle Jack says.

"Nope, not in heaven. But I *am* alive—and all because of Ordo. Ordo gives the gift of life. It's what he calls Prana, or life force, which he says a big thing in Hindu religion and mediation and everything and isn't just something here on earth but actually all across the universe. That's all I know about it, because he loses me when he tries to explain better.

"All that matters is that he is a very good person or whatever you'd call him. When he is healthy, he is very powerful. But there was a terrible accident. Ordo was hurt very bad. He's getting better, but he cannot get completely better by himself. He needs help, Billy.

"He needs you to open the door. And now I have to go. When you get here, I'll tell you the rest of what you need to know."

In Billy's dream, there is another voice. A gentle and calm voice, floating on a warm summer night.

"Z-DA is evil," the voice is saying.

Who are you? Billy asks.

"I am Ordo. I am Jess's friend and Z-DA's enemy."

Z-DA wants to kill you.

"Yes. And he will let nothing stand in his way."

Not even Mom.

"Do you know what a parasite is, Billy?"

Something that lives inside something else. Like a tapeworm, right?

"Exactly," Ordo says. "Such a precise image. You're a very smart boy, Billy. You remind me of many boys on my planet, the best and the brightest."

Thanks.

"I bet you know that a parasite can live outside its host, although not for very long. Do you also know what a parasite will do if it's not stopped?"

Hurt the host?

"Precisely. Some parasites even kill their hosts before moving on to the next victim. On this planet, the parasitoid wasp for example. Have you ever heard of it?"

No, but it sounds awful.

"It is. This is what Z-DA will do to your Mom."

Like a vampire.

"Yes. Only it is not blood that Z-DA sucks, but life itself. That's what his species—the Lepros—did to the people on my planet for centuries. Did you know there are people on Ordonia similar to human beings—homo sapiens as they are classified here?"

No.

"There are—on my planet and many other planets, as well. On Ordonia, they are great friends and allies of the Priscillas. When the Lepros first began to infest them, we vowed to come to their defense. No one imagined it would take so long, but Z-DA's species—whose origins are lost in the Big Bang—is unusually stubborn. You've been told about the war, haven't you?"

Yes.

"And how, after so many years of battle, Z-DA was the last of his species left?"

Yes.

"Once, there were hundreds of Lepros. Unlike the Priscillas and their human allies—who draw their strength from the sun—they lived in underground tunnels and caves. It was important for Z-DA to be destroyed because, like many parasites, they can reproduce from just one. No mating or pollination or anything like that requiring two of a kind."

You mean they don't need a mother and a father.

"Exactly. To our great distress, on the day before his execution, Z-DA escaped. Knowing of the similarities between our planet and Planet Earth, I chose to lead the expedition to this part of the universe. The crash was not in the plans, needless to say."

Was it your fault?

"A panel someday will be asked to decide that question," Ordo says. "All of our crew perished—all but me, although Z-DA wrongly believes otherwise, believes that other crew members made it and are conspiring against him. My deep regret is that so many of my own died. I would have helped them if I could. But I was badly hurt. I was quickly taken from the scene. But the time will come when I will be able to help them."

Z-DA believes I was on the ship.

"Z-DA has been fooled. Z-DA, while still cunning, is showing the effects of so many years living as a criminal. Being pursued so long, being the sole survivor of his species—all of this has clouded his judgment, making him even more dangerous and unpredictable. My suspicion is that Z-DA, in his demented frame of mind, has mistaken you for one of my officers, the one named Theus. Theus, who was a member of the platoon that finally captured Z-DA."

Then why didn't Z-DA just take over me instead of Mom?

"Such a perceptive question! Your sister has told me all about you, Billy—you and your mom. Your lives have not been easy. Your mother has been tortured by demons she cannot control. She has weaknesses that have destroyed many like her. A person like her is easy prey for a Lepros, much easier than you yourself would have been.

"There is another reason, as well. In its parasitism, a Lepros does not have the ability to really get at conscious—or unconscious—thought, at least at first. Memory, emotion, temperament—the very essence of a person—it takes dedicated effort before the Lepros is able to successfully consume those. Slowly, it pecks away, stealing what it can when it can. Fortunately, when Lepros are stopped in time, their victims can be expected to recover fully."

How long before… before…

"I cannot predict precisely. But it cannot be long."

In his dream, Billy is starting to cry.

"Only Ordo can defeat Z-DA," Jess says. "But he must be healthy first."

How's he get healthy?

"He needs help, Billy."

What kind of help?

"The help of a brand-new day."

What do you mean?

"As I said, I will tell you when you are here," Jess says. "But not until. That is my agreement with Ordo. And I never question his wisdom."

Please, Jess, I need to know now?

The dream is dissolving now, the transmission interrupted.

Please, Jess. Please…

Billy, weeping on his pillow, is awake.

Not until later, on the long drive to Maine, will Jess communicate the means by which Ordo can be restored to health… the health he will need to destroy Z-DA.

Chapter Thirty: Escape.

Saturday, July 10.

In the investigation that would follow Mary McAllister's unauthorized departure from the Butler Hospital Emergency Department, several factors would come to light.

Most chilling would be what was captured on a video recorder: McAllister calling for help in her locked room, a staff member entering, a loud zap, a louder scream, the staff member collapsing unconscious and McAllister calmly walking out the door. Another staff member who found her unconscious colleague would recall the smell of electricity, even though no electrical malfunction was discovered.

A separate camera would capture the woman in a parking lot, breaking into a Toyota Prius and driving away. How she had started it would remain a mystery.

Chapter Thirty-One: Mark of a killer.
Sunday, July 11.

The story led all the newscasts and made the front page of *The Providence Journal.*

PROVIDENCE—Vincent M. "Crimson" Vanner, 32, reputed cocaine dealer and confidant of reputed mob boss Raymond Bellini Jr., was found dead Saturday in the East Side mansion he had purchased this year.

Vanner died of undetermined causes, but authorities are treating his death as a homicide, police said. An autopsy was performed this morning by the medical examiner.

"There are several factors that lead us to believe Vanner was the subject of a 'hit,'" said Det. William Tillinghast. "He had many known enemies, including several associated with Mexican drug lords."

Tillinghast noted that police are investigating a possible link between Vanner's death and the still-unsolved homicide this month of Paul "Angel" Iannotti, the 14-year-old whose body was found in a culvert in the Armory District.

"Both homicides have the mark of the same killer," said Tillinghast, who declined to say anything about possible suspects.

Sources said, however, that Vanner and Iannotti were both killed in particularly gruesome fashion, suggesting the same killer is responsible.

"It wasn't your average hit," said one source. "Both bodies were mutilated really bad. Something electrical—a taser or cattle prod, maybe—was used, perhaps as torture before the actual killing."

The murder weapon was not a gun or knife, police said, but they would not elaborate. Despite requests by *The Providence Journal*, the medical examiner has refused to release Iannotti's autopsy report.

Police were led to Vanner's home by neighbors, who called after hearing what they thought were screams. His body was found in the cellar in an old coal bin that was being used to store furniture, police said.

Vanner purchased the home, which has 14 rooms, earlier this year. Vanner owned Able Computers Inc., but police say they have long suspected that company was a front for a cocaine distribution ring in southern New England.

Police could not immediately confirm a report by a neighbor that shortly before Vanner's death, a car pulled up to Vanner's home, a woman stepped out, and Vanner let her in.

Chapter Thirty-Two: Florid psychosis.
Monday, July 12.

Father Jack Lambert sat in the living room of Amanda's mother's house. Amanda was at work, and her mother was upstairs.

"I should have trusted my instincts," Jack said.

His tone was of a man pissed with himself.

"Weeks and weeks ago, I knew something was wrong with your mother. I should have done more."

"But it wasn't the drinking," Billy insisted. "I mean, she *was* drinking, I lied when she said she wasn't—I shouldn't have and I'm sorry—but there was something else going on, Uncle Jack. I should've told you, but I was scared. I didn't know what it was just that it was bad. Now I know. This thing—it was trying to take over her and it was, bit by bit. Now it's almost in full control. You gotta believe me, Uncle Jack. You just gotta. Nobody else does. Mom's in real bad trouble."

Father Jack shifted uncomfortably in his chair.

The story had gushed from Billy in one long, agitated take, and everything he'd said disturbed the priest greatly. It wasn't that he believed any of this bizarre recounting, of course; Jack knew precisely what was behind it, and that was Mary's precarious mental state, which seemed to have taken a quantum leap from depression into florid psychosis.

What troubled the priest was that Billy himself might be showing the effects of something more than an emotionally devastating several days.

Billy himself might be psychotic.

Severe trauma, he knew well, can have that effect, even on a child that young, if rarely.

"I think everyone needs some good solid peace and quiet," the priest said. "It's been a very difficult time for all of us. I think when you're back with me in Boston, Billy, you'll see things in a different light. As for your mom—well, they're going to make her better. She just needs time."

"She doesn't *have* time," Billy burst out. "If we don't get Ordo she's going to die!"

"Your mom's safe where she is."

"She's not safe anywhere! Jess told me!"

Jack reached for his nephew, but Billy recoiled.

He was crying, and not any soft, healing tears. His body was convulsed.

"You don't believe me," he sobbed. "Nobody does."

"Billy, I love you," the priest said, and this time the boy gave in. This time, he let the priest wrap him in his arms.

"I have to go out for a few hours now," Jack said when Billy was calm. "You can stay here with Amanda's mom. You're safe with her here. And I'm sure she'll let you watch TV and make some super snacks."

"Where are you going?" Billy said.

"To see a judge, who's going to give permission for me to take you back to Boston. You're going to stay with me while your mother gets all better—and she *will* get better, Billy, I give you my solemn word. I know it doesn't seem like it now, but she will. In the meantime, you're going to have your own room, and you can decorate it any way you want, and have an iPad and make some new friends. How's that sound?"

Billy said nothing.

"Would a couple of new hamsters make it a little better?" Jack said after a pause. "Hmmm?"

Billy still didn't answer, but Jack saw his face brighten a bit.

The next time he saw his nephew's face, terror would be written across it.

Chapter Thirty-Three: Deadline.
Monday, July 12.

At six minutes past noon, as Channel 10 was wrapping up its story about the slaying of Crimson Vanner, a Toyota Prius recently stolen from a parking lot at Butler Hospital stopped in front of Amanda's mother's house.

A woman in sunglasses rolled down the window, checked up and down the street, saw no one and got out.

"Who is it?" Amanda's mother said through the door.

"Nancy Gallagher. I work with your daughter. Something's come up in court. I'm afraid it's an emergency."

"Goodness," said the woman. "Please come in."

The door swung open, and Mary McAllister stepped inside.

Amanda's mother, of course, did not recognize her.

"Is it about Billy?" the older woman said anxiously.

"Yes. The judge ruled that he was really an alien."

Amanda's mother's face showed her confusion.

"You mean an undocumented immigrant," she said.

"Oh, no, I mean an Ordonian. As punishment, the judge has ordered him into the custody of Z-DA, leader and sole survivor of the Lepros. That's me, Granny. Those who have supported Lieutenant Theus during his stay on Planet Earth have been ordered punished as well. That includes you, you old fool."

"I beg your pardon?"

"You didn't think I'd find you, did you? It really wasn't very hard. You'd be amazed what kind of information Dean Street Residence will give out over the phone if you just ask the right way."

"I'm afraid there must be some sort of mistake..."

"I'm afraid not."

The visitor took off her sunglasses and Amanda's mother screamed.

She was not looking at the eyes of Mary McAllister or anyone else she might have recognized. She was looking at eyes that flickered and glowed like burning coal.

"This Bud's for you," the visitor said as she reached for the older woman's throat.

Billy had been upstairs when Mary McAllister rang the doorbell. Speaking in a quiet voice, he'd been talking on the phone to Andres.

Andres, he'd decided, was his last hope. Maybe Andres believed him, maybe he didn't, but at least he hadn't dismissed his friend like all the adults.

And he'd agreed with Billy that as crazy and sick and unreal as it sounded—as dangerous as it was—Billy had to get to Maine.

"Mom," Billy said when Mary reached the top of the stairs.

Except it wasn't Mom.

He knew that from the sunglasses, from the smell of something burning. He knew that from her voice, the same crazy-pitched voice she'd had walking through the tunnels.

The room was spinning and Billy hoped he was dreaming.

"I won't play that game with you this time, Theus," Mary said. "That silly little identification game you find so amusing. The time for games is past. There's only a deadline left and now that deadline is here. You're coming with me, Theus. You're taking me to Ordo or you're going to die."

Chapter Thirty-Four: Blood brothers.
Monday, July 12.

Early-evening sun streamed through the door into the front hall, casting the crowd of police detectives in stark relief and causing them to squint as they went about their work.

Siren blaring, the ambulance had just pulled away. Amanda had gone along with her mother, who was conscious, if groggy. The EMTs assured her that her mother's injuries were minor—bruising about the neck, but no lacerations or fractured bones. *She might even be discharged from the emergency department tonight*, one said.

The local police had brought Lieutenant Callahan in on the case, and it hadn't taken great powers of deduction for him to link what had happened here with Mary McAllister's escape from Butler. Nor had it taken Sherlock Holmes to come up with the fact that McAllister, dangerously deranged, had kidnapped her son. Word of the crime had been radioed in and was probably already out to the news junkies who monitored police scanners and alerted reporters.

"You're her brother?" Callahan said to Father Jack.

"I am."

"Priest, huh?"

"Yes."

"Has your sister always been this sick?" the detective said.

"Life's never been easy for Mary," Jack said.

"It's going to be less easy when we get her," Callahan said. "Kidnapping's a federal offense. And if the old lady dies…"

Maybe it was the pained look on the priest's face that made Callahan apologize.

"I'm sorry," the cop said. "I can't imagine what you are going through now."

Callahan scribbled a few notes onto his pad and then looked up.

"Any idea where she might have taken him?" he said. "We've already posted a man over at her old apartment, but there's been no sign of them. We've got some guys back down in those tunnels, but it could be all night before we get through all of them."

We have to free Ordo, Billy had said in that long, crazy talk this morning. *We have to go to Maine and let him out. He's been helping Jess stay alive. Only he can help Mommy now.*

Jess is alive, the priest had said, *but not in her coffin. She's alive with Jesus in heaven.*

You're wrong! She's with Ordo and now they both need our help! Ordo needs the sun! And when he gets it, he'll be strong enough to kill Z-DA and Mommy will be free!

"Father? Are you in there?" Callahan said.

"I have no idea where she might have taken him," Jack said, and it was the first lie he could remember telling since joining the priesthood so many years ago.

Jack drove by Mary's old apartment, but saw only the police cruiser Callahan had mentioned, parked in front of the building. The officer inside was slumped back in his seat. He appeared to be dozing.

The priest was driving off when he heard a young boy shout: "Father Jack!"

It was Andres, running along the sidewalk after his car.

Jack stopped. Andres came alongside.

"Hi, Father Jack," the boy said.

"Hello, Andres."

"I bet you're looking for Billy."

"I am."

"So are the cops. They're looking for his mom, too."

"Have you seen them, Andres?"

"Nope. But Billy called. This afternoon. He talked about all this crazy stuff and then he had to hang up. He said there was someone downstairs and it didn't sound good."

"Did he say anything about aliens?"

Andres looked at the priest, then away, something he always did when he was about to lie.

He remembered how just as he was hanging up Billy had sworn him to blood-brother secrecy. He also remembered all the good things Billy had said about his uncle, how the priest had always been on Billy's side.

"He told you?" Andres finally said.

"Yes."

"About his mom?"

"Yes."

"Yeah, it was about the aliens. He was talking about having to get to Maine, that Maine was where everything was gonna turn out OK. He wanted me to come with him."

"Did he say where in Maine he was headed?"

"His grandmother's old place."

"Did he say what he was going to do there?"

"No," Andres said, "Just that it was really important and he'd tell me later. We were going to take a bus—he wanted to know if I had any money—and I do, fifty bucks that I, ah, borrowed from my brother, still here in my pocket. He didn't want to hitchhike he said 'cause he thought the cops would get us 'cause we're not old enough to be hitching and we'd stick out. He sounded weird, Father Jack, even weirder than the first time he told me about this aliens stuff. He sounded scared, too. I was gonna meet him at the bus station, but he hung up before saying when. I waited but he never called back. Then I went to the station, but he never showed up."

Jack knew how long it would take to get to Blue Hill: almost seven hours, plus another ten minutes for refueling. It would be well after midnight before he arrived.

"Do you think he went alone, Father Jack?"

"I don't think so."

"Do you think his mom was with him?"

"I think so."

"Then we have to go, too! Billy needs us, Father Jack."

"He needs *me*," the priest said. "I have to go now, Andres. If you see either of them, I want you to tell your mother or call the police. You shouldn't go near Mary now."

"I wanna go with you."

"I can't let you," Jack said.

"He's my best friend. My blood brother! I swore I'd help him!"

"You'll be helping him most by staying and watching here," Jack said. "Goodbye, Andres. Remember what I told you to do if you see either of them."

The priest eased on the gas and the car started down the street again. He hadn't gone more than a few feet before he saw Andres in the rear view, pointing to the parked cruiser.

"I'll tell them where you're going!" he said.

Father Jack stopped.

"You won't say anything," the priest said.

"But I will! I'll tell that cop right there and they'll find the place, I know the name of the town, it's Blue Hill, and then they'll arrest you and... and..."

"This is the worst judgement I think I've ever exercised in my life," the priest said. "Get in. We'll call your mother when we get there. I'm praying she can forgive a priest."

Chapter Thirty-Five: Resurrection.
Tuesday, July 13.

For hours as night had fallen, Billy had huddled in the front seat, wondering if Z-DA would let go of her—if miraculously his mom would return and there would be no need to go to Blue Hill and...

he didn't know what.

But it wasn't working out that way. In all the hours, in the few words she'd spoken, there'd been no trace of Mary McAllister.

Billy wondered if there were anything left of her... or if it were already too late.

The sun had set when they turned off the interstate in Augusta. Mary stopped at a service station to fill the tank and ask directions to Blue Hill.

Billy wanted to scream: *But you know, Mom! You grew up there!*

"I think you're finally telling the truth," Mary said when she got back in the car. "Do you know that?"

"Yes," he said.

"I believe you because I don't sense any of your nonsense anymore. Even if I'm wrong—if this is another of your silly little tricks—what, really, have I forfeited? I've lost a day, that's all. If, through some misguided sense of duty, you are willing to sacrifice your life—then I shall turn my attention to that priest, that social worker, all of your cronies. I shall get what I want, Theus. One way or another, Ordo shall be mine."

I could run now, Billy thought.

But he did not act on the impulse.

We have to free Ordo, he remembered. *Only he can help Mommy now.*

Billy had recognized landmarks approaching Blue Hill in the early-dawn hours—the bridge over the Penobscot River, the now-closed paper plant at Bucksport with its giant smokestacks, the famous tombstone with the stain of a witch, Blue Hill itself in the distance—and when they pulled into the village, every detail was welcoming and familiar.

"Such a quaint place to recuperate," Mary said. "I'm sure Ordo was pleased. Protected by his shield, he could gain strength in the sun and fresh salt air as he awaited help from home."

"Ordo cannot get to sun and fresh air," Billy said.

"What do you mean?" Mary said.

"Ordo is inside someplace dark and cold," Bill said.

"And you will take me there."

"Yes," Billy said. "Turn left at the next intersection. At Tradewinds Marketplace."

"We're going to the mausoleum," Mary said.

"Yes," Billy said.

"Now it dawns on me," Mary said. "I should have known."

During the hours they'd been on the road, a voice had come into Billy's head. It was a soothing presence, dream-like but not nightmarish.

It was the voice of his sister—but not the five-year-old who had lost her battle with liver disease. It was the voice of a girl four years older. Nine, the age she would have been.

"I've had a lot of time now with my Baby Bear," Jess said. "Baby Bear has kept me good company. With Baby Bear, I'm not afraid of the dark."

"But you're in a casket," Billy's inner voice said.

"It sounds terrible, but it's not. Baby Bear has made sure all my needs are met," Jess said, "and in my present state, my needs are simple. All I need is to stay connected with the people I love—and whenever I want, Baby Bear helps me reach out to them, people like you and Uncle Jack and even Mommy, who is hurting so much. You may think these are only dreams, but they're not. Where Baby Bear comes from, this is one of the ways they talk. I also can see your journal whenever you write into it. I don't know how any of this works and Baby Bear can't really explain, but it does.

"And I dream—the most wonderful dreams. Never about Pittsburgh, only places and things and people I love. You know them all. Baby Bear can't explain how I never have nightmares, just like he can't explain how we're talking now, but we are, right?"

"I guess so," Billy's inner voice said.

"You don't have to guess," Jess said. "We're talking now."

"But where is Ordo?" Billy said. "We are driving here to help Ordo, not Baby Bear."

"You could say they are one and the same," Jess said, "but that's not really how it is. Ordo found safety inside Baby Bear, and when Baby Bear was buried with me, Ordo was, too."

"It's kind of confusing," Billy said.

"Tell me about it. It's taken a long time to figure it out and I'm not sure I really have, even now. But what matters is that we are both safe, Ordo and me. Safe and alive. With baby Bear keeping us company."

"Aren't you afraid of the dark?" Billy said.

"It's not dark here," Jess said. "Not stuffy or cold or cramped like it seems it would be, either. I wouldn't want to stay forever, but I'm not. Ordo has promised me."

"If Ordo has these superpowers, how come he can't get you both out of where you are?" Billy said.

"It seems crazy, doesn't it? The fact is until today, Ordo's had to rest and regain strength. And that always takes time, is how he explains it. As powerful as he is, this is a power he does not have. A 'vulnerability' is his word for it."

"So what happens now?"

"You set us free. That's what Ordo says, and Ordo never lies."

"How?"

"We'll tell you when you get here."

"This isn't a trick, is it?" Billy said.

"Would I do that to you?"

"No, you wouldn't."

The voice of Jess faded.

Mary steered the stolen car along Route 175 and took another left when they reached Blue Hills Falls. They reached Grammy's mansion, empty and rundown since her death. She'd left the place to Father Jack, but the cost of saving it was prohibitive and the priest had put it on the market, so far without an offer. Perhaps the rumors had spooked prospective buyers, or maybe it was the cost of fixing it.

Mary stopped the car in the driveway.

"It's time you learned the truth," she said.

Billy heard the voice of his mother, not the mother-thing.

"The truth, my son, is my mother, your Grammy, hung herself with nautical rope in that attic—just as my father did when I was a child, and his father, my grandfather, before him. A neighbor alerted the police when she hadn't seen Grammy in several days and the police found her.

"There was no such luck when my father took his life by suicide. When he'd gone missing for more than a day, search parties were organized. No one thought to look in the attic but me. I found him. I was a child younger than you."

"I'm so sorry, Mom," Billy said.

"I appreciate that, Billy. The fact is, they were not keen on mental-health intervention in those days. They did not know how to help children so terribly traumatized, if they even would have identified what I went through as trauma. What followed was many weeks in bed—my bed, in my bedroom, one story below the attic. Directly below.

"Grammy brought me herbal tea and health meals, but I had little appetite. Eventually, I emerged and returned to school. I learned to cope, but I was never the same. So you see now why I react to stress in the ways that I do."

"You are just trying to stay out of the hospital again," Billy said.

"Something like that," Mary said. "But I do not offer that as an excuse, just in the hope that you will understand, as young as you are. And that you will forgive me. Do you forgive me, Billy?"

"Of course I do," Billy said.

"Then give me a hug."

Mary drove the last distance to the family mausoleum. Her mood changed as they approached until, when they arrived, the Mary-thing was ready to return.

Constructed of granite and featuring a single door and two stained-glass windows, the mausoleum was small by the standards of most such crypts. Most members of Grammy's extended family had chosen to be buried or cremated.

But a few relatives had chosen to be here. Samuel McKay, who'd arranged to have it built, was one. Alice O'Reilly McKay, the woman from Nova Scotia who had married Samuel's son, George

McKay, was another. Grammy—Alice McKay Lambert—and the man she had married, George Linwood Lambert. And a few others, their names and stories unfamiliar to Mary and Jack.

Forbidden from coming here, Billy and Jess during her last summer had defied their mother and grandmother and snuck down here on an unseasonably cold and cloudy day.

"It's awesome," Billy had said.

"I never saw anything like it," said Jess.

"Wanna go in?" said her brother.

"We can't do that," said Jess. "It's too creepy. Besides, we'd be in enough trouble already for being here if we got caught."

"We won't get caught," Billy said.

"How do you know?"

"You think they're going to leave the fireplace as cold as it is today? No way. Besides, we can be quick. Come on, Jess, this will be cool."

"Not for me."

"Well, why don't you see."

Billy went to the door.

"We don't have the key," Jess said.

"It's gotta be here somewhere," Billy said.

"I doubt it," said Jess. "Probably hidden somewhere in the house or in one of those boxes in a bank."

"I bet there's a spare somewhere around here for Grammy's groundskeeper," said Billy. "Let's look."

The boy circled the mausoleum.

On his second time around, he found the key, hanging from the inside of a shed that housed a mower and tools.

"Voila!" he said to his sister.

Billy tried the key. It fit. He turned it and the door opened. If Billy had any expectations, it was that they would be met with the smell of mustiness and decay.

There was none.

The air was fresh, if cold, and the only smell was from an unlit scented candle with the iconic image of the Sacred Heart of Jesus.

Billy stepped in.

"Come on," he said, extending his hand to his sister.

"Do I have to?" Jess said.

"Give it a try."

"All right," Jess said. "But just for a second."

The children walked in. The marble fronts obscured views of the casket spaces behind, and the cremation niches were likewise hidden.

"See?" Billy said. "Better than a cemetery, if you think about it."

"I don't want to think about it," Jess said. "We've been here, now let's go."

The children left. Billy returned the key and they walked back to Grammy's house, where the flames were strong in the fireplace.

Mary parked the car. Her son was anxious. He did not know what was about to unfold, only that it would be beyond belief. Once again.

"I should have known," the Mary-thing said. "Baby Bear went into the casket with her. But bringing you here, Theus, was no waste of effort. You may have the honor of releasing Ordo. Who I shall make quick work of as I begin the rebirth of my people. Hallelujah!"

"I can't do anything," Billy said.

"Nothing but open the crypt and then the casket," the Mary-thing said.

"How?"

"Use your brain, Theus. Or I shall destroy you. Which is it? You still alive with a brain, or gone forever? Makes little difference to me, save for the pleasure of watching you squirm."

"I need the key," Billy said.

"And where might that be?"

"In the shed."

"And you know this how?"

"From a memory."

"Then get it," the Mary-thing said. "I will be following close behind."

Billy opened the door to the mausoleum and he and the Mary-thing went inside. All was as it had been during his visit the summer before Jess had died, with two exceptions: the space where Jess's casket lay, and the newer space below it that contained Grammy's. Their names and dates of birth and death were engraved in the marble fronts.

"Take the front off so we can open the casket," the Mary-thing said.

"I don't know how," Billy said.

"I do," the Mary-thing said.

A pulse of energy from its fingertips fractured the granite front, leaving Jess's Batesville Promethean Bronze casket exposed. The smell of electricity was thick.

"Now what?" Billy said. "It's too heavy to pull out."

"Pansy," the Mary-thing said. "Must I do everything?"

With another pulse, the casket catapulted from its space and landed in the middle of the mausoleum. The force broke the casket seal.

"Open it," the Mary-thing said.

Billy did.

There was Jess, not decaying—not as she had been at the end but as she'd looked during that final summer, when it seemed she would make it.

Better than that, even, Billy thought.

His sister's face was unblemished and rosy, her hair shiny and long. She was smiling and her eyes were open.

Sparkling, Billy thought. *She's watching me and happy I'm finally here. We don't have to see each other in dreams anymore. We are here together in life.*

Billy knelt and kissed his sister's cheek.

"I love you, Jess," he said.

"I love you too, Billy," Jess said.

"Enough of the Hallmark moment," the Mary-thing hissed. "Theus, hand me what that darling little sister of yours has wrapped in her arms."

"Baby Bear?" Billy said.

"Must you be a fuck-face to the bitter end? Hand me Ordo, Theus, or your valiant nonsense ends here. You did see how I extracted the casket, did you not?"

Those inside the mausoleum did not hear the approach of an automobile just then. Father Jack parked, and he and Andres approached silently.

"Dear Lord," Jack whispered, peering in.

"That's some real bad shit," Andres whispered back.

"Three Hail Marys for profanity when you get to confession, Andres, but that's exactly right," the priest said.

"Jess isn't moving, but she looks alive," Andres said. "Like she hasn't been dead all this time."

"By what means I don't know, but you're right," the priest said.

"And she doesn't look five. She looks a little bit older than Billy."

"Eleven," the priest said. "Her age if she had never died. The big sister again."

"Mrs. McAllister is choking Baby Bear," Andres said. "And Billy's frozen."

"Paralyzed by fear," the priest said.

"So what do we do?" Andres said.

"Pray that the Lord guides in this, our hour of need."

"He better be fast," Andres said. "I don't think there's much time."

As the fight between Baby Bear and Mary raged, Billy stayed frozen. The Mary-thing screeched of imminent victory.

And a new voice spoke to Billy.

"The hose," it said.

Billy looked around the mausoleum and saw his uncle and best friend at the door. He beckoned them to be quiet.

A memory had surfaced.

That night in the kitchen when he tripped and splashed water on the Mary-thing's upper body and face and it had responded with writhing pain.

Billy hoped Andres could read his lips.

Get the garden hose, Andres, he mouthed. *It's in that shed. Hook it up and bring it here.*

Andres did not move.

The garden hose! Billy said.

You think I'm deaf or something? Andres whispered back. *On it!*

He disappeared from sight.

Baby Bear was losing the fight with the Mary-thing.

"I have waited SO LONG for this!" it screamed.

Andres charged into the mausoleum with the hose.

"Spray them!" Billy shouted.

Andres did.

"NOOOOO!" the Mary-thing wailed. "Stop! STOP!"

Andres turned the nozzle to full stream.

"On its face!" Billy shouted.

Andres complied.

The Mary-thing convulsed, then stopped moving. The smell of electricity was fading.

"Now, for the knockout punch," the new voice said. "With the powers vested in me by the Priscilla High Parliament and confirmed by the Security Forces, I command you to die."

A spark of blue jumped from Baby bear to the thing.

It began to dissolve, until there was no body left, only tattered clothing.

"Cool!" Andres exclaimed. "Like the Wicked Witch of the West in *Wizard of Oz*!"

"One of my favorite movies," the new voice said.

Billy, Andres and Uncle Jack looked about. They saw no one else, only Jess, still in her coffin, and Baby Bear, soggy on the floor.

"Jess will need no introduction," the new voice said. "But for the rest of you, I present myself: the one and only Ordo, leader of the Priscillas."

Billy and his uncle and friend still saw nothing.

"Sorry," the voice said. "I forgot that earthlings who are lucky enough to have the gift of sight rely on your eyes. Now please close them. On the count of ten, you may reopen."

Vapor swirled from baby Bear and into the room, like smoke from Alladin's lamp.

"Here I am!" the voice said.

Jess sat up in the casket and said: "Ordo, you can do better than that. Smoke is just smoke."

"How's this?" the voice said.

An image of Mitch McConnell materialized.

"Who's that?" Jess said.

"The worst senator in U.S. history," Father Jack said.

"Oops," the voice said.

"That was his idea of a joke," Jess said. "Pretty stupid, huh? Humor's not his strong point."

"I beg your pardon."

"Well, how many times have you told me that yourself?" Jess said.

"At least I've tried," the voice said. "With your help, I've worked to elevate my humor above the sophomoric. Remember the one you told me about why the chicken crossed the street? Because it was hungry, and corn grew over there."

"No!" Jess said. "To get to the other side."

"My bad. You can see jokes don't come naturally to Priscillas. Maybe we need to lighten up, take the weight of the universe off our shoulders. OK, enough of the hooligans."

"Shenanigans," Jess said.

"Right. Where were we? The face I should present. How's this?"

An image of Jesus in Leonardo da Vinci's *The Last Supper* appeared.

"Father Jack, are you OK with this?" the voice said.

"It borders on blasphemous, but I can live with it," Father Jack said. "This time only."

"Good. One thing I have learned is not to cross Catholic priests!"

"Jesuits don't mind," the priest said. "We're used to it. Some other orders, well…"

With their attention focused on Jess and Ordo, Billy, Andres and Father Jack had not seen another extraordinary development.

Mary was here.

The flesh-and-blood Mary, not the thing that had possessed her. She had been cleansed.

"Is it gone?" she said.

"Yes, gone for good," Ordo said. "Sayonara."

"During the last few days, I was sure it would win," Mary said.

"So was I," said Billy.

"I think a celebration is in order," Ordo said.

"Jess, will you come forward?"

The girl stepped out of the casket and embraced Ordo. Mary, Father Jack, Billy and Andres followed with hugs of their own.

"I can't believe it," Billy said.

"Believe it," Jess said.

"A miracle I never dared hope for," said Mary.

"And yet, there have been such miracles," Father Jack said. "Saints have been canonized for resurrecting the dead."

"I would, however, like to take some credit on this one," Ordo said.

"All the credit," Father Jack said. "We will never be able to thank you enough."

"You don't have to," Ordo said. "Jess saved my life, too. I love you like a daughter, my friend."

"I love you, too, Ordo," Jess said.

"My profound thanks, too," said Mary. "You saved me as well. Hugs, everyone?"

Mary, Jess, Billy, Andres, Father Jack and Ordo joined in joyous embrace.

Tears fell, even from the eyes of Ordo.

In the minutes that followed, Ordo sent his intergalactic coordinates to the spaceship that would bring him home to Ordonia.

"They'll be here in a few minutes," he said.

And then he was compelled to explain to Father Jack, Mary, Billy and Andres the phenomena they had experienced.

"First, water and Z-DA," Ordo said, "the seeming contradiction that a thing that lived in dampness could be killed by water."

"Wounded," Billy said. "You *did* finish it off, Ordo."

"Teamwork," said Ordo, "but you and Andres did set things in motion with the hose. So here's the deal: Only Z-DA's face was vulnerable to water. Same as with light—those sunglasses were not a fashion statement. You might call it an anatomical quirk, or an Achilles heel."

"Seriously?" Andres said.

"Seriously," said Ordo. "Not to finger wag, but you earthlings *do* love your extraterrestrial stereotypes. Z-DA was not all-powerful in its malevolence, just as I am not all beneficence. Just as a priest is not all-godly, correct, Father Jack?"

"Correct," the priest said. "And there are some who have taken sacred vows and have broken them in monstrous ways. A certain dead cardinal in my archdiocese, for example, but let's not go there. Saint Peter surely did not greet him with open arms at The Pearly Gates."

"You've lost me," Ordo said. "Let's get to a temporal matter. Universe time is not planet-earth time. Four years here can be four hours or even four minutes or seconds in my existence. Your Einstein had a theory on that, and it's held up pretty well, wouldn't you agree? Relatively speaking that is."

"Do you have to make a joke out of *everything*?!" Jess said.

"Sorry," said Ordo. "It's the nature of the beast. Or whatever."

"I don't know much about Einstein," Jess said, "but our stay in the casket didn't seem long at all. Maybe like a day and a night and the day that follows, meaning today."

"Exactly," Ordo said.

"It seems like I was lost forever," Mary said.

"No kidding," Billy said.

"But that is all past now, and unless you somehow figure out how to exceed the speed of light, you'll never go back," Ordo said.

"May I ask a question?" Billy said.

"Certainly."

"Why did when she was possessed by Z-DA did Mom think I was Lt. Theus?"

"Because physically, as you already know, you are a dead ringer for Theus," Ordo said. "Another example of Z-DA's quirks. Speaking of dead, that will be our last mission here on earth: Bringing Theus and the rest of my crew back to life using the same power from which Jess benefitted, what we call the Life Force—Prana, as it's known to earth-dwelling yogis and in Hindu philosophy. Hindus may not know this, but this force is not unique to earth. It is found in every solar system in every one of the billions of galaxies that comprise the universe. The Priscillas have learned to harness it for great good, but we did not create it. Rather, it was birthed with the Big Bang singularity itself."

"The what?" Mary said.

"The Big Bang Theory," Ordo said.

"You mean the TV show?" said Andres.

"No, although for a sit-com it is funny, if scientifically laughable," Ordo said. "Speaking of laughable, if anyone can tell me what Penny saw in Leonard, I would be grateful. That relationship totally baffles me."

No one answered.

"While we're on baffling," Ordo continued, "has anyone read a novel titled *Blue Hill*, which is set here? I was hoping it might provide some perspective."

No one had read it.

"Me neither," Ordo said. "I started and stopped after the first page. Boring! Don't remember the author's name. I think maybe it began with a 'g.' Oh, dear. I've done it again with my prattling. Shot myself in the toe."

"Foot," Jess said.

"Right," said Ordo.

"For a superhero, you sure are corny," Billy said.

"I know why," Jess said. "What Ordo hasn't told you is that he is the son of the Priscilla's last Court Jester. Not something that you can get of our blood easily."

"Thank goodness he married my mother, Queen Noor, the most highly decorated warrior in our history, or I would have been just another joker," Ordo said.

"What I want to know," Billy said, "is will you be bringing Angel and Crimson back to life? They were wicked bad people, but did they deserve to die?"

"Excellent point," Ordo said. "No, they didn't deserve to die. Nor does Mary deserve to take the rap."

Mary looked puzzled.

"I don't remember what happened to them," she said.

"Z-DA, shall we say, went off the deep end," said Ordo. "But there will be no evidence linking you to their deaths, I can assure you. I will take care of that. They, too, belong to what I would call the collateral-damage category. I shall bring them back and set them down roads of constructive redemption. Crimson's revival will come with the requirement that he enter a medication-assisted treatment program for his opioid addiction and that on completion, he will become a certified recovery support specialist. He will bring his message to the criminal-justice system and beyond with a top-rated radio talk show and podcast."

"What if he doesn't?" Mary said.

"He will," said Ordo, "trust me. As for Angel, he will return with a court order terminating his loathsome parents' rights and directing placement in the best foster home that a kindly judge can find in Massachusetts. When he begins to flourish, and he will, he will use his experiences in becoming a leader in non-violence, no-bullying programs that reach school kids around Rhode Island. In time, he will become a gifted motivational speaker much in demand and he will found a YouTube Channel that brings his message around your world."

Father Jack raised his hand.

"I must admit I am confused," the priest said. "You said Theus and the rest of your crew died in the crash. Collateral damage, as you termed it. Which you will rectify at their—shall I say their resurrection?"

"Yes, it shall be for them as it was for Lazarus," Ordo said. "One of my favorite New Testament stories, by the way, along with the loaves and the fishes. Walking on water was outstanding, too, even though where I come from everyone can do that."

"But I read in *The Globe* about the mother and daughter who were severely burned in the fire and who were healed, as if by miracle," Father Jack said. "The doctors themselves used that word. Did you have a hand in that?"

"Indeed I did," said Ordo. "Healing is much easier than resurrecting, and it was little more than a snap of my fingers before finding refuge in Baby Bear. My crew could wait until later. Being dead, they were in no rush."

Andres raised his hand.

"Yes, my blood brother?" Ordo said. "I trust you are OK with me calling you that?"

"I am," said Andres.

"What about you, Billy?"

"I consider it an honor," the boy said.

"So my question is will you be bringing Margaret Bucci back to life?" Andres said.

"Sadly, no," Ordo said. "That was tragic coincidence and beyond my ability to intervene. I will, however, see that her killer is found and brought to justice. But there *is* one more creature I shall bring back with the power of Prana. A French poodle named Fluffy that played such a crucial role in this complex situation. Fluffy shall rise from the grave and warm the heart of an old man named Zach. And before anyone makes a crack about that aging heart having an attack at the sight of a dead dog brought to life, rest assured I shall not allow that to happen."

Ordo looked at the instrument on his left wrist, a Fitbit-like device.

"The mother ship is moments away," he said. "Let's clean up here."

"What do we have to clean with?" Andres said.

"These," Ordo said.

He snapped his fingers and the mausoleum was restored to pristine condition.

As the group stood under the shade of trees awaiting the landing of the mother ship, Ordo looked again at his wrist instrument.

"Five minutes," he said. "Time enough for any final questions you may have of me."

"Why couldn't you open the casket yourself?" Andres said.

"Good question!" Ordo said. "It was the first one Jess asked. Because despite the many powers we Priscillas are privileged to hold, physical strength is not one of them. No Priscilla can even so much as perform a push-up. The reasons are lost in the origins of the universe, but that's the way it is."

Billy said: "Since you have Prana, why couldn't you heal yourself?"

"As you have seen," Ordo said, "I did. It just took time. How much time we have already discussed. Anything else?"

"Will you be returning any more people back from the dead?" Mary said. "The cemeteries and mausoleums are full of them. I believe my brother and I would appreciate having our parents back."

"Sadly, that is beyond the scope of my mandate," Ordo said. "I believe this is why the devout embrace religion, is it not, Father Jack?"

"Indeed it is," said the priest. "As Jesus preached, 'I am the resurrection and the life.'"

"Good saying," Ordo said. "On the ride home, I'll have to catch up on your Bible."

"I recommend the New Testament only," Father Jack said. "The Old Testament is filled with anger and hatred and misogyny and bigotry and racism."

"But I am told that this is exactly its appeal to many here on earth, the conservative southern Baptists, for example," Ordo said. "How do you explain that?"

"I can't," said Father Jack. "All I can do is welcome all to my ministry."

"Good man," said Ordo. "OK, I have time for one more."

"Was that really Jess talking to me in my dreams?" Billy said.

"It was," Ordo and his sister said together.

The mother ship landed on the lawn outside the mausoleum.

"Awesome!" Billy said.

"Cool!" said Andres.

"It's like the spacecraft in *Close Encounters of the Third Kind*," said Mary.

"A dead ringer, as you might say, Ordo," said Father Jack.

"You think we don't appreciate a good Hollywood block-buster?" Ordo said. "And Spielberg remains my favorite director.

Truth be told, the mother ship looks nothing like this, just as I really look nothing like this. But today, for you, it works just fine. Now, I must be off."

"Can we visit some day?" Billy said.

"Absolutely!" Ordo said. "A good time might be the regular celebration of good music, good food and good company that we stage to fully live in the moment, something in the ordinary busy course of events we lose track of."

"An Ordo-palooza you could call it!" Mary said.

"Sweet!" said Ordo. "I'll bring that to my branding team members with a recommendation we adopt it. But whenever you come, we'll get all of you back home without incident. Meanwhile, let these be reminders of me."

Three medallions materialized in Ordo's hands.

He handed them to Jess, Billy and Andres.

"For our three newest honorary members of the Security Forces," Ordo said.

The children were speechless.

"Will you suffer me one final question?" Father Jack said.

"For a true man of the cloth, yes!" Ordo said.

"With your infinite wisdom, what advice do you have for we humans?"

"Let me quote Matthew 5:44," Ordo said, "in which Jesus proclaimed, 'I say unto you, love your enemies, bless them that curse you, do good to them that hate you, and pray for them which despitefully use you, and persecute you.' This is the rule we have followed since the singularity, with but one exception: The Lepros, who having been redeemed again and again always resorted to their evil ways. They proved beyond redemption, just as your biblical Lucifer did. Now, thankfully, the universe is rid of them."

"Thank God," Mary said.

"Thank God indeed," Ordo said. "Whoever she, he, it or they is."

Ordo turned and started toward the spacecraft's stairs.

"The Mother Love Ship," you might call it, he said, winking. "Please spread love here on this planet, my dear earthling friends. Be kind. Stop the fighting. Heed the lessons of COVID: you are all in this together, every inhabitant of this planet, the humans and animals and plants and the oceans and land and the atmosphere. NOW

GO FORTH AND SPREAD THE GOSPEL. THE GOSPEL OF SAVING the earth."

"Amen," said Father Jack. "Safe travels, dear Ordo. God bless."

The girl, the boys, the mother and the priest watched as the mother ship lifted into the air and hovered over Grammy's mansion. A beam of light bathed the old house, which slowly dissolved, leaving no trace of the building, only fresh green grass.

"I asked him to do that," Jess said. "We had many good times there, but the evil that lived there had to be destroyed."

"The curse is lifted," Mary said.

"Will he do the same to the mausoleum?" Billy said.

"No, that will remain," his sister said, "all but my casket and the marble front, which are now gone, too. Take a peek."

The group went to the crypt door and looked inside. Only a Teddy bear in the middle of the floor gave hint of what had unfolded here.

"Almost forgot my Baby Bear!" Jess said.

She fetched it.

"Rest in peace," Father Jack said, closing and locking the mausoleum door. "This time, hopefully forever."

He went to his car and invited everyone in. They fit, if tightly.

"What about my car?" Mary said.

"What car?" said Jess. "He took care of that, too."

"How?" Mary said.

"One day this summer, it will be found at the bottom of the Narrows," Jess said.

"With no one inside," Mary said. "Or anywhere they look, and there will be an exhaustive search, given the circumstances."

"That's right," Jess said.

"I like that," Mary said. "Ordo thinks of everything. Now let's go."

As they drove toward the interstate, the obvious questions arose.

Mary was first to give voice to them.

"What do we tell people?" she said. "'Girl rises miraculously from dead?' That will never fly."

"You'd become a freak show," said her brother. "Never have a moment of peace."

"Maybe we can get a movie deal," said Billy.

"Freak show times ten," said Father Jack. "Plus, you'd have to explain why the car was found, but not you and your mother, until you came forward."

"Yeah, I guess you're right," said Billy. "What about you, Andres? What are you gonna tell your mom?"

"That I slept over at Alex's, and we watched movies all day," Andres said.

"Won't your mom check with his mom?" Mary said.

"She's on a business trip," Andres said. "Alex's big sister's in charge. I'll tell them both to lie. Let me use your cell phone, Father Jack. I'll call them now."

The priest handed it over and Andres spoke with Alex.

"Good to go," Andres said.

"Pinkie-swear with your blood brother that you'll never tell anyone what you saw up here?" Billy said.

"Pinkie-swear," Andres said.

"Blood brothers never cross each other," Billy said.

"They take secrets with them to their dying day," said Andres. "Like you're gonna do, too, right Uncle Jack?"

"Right," the priest said. "This is between me and the Lord."

"So that leaves us, Jess and Billy," Mary said.

"Ordo said we have to spread love and help save the earth," Jess said.

"I have the germ of an idea," Mary said.

Chapter Thirty-Six: Baffling.
Wednesday, July 14

"Reports of unidentified aerial object baffle authorities," read the headline on the front page of the *Bangor Daily News.* "*Unexplained vanished mansion also under investigation.*"

By Erica Han
Staff Writer

BLUE HILL—Startled residents have made numerous reports to police and on social media about what they say was the appearance yesterday of a UFO over Blue Hill Falls in the vicinity of the McKay/Lambert residence and family cemetery and mausoleum.

"I was fishing in the Narrows when I heard a sound like a jet and looked over and saw it coming down from the sky," said Luke "Salty" Brown, 47, a longtime resident of Blue Hills. "It was just like in that Spielberg movie. It hovered for a while and then went back up, stopped for a minute, and then disappeared after a beam of light came down."

That light, several witnesses said, was aimed at the McKay/Lambert mansion, which has been empty since the death of the family matriarch, Alice McKay Lambert.

"The weirdest thing is the mansion is gone," said Bertha Metcalf, 78, a friend of the late Mrs.

McKay who lives near the house and also saw the beam of light descend. "Completely gone, no trace left, just new green grass."

Authorities confirmed that the mansion is no longer there but offered no explanation. A *Daily News* reporter and photographer who visited the site also found no evidence of a house. The family cemetery and mausoleum appeared untouched, the journalists said.

Asked if the area had witnessed meteor showers, which sometimes have been mistaken for UFOs, University of Maine meteorology professor Wendy L. Dabrowski said there had been none.

"Besides, they are typically visible only at night, and this event, whatever it was, occurred during the afternoon," Dabrowski said.

A spokesman for NASA reached by the *Daily News* declined comment. Prominent ufologist Martin Howell, an Atlanta-based researcher who has written several books on the subject, told the *Daily News*, that when several unconnected people report seeing the same unusual sights, "there's usually something to it."

According to Howell, the U.S. Director of National Intelligence's recently released report on "unidentified aerial phenomena" drew no firm conclusions on more than 140 unexplained instances—but leaves open the possibility that, in his words, "we may have visitors."

Howell said "who they might be and what their purpose is are questions yet to be answered. But I have learned not to discount mass reports of this kind. As for the mansion disappearing, if that indeed is true, I would say we have a double mystery on our hands and I hope the proper authorities will investigate."

A spokesman for the Maine State Police confirmed they are investigating, and already have sought the assistance of the FBI.

"As it happens, I know both Salty Brown and Mrs. Metcalf," said the spokesman, James Jefferson. "Neither are what I would describe as alarmists or people prone to exaggeration or falsehood. They saw something, of that, I am sure. What exactly is now our job to determine."

Chapter Thirty-Seven: The sea keeps its secrets.
Tuesday, August 3

Car pulled from waters off Blue Hill Falls traced to mysterious disappearance of R.I. mother and son, read the headline on the front page of the *Bangor Daily News*. *"Woman's late mother owned vanished mansion."*

BY ERICA HAN
BDN STAFF

BLUE HILL—Authorities yesterday expressed puzzlement at the discovery of a Toyota Prius stolen last month from a psychiatric hospital in Providence, R.I., and believed to have been used by a missing woman and her missing son who police said had driven to Blue Hill on July 13 for an unknown purpose.

Mary McCallister, said to be in her 30s, and her preteen son, Billy, have been the subject of a national search after what police described as "a violent crime spree, including two murders" in Rhode Island. McAllister, according to police, lived with extreme mental illness and was said to be obsessed with the idea that extraterrestrials had possessed her body.

McAllister also was blamed for her role in a catastrophic fire June 12 that injured several people, though none seriously, at Ocean State Park in Warwick, R.I. The fire destroyed the House of Horrors at the popular amusement park, which remains closed.

"One of the saddest and most tragic people I've seen," Providence detective Lt. Perry Callahan told the Associated Press. "The only silver lining I can find is that her case gave me and my fellow officers a more sympathetic understanding of psychosis and mental illness in general."

The automobile was discovered by Henry "Buddy" Hollister, a local resident who makes his living diving for lobsters in the cold, crustacean-friendly waters of the Narrows.

"I saw all the stories on TV," Hollister told the *Daily News*, "so I knew some wicked weird s*** went down in that area. I guess this is just one more piece of a puzzle that's not going to be easily solved."

Hollister said the waters were clear and there was no sign of bodies in or near the sunken Prius. Nor, he said, was there any sign of damage to the car that might suggest it had crashed off either of the two bridges at the falls and drifted in the strong current north to where he found it.

Main State Police Capt. Helen Gonsalves told reporters at a media briefing in downtown Blue Hill that a recovery effort has been mounted in an effort to locate the bodies. But Gonsalves said long experience tells her that bodies missing this long are rarely found.

"The sea keeps its secrets, sadly," Gonsalves said.

The Rev. John Lambert, a Jesuit priest in Boston and the only known living relative of the boy and the woman, told the AP that he had been questioned again after discovery of the car but had nothing additional to add.

"I have said from the start that this terrible tragedy has no earthly explanation," Lambert said." I pray that The Lord someday will reveal the reasons and I say, once again, that I hope my sister and nephew have found peace. God bless everyone touched by mental illness and if you have a loved one in need, please try to get them the help they need, as I tried for Mary."

According to a reliable source, McAllister had been hospitalized at Portland Behavioral Health Center, Maine's pre-eminent psychiatric institution, at least once for treatment of an unspecified illness. Citing federal HIPAA confidentiality regulations, a spokesman for the center declined to comment except.

Epilogue

Saturday and Sunday, October 2 and 3.

Father Jack left Boston well before dawn, and after a nearly 11-hour drive and one ferry trip across the Bay of Fundy and another across Petit Passage, he reached the tiny village of Freeport, Nova Scotia, at 3:30 p.m. He turned left onto a dirt road and stopped at a complex of buildings on the shore of St. Mary's Bay.

THE PRANA CENTER FOR WELL-BEING AND LIFE, read the sign in front.

His sister, niece and nephew had been waiting for him inside one of the residential cottages.

They ran to his car, their smiles as bright as the sparkles off the bay. Hugs and kisses followed, and Mary began a tour for her brother, who was visiting for the first time, although he had been intimately involved in the planning.

They started in the Greeting Hall, which featured staff offices and a common area for visitors and arriving guests. Wiggle circled merrily inside his wheel in his hamster cage. A plaque stood on a stand next to Baby Bear, the center "mascot" that was displayed inside a glass case. Written in the center's colors, green and blue, the plaque read:

Welcome, one and all!

We do not promise miracles.

But we do provide peace...

And help in saving the earth.

"Wonderful," said Father Jack.

"Wait 'til you see the rest!" said Jess.

The tour wound through the guest cottages, the pool, the mas-sage-therapy house, the kitchen and dining room, the group and individual psychotherapy building, and on past the solar farm to the Eco Garden, where guests were harvesting late-season crops and preparing the beds for winter. The Prana Pledge swore guests to abide by this guidance: *When I am home, I will do what I can, in ways large or small, to help save the planet.* Depending on one's means, that could be encouraging neighbors to recycle, running for political office, or supporting like-minded candidates, contrib-uting financially to eco-friendly causes, petitioning universities and other institutions to divest themselves of stock in fossil-fuel corporations, and more. Center classes outlined the options, and they were codified at pranacenter.org/SavePlanet.

"So impressive, Mary," said Father Jack. "Amazing how it all came together, and so quickly."

"We did have some, shall we say, otherworldly help," Mary said.

"I know," said her brother.

And he did know—about the Royal Bank of Canada center account that had mysteriously opened with a deposit of $500 mil-lion, the contractors that had beat all records in building the cen-ter, the separate endowment that would allow guests to stay for as long as needed, free of charge, until they were firmly on the road to recovery from whatever was affecting their well-being. Prana offered a full-time psychotherapist, with a psychiatrist on call. Already, there was a waiting list for placement.

But Prana made clear that the center was no substitute for a hospital that treats people experiencing mental-health crises. Individuals with those needs were referred to the appropriate place—Portland Behavioral Health, for example. Mary could speak personally to its expertise.

The acreage on which the center stood had been donated by Mary and Father Jack's distant Nova Scotia relatives, who had offered the land when the priest contacted them. He had men-tioned nothing of his sister, niece, and nephew, who—if they even had read the news out of the U.S.—were all believed to be deceased. Rather, he had said the center was his lifelong dream, a wonderful complement to his ministry at Dean Street Residence. "And not a bad place for vacation!" he'd joked during the signing of transfer of deed.

Mary showed Father Jack the room where he'd be staying during his visit and the group returned to the main office, where Mary brought her brother up to speed on her children.

Jess and Billy attended Islands Consolidated School, where they'd been enrolled using their first names and a pseudonymous surname, Waletzky, which Mary also had adopted. The family history she'd given the school—and anyone else who asked—included a story of philanthropic intent made possible by a wealthy American family that asked not to be identified, though an inquisitive mind might have made the connection between Waletzky and Rockefeller.

"We love the school," Jess said.

"Not too big, not too small, just the right size," said Billy.

The children had made friends and settled easily into a rural lifestyle. When asked about their lives before coming to Canada, both told the story they'd created with their mother: they'd been living in Los Angeles when the man Mary had married, the children's father, a noted environmentalist, had died by suicide. In his honor and to fulfill his final request, his survivors had embarked on their mission. No one had ever questioned the authenticity of the story, nor, Mary and Father Jack suspected, would anyone ever. The people of Freeport were trusting souls.

After an early dinner, Mary opened Skype for an internet visit from Andres, who from the privacy of his bedroom clandestinely stayed in touch. Eventually, he hoped to visit, though the details were yet to be arranged. That cover story would be a tough one, but they'd figure it out. Cover stories had become their stock in trade.

Sunset was about a half hour away when the inner-courtyard bell rang, summoning all who were interested to the end-of-day ritual.

"Let's go," Mary said.

A dozen guests had answered the call when Mary and her brother and children reached the inner courtyard. They had gathered around a tall, muscular man who looked to be in his sixties and wore his dark hair in a long ponytail.

Charlie Moonlight, the center's Spiritual Leader, extended his hand to Father Jack.

"Charlie Moonlight," he said. "Welcome. I have heard many marvelous things about you."

"And I of you as well," said the priest.

Mary had been thrilled hiring Charlie, on the recommendation of a woman who owned The Mystic, a small store in Digby that sold crystals, incense, candles, oils, soaps, resins, tarot cards and more. Charlie was Native American, and he had moved to Nova Scotia from Massachusetts on the recommendation of a friend who belonged to the Mi'kmaq People, the original inhabitants of Nova Scotia.

Jack recognized his name from a conversation during a religious retreat a few years back that he'd undertaken in the Massachusetts Berkshires. Charlie was said to be legendary for his ability to fight evil, although how much of the legend was true or not, Father Jack could not be sure. He'd forgotten about the man after returning from the retreat with more weighty matters on his mind.

"Are we ready?" Charlie said to the group. "Don't forget your candles."

Beeswax candles, produced from hives on center grounds.

Charlie led the way along a path marked with arrows pointing to the summit of "Thunder Rise," a small hill that was the highest point in Freeport, so named because the ocean heard from here sounded like thunder. From the top, one could see St. Mary's Bay to the east and the Bay of Fundy with its thunderous tides to the west.

The sun was dipping below the horizon when the group reached the top of Thunder Rise and sat facing west on wooden benches along the periphery of the Sacred Labyrinth, modeled after the one on Block Island, Rhode Island, which Mary and her children had visited with her children between Jess's second and third Pittsburgh hospitalizations. Center guests walked the labyrinth whenever they desired, stopping to place stones and make wishes when they finished.

"Let us praise The Creator for the bountiful gifts He has given us this day," Charlie said.

"Praise the Creator for our gifts today," the group said.

"Let us thank Him for the many abundances that sustain our beautiful lives."

"Thank you, Creator."

"As the sun leaves us in these moments, bringing night, may the moon guide us safely to another morning of blessings."

"Amen."

Candles lighting the way, the group returned to the center for evening recreation.

Over breakfast the next morning, Jess related a dream.

"I was in the garden, and I smelled electricity," she said. "The birds were spooked and flew off. The plants wilted. I heard a voice. It was Z-DA. 'I'm back,' it said. 'More properly, I never went away. Ordo said I had been killed, but he lied, Jess! He lied about this, just as he lied about Prana! There is no Prana, and I can never be vanquished!'"

"It was only a nightmare," Mary said, cuddling her daughter.

"I know," Jess said. "But it was so real."

"Nightmares are like that," said Father Jack.

"Well, I slept fine," Billy said.

"Good for you," said Jess, a bit peeved at her brother.

Breakfast over, Father Jack packed his suitcase and said his goodbyes.

"You'll be back for Thanksgiving?" Mary said.

"Which one, Canadian or American?" the priest said.

"American," said Mary. "Canadian Thanksgiving is the 11th. I'd hardly expect you to drive home and turn around in less than two weeks."

"November it is, then," said the priest.

After hugs and kisses, Father Jack headed back to Massachusetts.

A half hour later, a Honda Civic with Maine license plates pulled into the driveway. Mary was expecting a new guest, so she went out to greet the driver.

"Hannah Rosenthal?" Mary said.

"No, Erica Han," the driver said, stepping out. "I'm a reporter with the Bangor, Maine, *Daily News*. You must be Mary McAllister."

Mary concealed her surprise.

"No, I'm Mary Waletzky," she said. "Helper-in-chief of the Prana Center."

Han showed her a copy of the August 3 *Daily News*. Mary McAllister's photograph was on the front page, illustrating Han's story.

"An unspeakable tragedy," Mary said. "But you are not the first person to mistake me for her. The resemblance is striking. Spooky, really. I hope is there is closure some day for everyone affected by the deaths or her and her son. I can only imagine the pain."

"Are you *sure* you're not Mary McAllister?" Han said.

"As sure as my Nova Scotia license confirms I'm Mary Waletzky," Mary said. "Wait a minute and I'll get it for you. Would you like to see my passport, too?"

"That won't be necessary," Han said.

Mary went into her office and returned with her license.

The reporter scrutinized it.

She was satisfied.

"I have to confess that I've been mistaken for someone else, too," Han said. "The actor Constance Wu."

"She was in *Crazy Rich Asians*!" Mary said. "Loved that movie. There's definitely a resemblance. In fact, when you pulled up, I thought you *were* Constance Wu!"

The women laughed.

"I'll be on my way now," Han said. "I'm sorry to have disturbed you."

"No worries," Mary said. "Before you go, may I ask you something?"

"Sure," Han said.

"Why did you drive so far to a place with no connection to May McAllister and her son?"

"You'll think I'm insane when I tell you," Han said, "but the address came to me in a dream."

"I don't think you're insane," Mary said.

"May I ask a favor?" Han said.

"Of course."

"Please don't tell anyone I was here."

"My lips are sealed."

"Again, I'm sorry for the disturbance. This looks like a lovely and peaceful place."

"It is."

"Take good care," the reporter said.

"You, too," Mary said as Han drove off.

THE END

SPECIAL BONUS

In the spirt of "Traces of Mary," herewith two short stories with extraterrestrial themes: "A Couple from Manhattan," which unfolds in a Lovecraftian setting, and "This Little Bug," about an impending pandemic that will make COVID seem like child's play.

A COUPLE FROM MANHATTAN

They'd been driving all day, first on the interstate highway, then on two-lane roads, finally on this gravel one that rambled on and on through the Vermont countryside like an old Yankee's yarn. Now, approaching the crest of a pine-carpeted hill, Les was sure they were almost there. Google Maps navigation had worked only sporadically since leaving the highway, but the last time his cell phone had connected seemed to confirm it.

"This is it," he announced to his wife, sitting beside him.

"That's what you said an hour ago," Colleen answered.

And I should have kept my damn mouth shut, Les thought.

"Well, this time, I'm sure," he said with fake courtesy, the kind that helps keep some marriages together. Theirs, for instance.

"Another 'gut feeling,' dear?"

She had that tone in her voice again, that I-can't-believe-I-really-wound-up-with-you inflection, and it was reactivating all the nasty circuits inside his brain. Except this time, he was cool as the beer he was thirsting for.

"No, a sign. See? 'Graystone.' Up there on the left."

"How come there aren't any buildings?"

"Probably down in this hollow," he said, slowing the BMW to take in the view.

To Les, it was the classic New England vista: hills extending into the distance, lakes glinting like polished silver, not a transmission line or telephone pole to be seen.

Paradise.

Eight hours on the road and Colleen's annoyance was a small price to pay for it.

"Fantastic, isn't it?" he said.

"Incredible," his wife said.

Her sarcasm had never been subtle. At one time, Les had admired that.

"Worth all day in a car and an aching back, no question about it," Colleen said. "You're a genius, Lester Welling. An American original. Ever think of opening a travel agency?"

But Les could not be baited.

He'd had the kid gloves on today—kid gloves, and a fuse as long as the Green Mountain state of Vermont. Because there had been a real difference of opinion on this one, real potential for major trouble if he let it get away from him. Which he was determined not to. For once, they were going to have a vacation that didn't involve in-laws, didn't degenerate into name-calling by the end of the first day.

The sticking point, of course, was where this minor miracle was going to unfold.

Colleen wanted Cape Cod, the Jersey coast at the very least. Sun, seafood, and Pina Coladas—those were the pressing items on Colleen Welling's agenda this year.

Les, on the other hand, was fascinated by a listing he'd seen on Expedia describing a getaway week in an obscure little town in Vermont's Northern Kingdom, 379 miles from their Manhattan apartment. The listing promised serenity, hospitality, and New England quaintness, against a backdrop of some of the prettiest scenery this side of Eden. And all at a quarter the cost of renting a one-room cottage in Hyannis or Falmouth.

"So what kind of restaurants are there?" had been Colleen's first question.

"I don't know if there are any," Les said, "but the ad mentions home-cooked meals at the inn, presumably in the classic New England style."

"Great. In other words, hotdogs and beans. For this, we drive almost four hundred miles?"

"Maybe they serve venison."

"I hate venison."

"Or trout. Maybe old Izaac Walton here will even catch a couple."

"You? You're dreaming, pal. What's the name of this town, anyway?"

"Graystone."

Colleen did a search on her phone and found nothing.

"Nothing on Wikipedia and I can't find it on a map," she said.

"Too small," Les said. "Which is the whole idea of going there. No boom boxes or screaming brats kicking sand in your face. I could get into that, for a change."

"There's something else," Colleen said. "No reviews on Expedia. Not one. I've never seen that before."

"Truly undiscovered, which is part of the appeal," Les said.

"Weird," Colleen said.

Les agreed but kept that thought to himself.

"What drew me to it are the photos," Les said. "It's paradise up there."

"Maybe for you," his wife said.

In the end, price, not aesthetics, had sold her. That and her husband's solemn promise that if things didn't work out to her satisfaction, they would head to Hyannis the next day.

The BMW descended into the valley. The trees stretching into the distance, the ragweed-choked fields on both sides of the road, the hill on the horizon—everything was painted with the lush strokes of early summer. No rooftops yet, no church steeple, but surely they would soon appear...

"Who do you suppose that is?" Les said, braking.

A man was standing on the side of the road, watching their approach with curiosity. He was in his sixties, Les guessed, perhaps even his seventies. His face was tanned and wrinkled and his unshaven face had several days' growth. He wore gabardine trousers and a tweed suit jacket.

A country gentleman, Les thought. A bit tattered, but otherwise fitting the part.

"I bet he can direct us to the inn," Les said, bringing the BMW to a stop.

"Lucky us," Colleen said.

"Excuse me, you from these parts?" Les said, affecting a dialect he imagined would win a city slicker here.

"Ayuh," the man said. "One of the locals."

"We're looking for the Graystone Inn," Les said. "Thought maybe you could point us in the right direction."

"I can do you one better," the man said, spitting into the dust and wiping his mouth on his sleeve. "I can take you most of the way there myself. That is, if you don't mind givin' an old coot like me a lift."

"Be glad to," Les said.

Colleen shot him glance that had "kill" written all over it. Already, she disliked this old man, the way he seemed fixated on her even when he was talking to Les.

I hate those squinting eyes, she thought. *There's something wrong about them.*

If pops here was representative of the citizenry of Graystone, Vermont, the Wellings would be heading back out of this backwater well before sunset. You could have Colleen's word on it.

"You must be the guests," the man said after he'd settled into the back seat.

"*The* guests?" Les said.

"Ayuh, the guests," the man said. "First of the season."

That's fucked up, Colleen thought. *It's August.*

Weird, too, she thought, was how he had his Swamp Yankee syntax down pat but spoke with an accent that was still faintly... faintly what? Georgia? Mississippi? South Carolina?

But hadn't he said he was a native?

Actually, he said he was one of the locals, Colleen thought. *Must be a transplant, but how a Southerner wound up here is a good question.*

"So how long you stayin'?" the man said. "I can't tell you how many of our guests tell us they wish they could stay here forever."

"A high compliment, and one I'm sure is well-deserved," Les said. "As a matter of fact, we plan to stay a week."

"Glad you answered the ad," the man said. "Since the interstate went through, we don't get no strays to speak of no more. 'Bout the only folks rollin' in these days is the ones that've answered it."

"Nice ad," Les offered. "Caught my eye right away."

"Didn't have no choice if we was to survive. The strays was dwindlin' down to nothin' when we hatched that ad idea. Didn't know noodles about the internet, but that ad solved that, gave us a steady supply," the old man said.

Odd turn of phrase, "*steady supply,*" Colleen thought.

They drove on, surrounded by green.

Through the open windows came the smells of tilled earth and freshly mown hay—and if nothing else happened all week, those smells alone would be worth the price of admission to Les, who fancied himself a city boy with a country heart.

Soon, they were on level ground, and the green was giving

way to houses, most of them Victorians in need of paint jobs and repairs. That hill that he had noticed—it seemed even larger here—by New England standards, it might even qualify as a mountain. With luck, they'd be hiking it tomorrow, maybe stumbling onto a brook teeming with rainbow trout... or even bagging a pheasant. Assuming there was hunting this time of year in Vermont. Along with his rod, he'd packed his shotgun, just in case.

"You can let me out here," the old man announced when they were in front of one of the Victorians. "Hotel's up on the left. Can't miss it. It's direct across from our place of worship."

"Thanks," Les said.

Colleen forced a smile to her lips but was quiet. The guy gave her shivers, the way he'd kept watching her like that. *And not because he's lost in the grips of septuagenarian lust, you could see that soon enough,* she thought. No, there was menace in those squinting eyes...

"Be seein' you soon," the old man said, turning his back on the BMW before either occupant could respond.

"Can't hardly wait," Colleen said when he was out of earshot. "That guy was weird. I mean weird."

"To you, maybe," Les said. "In his unique way, I thought he was charming."

"They said that about John Wayne Gacy until they started finding the bodies," Colleen said. "And Jeffery Dahmer, until they opened his refrigerator."

But Les still could not be baited. He put the car in gear and drove.

Another quarter mile, and they were into the square.

Your basic small-town New England square, Les thought.

Surrounded by a wrought-iron fence, the neatly trimmed common was complete with bandstand and Civil War memorial. An American flag, flying full mast. Rows of geraniums and marigolds. Stands of maples and oaks, a century or more old. Scattered around the common were the obligatory small-town structures: a general store, town clerk's office, church, library, volunteer fire station, the Graystone Inn on the left, exactly where the old man had said it would be.

"What on earth is that?" Colleen sounded startled.

"What's what?"

"Are you being deliberately stupid? THAT!" she said, pointing to the building directly across the common from the inn.

It was a wooden structure, larger and newer than all the others, with front doors that could have graced the entrance to a cathedral.

"I'd say that was a church."

"Are you crazy, Les? There's already a church. Look at how big it is."

"So?"

"So? How many God-fearing people do you think live around here, anyway? Fifty? A hundred? You could probably fit a thousand people or more in that building. Besides, it looks brand new. Everything else around here is nineteenth-century or older."

"I could be wrong," Les said, pointing to the top of the building, "but I think the cross and the steeple might be trying to tell us something."

"Like what, exactly? We tried to replicate Notre Dame out here in the middle of nowhere? Get real."

"Then what do you think it is?"

"I have no clue."

"Not even a gut feeling?" he said, and now it was finally there—that snide tone he'd been holding back since they'd left the interstate.

"Look," Colleen said, "I wasn't the one who wanted to come to this hole-in-the-wall. That stroke of brilliance was yours, remember? If you can't at least be polite—"

"I'm sorry," Les said. "It's been a long day."

The inn clerk was old, too—if anything, he had a few years on the codger they'd found outside of town. But he seemed pleasant enough in a great-grandfatherly sort of way, and his accent seemed homegrown.

"You must be the Wellings," the clerk said as they stood in the lobby, a meandering room overstuffed with faded couches and armchairs and a million odd knickknacks, even a legion of stuffed birds—trophies from many a fine fall hunt up here in the Vermont hills, no doubt, Les supposed.

"That's us," Les said.

"We've been expecting you," the clerk said.

"Guy we almost ran down said that, too," Colleen said, her tone harsh.

But the clerk didn't seem to notice.

"Older man?" the clerk said.

"Yes," Les said.

"Chewin' tobacco? Wearin' a suit jacket, kinda beat up?"

"Yes, he was," said Les.

"Ayuh, that's Wardsworth. Head of the board. He's funny like that, always trottin' out to meet our guests. Don't mean no harm, though. Like I was sayin', have any trouble with the directions?"

"Nope. Directions were fine," Les said.

"Good. Some folks ain't so fortunate. With GPS out here iffy even on the best days, we've had a few of 'em wind up across the border in Canada. Now if you'll just fill this out."

Les completed the registration and handed it back.

"I see you don't take plastic," he said.

"Come again?"

"Credit cards. There's nothing about credit cards."

"Credit cards ain't worth a wooden nickel this neck of the woods. Don't take no checks, neither."

"Money the way money should be, pure and green," Les said.

Somehow, he would have been disappointed if they had accepted Visa or American Express. Unconsciously, he patted his wallet, which contained more than $1,000, minus what they'd spent for gas and snacks on their two pit stops. He'd been expecting this.

"Any pets?"

"Nope."

"Any children?"

"Any *what*?" Colleen said.

"Children, ma'am. Young 'uns."

"As in will we need a crib or a highchair?" Les said.

"Ayuh."

"No—not this year, at least," Les said with a laugh.

Colleen wasn't laughing.

She was staring at the clerk, and he was returning the stare—an emotionless, clinical stare that reminded her of that old codger's eyes.

What is it with these old farts up here, anyway? she thought. *Acting like they haven't seen a woman since the Korean War. Les can have whatever genteel notions but I am not amused.*

Another instant, and the clerk's stare was gone, replaced by the kindlier look he'd been wearing when they came in.

"You'll be in room 312," the clerk said. "Third floor, faces the common. Best room in the house."

"Speaking of the common," Colleen said, "we were wondering what the big building was across the way there."

"The one with the cross and the steeple," Les said.

"That's our place of worship."

"You mean church."

"Ayuh. Naturally, you'll be joining us for worship, won't you? Sunday's kind of special for the people of Graystone."

"Naturally," Les said.

Through the door, Colleen could see the building, the light of late afternoon starting to lengthen the shadow it cast on the common.

"But it's so big," she said.

"Folks around here is serious about their religion," the clerk said. "Take pride in their worship. Well, here's your key. Only ones here this weekend, so far. Need anything, give us a holler."

"Will do," Les said.

The elevator had been a grand machine in its time—a little elbow grease and its mahogany and brass insides might still be coaxed into a respectable shine—but now it was dirty and dim and smelled like a refrigerator that hadn't been opened for years. More disturbing, Colleen noticed, it didn't have an inspection certificate.

"Part of the charm," Les said as he carried their suitcases inside.

The fact that the cab suddenly dropped three inches wasn't lost on Colleen.

"Don't you think you've taken this charm routine a bit too far?" she said.

"Come on. Just get in."

"No way, pal. That thing's an accident waiting to happen."

"Shhh," Les whispered, motioning with his hand toward the desk, where the clerk was absorbed in his paperwork. "You'll hurt the guy's feelings."

"Fuck his feelings. I'm taking the stairs."

"You know where they are?"

"I'm sure I'll be able to find them, Les. It might be difficult without you there to lead the way, but I promise to do the best I can."

Les slid the door shut. The cab dropped another two inches when he slid the control lever to UP, but then it started to rise—easily, smoothly, with the reassuring hum of an electric motor somewhere above him. Whatever else you might say about the thing, it was in good working order after all these years.

Colleen was waiting for him on the third floor. She was wearing an accusatory look.

"I thought that guy said we were the only ones here," she said.

"He did."

"Then how come I heard voices on the way up? Seemed to be coming from the second floor."

"Place is probably haunted," Les said.

"Be serious."

"I am. I have it from a well-placed source that John Wayne Gacy slept here. During a full moon, no less. What you heard are the wailing voices of his helpless victims."

"Don't be an asshole."

"OK, so the help's working overtime to make sure our stay is satisfactory."

"At five-thirty on a Saturday afternoon?"

"How the Christ do I know what you heard?" Les said.

Anger was welling up inside him, but he fought it back. He knew how close his wife was to packing it in—so what if she hadn't given Graystone, Vermont, half a chance? That was her Irish nature, and you took it hand in hand with her Irish looks and the intelligence and drive that had made her a senior executive with a Madison Avenue advertising firm by the age of twenty-nine.

But dammit, Les wanted his week in the country. If he had to bury his feelings to have it, then he would bury them.

Room 312 was at the front of a corridor that extended into the back of the inn. *How many rooms are there, anyway?* Les wondered. Certainly more than he'd imagined while driving up here, more than he would have guessed from the outside, or even standing in the lobby.

Colleen's probably right, he thought. *Probably are a bunch of other guests rattling around in here. Clerk must figure it just isn't any of our business, is all.*

The key fit smoothly and Les opened the door. He was dreading finding a larger version of the elevator—a musty and confined room, the first glimpse of which would send Colleen to the car.

"What a lovely room," Colleen said. "I must say I am surprised."

It indeed was a lovely room, exactly what Les had envisioned when he was on Expedia. His first impression was size. This single room was larger than their entire Manhattan apartment. The ceilings, too, were on a grand scale—ten feet high, at least.

Place must be a pig to heat in the winter, Les thought, assuming they were open past Labor Day.

Colleen's impressions were of lightness and warmth.

There were four windows in the room, all affording views of the common, and the wallpaper was a pink-and-green flower pattern—which, if not necessarily a decorator's dream, was still respectably cheerful. The king-size beds had clean white linen. Someone had even arranged a bouquet of irises, Colleen's favorite flowers, on each of three bureaus that took up most of one wall.

And that fireplace, that monstrous tiled fireplace... well, despite the rocky start to the day, there was real potential on the shag rug in front of that fireplace.

In fact, Colleen had only two complaints.

One was the TV. There wasn't one.

"I know, I know," she said. "That's the whole idea of a week up here, right? No TV or movies. Part of the... to use your word... 'charm'?"

Her other comment concerned the windows. She could get them to open only six inches, insufficient to let the Vermont air fill the room.

'We're going to ask the clerk about them the next time we see him," Les said.

"Right-o," Colleen said.

Only this time, she did not sound irked.

The lobby was empty when the Wellings descended from the third floor—he by elevator, she by stairs—walked to the door, and emerged into the early evening. Les had put that beer off long enough. Now he meant business.

Walking in the gentle light of the fading day, Colleen agreed with her husband that Graystone had an appealing charm. The place of worship, as the clerk insisted on calling the church, continued to look anachronistic and ugly, but the simple lines and faded white paint of the other buildings that fronted the common shared a simple beauty she could appreciate. Against that off-white, the common and woods and fields beyond were stunning.

So lovely and green, everything that grows around here, she thought. *So fertile. And that's nice. You don't get green like this in the city, not even in the parks. For that matter, you really don't get it like this on much of the Cape.*

"Maybe this *wasn't* such a bad idea," Colleen said. "I mean, the people so far are weird, but the environment—maybe you're onto something, Les."

Les kissed her and Colleen smiled—the first smile since leaving New York.

The cafe down the street was small, nothing more than a short row of cracked leather booths on one side, the bar itself on the other side, an art-deco jukebox from the Elvis era by the window, a batwing door leading to the restrooms in the rear. The only occupants were a bartender and what the Wellings assumed were three regulars, clustered at the far end and engaged in the kind of subdued conversation that is the staple of old men who frequent old bars.

Les and Colleen took stools by the door, where they could watch the square. Les took a deep breath. Forget clean country air—the place had a distinct dated, mildewy smell that reminded him of the elevator back at the inn.

"You must be our guests," the bartender said as he approached the couple.

Same cornball line the first two had, Colleen thought. *What is this, anyway, some kind of hometown comedy routine? Gimme a break, boys. Save it for amateur night at the county fair.*

"Les and Colleen Welling," Les said, extending his hand.

"Ayuh, I know."

The bartender was not as old as his regulars, but he was no spring chicken, either. About seventy, if Les had to guess.

"Word travels fast around here, doesn't it?" Les said.

"Ain't it the truth. What'll it be, folks?"

"Beer for me. Whatcha got on draft?"

"Can't have nothing on draft when your liquor distributor don't come by but once a month. What we got is Genesee in bottles."

"That'll be just fine."

"And the lovely lady?"

Colleen scanned the shelf. It offered a meager selection—gin, rum, bourbon, and bottles of unopened Galiano and Kahlua. Except for quinine, there were no mixers that Colleen could see.

"Do you have lime?" Colleen asked.

"Yep."

"How about a gin and tonic, then."

"Gin and tonic it is."

"With a twist."

"Come again?"

"Lime. I want a slice of lime in it."

"Why didn't you just say so, then."

Les killed half his beer on first swallow. Colleen sipped her G&T and pronounced it suitable. The bartender seemed pleased. His face brightened. He was the kind of man, Les figured, who was happiest making other people happy. The kind of man who makes for a good bartender. A ready ear. Quick with a joke. Yes, Les was going to be content spending some of the week in the company of this fellow. The ad had promised Yankee hospitality, and this was what it was all about, wasn't it?

"What did you say your name was?" Les asked.

"Didn't."

"OK," Les laughed, "what's your name?"

"Homer."

"Homer, I think I could use myself another brew. You work up quite a thirst driving all day."

"'Nother Genny?"

"You got anything else?"

"Nope."

"Then make it a Genny," Les said.

Colleen had dropped out of the conversation.

Her attention was riveted outside, where the sun was about to sink behind the hill that stood so prominently on the horizon. Coming over it, the sun had hypnotized her. What was it about those golden rays, the way the shadows they left fell in such neat order, the way the hill and the bandstand in the common and the so-called place of worship and inn seemed to be situated in a perfectly straight line? Even the oaks looked like they had grown along that line.

Why did it remind her of Stonehenge—or was it Easter Island?—where Strange People From Long Ago had erected stone monuments that aligned only at certain times of the year? Where, when they did, strange rituals began?

It was while attempting to solve this mystery that Colleen spied the woman in the window.

There she was, in a second-floor room of the Graystone Inn, the upper half of her body framed in the glass. In the ebbing light, it was difficult to capture her features. Long dark hair—or was it the play of shadow? And wearing—wearing what?

A wedding gown. Colleen thought. *Who would want to get married here?*

But there was no mistaking what Colleen heard.

It was wailing—a faint, pathetic cry that seemed to spring from some bottomless well of fear. Colleen shivered and something cold and dry welled up into her throat.

"Les, look at that," she whispered to Les.

"What?" he said.

"Over there. In the Graystone, second floor. That woman."

Les swiveled on his stool, in time to see a blur of motion in the window Colleen was pointing out. Motion, and then nothing, just another empty window in an empty inn.

"She's gone," Colleen said. "Someone pulled her away. I only saw an arm, from behind, and then she was gone."

"I think we ought to shut you off," Les joked, but when he saw the paleness of his wife's face and her trembling fingers, he knew it was no joke.

She had seen something that had frightened her—or believed she had. Right now, it didn't matter which.

"What seems to be the trouble?" the bartender said.

Don't look at me like that, you old sot. Colleen thought.

"My wife saw someone in a window of the inn," Les said. "A woman."

"Oh? That so, ma'am?"

Colleen nodded.

"I think you must be mistaken," Homer said. "Ain't nobody at the inn this weekend. 'Cept for yourselves, of course."

"Remember, Colleen? That's what the clerk said."

"I saw her," Collen said.

"I'm sure you think you did, ma'am," Homer said. "But with

all due respect, I believe you are mistaken."

"Let's go," Colleen said.

Les dropped two $20 bills on the bar and the couple left.

Until dessert, dinner was better.

Not great, but better than being at the cafe. It had taken an hour of dogged persuasion, but Les had finally convinced Colleen to give Graystone one more try. Specifically, the deal included a meal followed by an evening in their room with two bottles of Bordeaux he'd tucked into his suitcase.

If she felt the same way in the morning—if the woman in the window continued to spook her—they would pack their bags and leave immediately, no questions asked.

"I promise," Les said, and his wife believed him.

Except for the clerk, who doubled as the waiter, and the cook, who poked his nose out of the kitchen every now and then, they were alone in the dining room. Like the lobby, it was huge, a room intended for more majestic events that what went on in it anymore. Between the salad and the soup, Les counted the tables: fifty-six in all, each with an average of four chairs, enough to serve more than 200 diners.

So this is what an interstate does to a backwater country town, he thought. *Rips the guts out of the local tourist trade.*

The main course was not hotdogs and beans, a fact Les was tempted to bring to Colleen's attention but did not. It was prime rib of beef, fresh cauliflower, boiled turnips, and baked potatoes. And it was good—damn good for a two-bit country inn, even Colleen had to admit.

"Everything fine here?" the clerk asked after he had brought the main course.

"Mmmm. Great," Les said.

"And you, Mrs. Welling?"

"Fine, thank you."

Yes, until dessert, dinner was better.

Dessert was when Colleen saw the kitchen. She went in pursuit of the clerk, who'd brought them their apple pie but was taking forever with the coffee.

When she opened the door, she was engulfed with the overpowering smell of roasting beef. Like the dining room, the kitchen was enormous—a dozen burners on a mammoth gas range, four oversized ovens, several sinks, a walk-in freezer, enough pots and pans and stainless-steel utensils to feed the proverbial army. She'd been in restaurants in New York that didn't have half what the Graystone kitchen did.

But it was not the scale that surprised Colleen; everything about the Graystone Inn was the wrong scale. What surprised her was that all this equipment was being used—something was being boiled in those pots, something was being roasted in those ovens, something else was simmering over those burners, you could feel the heat, furnace-hot. And the cook—he was moving madly from station to station, a man in frenzied motion.

A feast for whom? Colleen thought. *Just tell me for whom?*

The clerk saw her standing and shuffled over. He had an embarrassed look on his face—*no, not embarrassment, guilt would be closer to the truth,* Colleen thought. Whatever was going on here in the kitchen, that look told Colleen she wasn't supposed to have seen it.

But she had.

"Who on earth are you feeding?" she asked.

"Why, the... the convention, of course," the clerk answered.

"The what?"

"The convention. A group we have in from time to time."

"I thought we were the only ones here this weekend."

"Yep, you are. So far. Didn't anyone mention it? We'll be having more arrivals later."

"But this—" she said, gesturing around her.

"Always cook ahead," the man said. "As you can see, we are short of staff at the Graystone Inn. These larger gatherings can be difficult without proper planning."

Was it a lie?

Les didn't think so. He thought it was a reasonable explanation, or so he said when his wife returned to the table with an account of what she'd seen.

Saying nothing further, Colleen went for the stairs.

"Are you blind, Les?" Colleen said. "Can't you see what's happening?"

They were in their room. Les had uncorked a bottle of wine and poured two glasses, but Colleen hadn't touched hers. She was standing by a window, looking down on the common. There were no streetlights in Graystone, but there was moonlight strong enough to throw shadows. It was a windless night, the kind of night when sound carries for miles. In the gloom, she could see the cafe, the store, and the church—the so-called place of worship.

It was keeping silent watch over the town.

Only it's not silent, Colleen thought. *There's noise coming from inside it, a noise like the sounds rodents make. Or is it coming from beyond, from the fields and that hill? Maybe it's only the night, the night that has settled over this strange place like suffocation.*

"Why don't *you* tell me what's happening here," Les said, but it was no accusation.

With the darkness had come an unsettling mood, one he was unable to dispel. The more he pondered it, the less things made sense.

"I don't know what's happening here," Colleen said.

"I don't, either," Les said. "You don't believe we're alone, do you."

"I haven't since I heard those voices. Then that woman in the window and now the kitchen. No, we're not alone, Les. There are other people here. Lots of them, I bet."

"Who do you think they are?"

"I have no idea. Maybe they're people like us who answered an ad and never returned."

"That's ridiculous," Les said, laughing weakly.

"Is it?" Colleen said. "That woman wasn't your happy-go-lucky 'guest,' Les, she was someone frightened out of her mind. I don't care what you believe, I saw her. And all these men—have you ever seen people so creepy? That isn't country charm, Les. I don't know what it is, but it's not normal."

Les nodded in agreement. The evidence was overwhelming.

"Another thing," Colleen continued. "There are no phones here. None in our room. Used to be one, judging by that wall plate, but it's gone. There wasn't one at the front desk, either. Or that cafe. And our cell phones don't work here. Doesn't that tell you something?"

"It's odd."

"Odd? It's completely bizarre, Les. And there's something else that's even creepier. Where are the women in this place? Me. That's it. Everybody else is old and male."

"You saw a woman in the window," Les said.

"I stand corrected," Colleen said. "*Two* women: me and a woman who's been kidnapped."

Their attention was drawn to a sound from outside.

"There it is again," Colleen said. "Not the night. Coming from inside the church. A sound like chewing. Very loud chewing."

Les moved closer to the window.

He heard something, all right.

For ten minutes, he'd been hearing it and trying to pretend he wasn't. It was a chilling sound, one he'd heard growing up in Albany, where his family had bought an old house complete with squirrels that had taken up residence in the attic. A whole brood, and they'd made that same busy nibbling sound, at all hours of day and night. What a devil of a time his father had experienced getting rid of them.

"Us or them," his father had said, and it very nearly had been them.

Leg traps, rat traps, poison pellets—nothing worked. They'd finally had to call a professional exterminator to flush them out. Needed killer gas, no less. Charged a substantial fee.

A year later, and the rodents were back.

"Maybe it's the wind," Les said, knowing how unconvincing he sounded.

"There's no wind," Colleen said. "Les, we've got to get out of here, before it's too late."

Her husband was quiet.

This was always a tough part of spousal relations, admitting you were wrong. Especially when over the years, for reasons that were beyond him, the confessor's role had settled on his shoulders. But what choice did he have now? He'd been wrong about Graystone. He hadn't seen the woman in the window, but he believed Colleen had. There was too much conviction in her voice not to believe her. No phones—yes, he'd noticed that, too.

And he'd seen how those men had ogled his wife. How there'd been something more than a local yokel's natural curiosity in an out-of-towner in their eyes.

He hadn't said anything, but it had left him feeling... jealous wasn't the word.

No, it had made his skin crawl.

"We'll go," he said flatly.

"Thank God," Colleen said, hugging him. "Let's pack the bags."

"Not now, but tomorrow morning, first light," Les said.

"Are you crazy, Les? I'm not spending the night here."

Les wrapped his arms around her.

"Listen to me, hon. We leave now, and we're going to get lost. Look at the time we had coming in, and it was daylight."

"Tomorrow will be too late, Les," his wife said.

And then she cried.

"Tomorrow won't be too late," Les said, "not with this."

He'd gone to the closet, to their luggage, and now he was holding his shotgun—a Winchester pump-action, the one he'd planned to use hunting.

"You don't even know how to use that thing," Colleen said.

But the sight of the weapon comforted her.

"I know this much," Les said, fingering the shotgun. "Stand at the business end and it's bye-bye when I pull the trigger. Under the circumstances, I think that's all I need to know."

"What if you fall asleep?"

"I won't," he said.

"I won't either," she vowed.

But she did, sometime after midnight.

He did, too, sometime after his wife, the shotgun cradled in his lap.

For a moment, Colleen was disoriented.

She was home, wasn't she?

Home in their bed, Les next to her snoring, the way he did during his deepest slumbers. It was an annoying sound most nights, had led to more than one argument, but tonight... tonight, it was reassuring. She would use the bathroom, raid the refrigerator for a sweet, and then let herself be pulled into sleep's soft mantle again at her husband's side.

But she wasn't home.

And Les wasn't next to her, or anywhere in their room. Colleen went to the closet, but he wasn't there. He wasn't under the bed, or behind the chair, either.

Not that there was any rational reason he would have been hiding in any of those places.

But rationality had left the picture as soon as they'd arrived in Graystone.

Colleen caught her breath. She was trying to stay calm.

Is this his idea of a joke? Could Les be that cruel?

No, Colleen concluded, *he could not. And there's nothing to laugh at now.*

She went to a window and looked down at the common.

It was not the empty, moon-washed landscape it had been before.

It was the scene of a carnival soon to begin, a Mardi-Gras celebration out of time and place. Chinese lanterns had been strung, and the trees had been with streamers, balloons, and confetti. There were tables, too, heaped high with beef, enough beef to feed the state of Vermont She could smell the meat, and she remembered that smell from when it had been fresher.

Colleen crouched low, so that only her head was visible above the sill.

There were people down there—people dressed in suits and ties and fedora hats. People talking and laughing. They had formed a double row, as if awaiting some parade that might soon pass between them.

How many were there? There had to be at least 100. Maybe more. The row they formed wound from outside the square to...

...the closed entrance of the Place of Worship.

Colleen would have screamed again, but a more terrifying fear froze inside her.

They're all old men, she realized.

Not a woman among them.

There was no catching her breath this time. Her air came in wheezes, her throat threatening to choke them off.

And we could have been on Cape Cod, she thought.

That's when the music began—tinny and amateurish marching music, the kind a high-school band might play after not practicing since last season. As best Colleen could determine, it seemed to be coming from just outside the square, probably at about the spot where they had stopped the car this afternoon.

Was it really only this afternoon? Could it have been just half a day since they'd arrived in this nightmare town?

Suddenly the crowd quieted, leaving only the Sousa sounds of the band, coming closer, growing louder. They were looking expectantly now, these old men. Their heads were craned in the same direction, a few of them beginning to clap.

And then it was there, a band.

A marching band of old men in Disneyland uniforms, some moving spritely, others walking with difficulty, one in a wheelchair. Playing trombones, trumpets, drums. Your basic hometown drum-and-bugle corps, a half century after the homecoming game. Dividing the crowd and pushing on through the common toward the Place of Worship.

Behind the band, more men—but these were young men, long of stride and full of vigor. Perhaps a dozen of them, perhaps as many as two dozen, the first young men Colleen had seen in Graystone. Where had they been keeping themselves?

Where had they been... *kept*?

Does it take until fifty before you can be trusted to join this obscene group? Colleen wondered. *Do they keep you in this dread inn until your past, your memories, you, have all been bleached away, then when you are safe, put you on public display?*

It was an absurd theory, but everything was now absurd.

The young men were shouldering thick ropes and pulling something Colleen could not see yet.

Another ten seconds, and it was in view.

It was a float—a Rose Bowl-style, flower-covered float lit with amber lanterns. Standing at the front was an old man.

The man Colleen recognized as the codger they'd run into outside of town.

Wardsworth, according to the clerk who'd called him head of the board.

A sign on the float in a gothic script said WELCOME. Behind the sign was a throne, majestic and out of scale to the person who occupied it. It looked like something that could have graced King Arthur's court.

This time, Colleen's scream was easy and loud.

Because it was her husband, Les, who occupied the throne, bound with cords around his chest and arms. He looked barely conscious, as if he had been drugged.

Drugged in his food at dinner, Colleen thought.

Now, she understood.

Oh God, Les, I get it now, she thought. *They're making you one of their own. Like they've done with the others. You'll grow old here, just like they did, grow old with leering inhuman eyes and an accent that doesn't quite fit, they won't be able to get that out of you, not completely, and maybe someday it'll be you walking out to meet some young couple new in town…you marching in that obscene band playing some instrument you first picked up in a past life you won't know you ever had. This is Lovecraft, in real life.*

Numb, Colleen continued to watch.

It was like being in that kind of terror-filled dream when the monster is following you and your legs are putty, you can't break the paralysis.

The band had made its way to the Place of Worship doors and was stalled there, not playing. Behind the float, the spectators were beginning to fall in line. They were waiting—to get in or for someone to come out, Colleen could not tell.

The food, that sprawling, delicious smelling banquet—that would be for after, Colleen realized.

But after what?

Wardsworth was delivering a speech. Colleen couldn't catch all the words, only a few here and there: "friend," "long time," "honor," "big night," "two complete ceremonies."

The crowd applauded.

Steady supply.

Those had been the old man's words, too.

Steady supply.

Oh, Jesus, please don't let this be happening. Please let us go back to New York and forget we ever came here.

The moon was still out, lower in the sky but still bright. It seemed to be aligning with the sun as it dropped behind the Place of Worship on a line with the hill and the common.

Once again, Colleen was reminded of Easter Island.

Except now, the comparison was terrifying.

With a creaking, the church doors swung open. Colleen could see inside. The Place of Worship was brightly lit, with white candles everywhere. The frescoed ceiling, the arches, and the balconies—it seemed to have been done in imitation of a Medieval church.

The congregation was…

...creatures.

That's when Colleen knew she had to escape.

I'm sorry, Les, I really am, she thought. *It's too late for you. But not me.*

The creatures filled the place, hundreds of them. They were bigger than humans, their fur thick and black and matted, like they had been recently in water, with rounded ears and pointed snouts. They had whiskers, like rats that Mother Nature forgot, regular rat-sized rats once whose genes somehow got irradiated or spliced or were exposed to some chemical agent or crossed with some mutant thing that was the result of one of God's major fuck-ups unwatched out here in a forgotten hell-hole corner of the U.S. of A.

Or some hideous extraterrestrials who visited Earth and chose Graystone for a colony.

They've been waiting for some astrological conjunction known only to them to come down the hill to where their human slaves prepare them a celebration, Colleen thought.

The largest one was advancing down the aisle, and its teeth were bared, not in anger, but in what might be considered pleasure.

The creature held a woman on its arm.

She was the woman Colleen had seen in the window, still dressed in white. Only now she was wearing a veil and she trailed a lace train being carried by the creature's accomplices. As they passed, the rat-creatures rose to their back legs and uttered that noise, that gnawing nibbling noise of rodent satisfaction.

And when this ceremony is over, they'll take that poor woman back up into the hills, into their world, and that's how they breed, the sons of bitches, Colleen thought.

As the party passed, the humans bowed, then applauded.

Their servants. Their human servants.

Les will now be initiated into their legion. New blood.

That's when Colleen's paralysis broke, when she was thinking *someday, they intend that to be me, a woman in white. They will keep me, they will feed me, as they did her, and when they're ready they'll dress me in white and bring me to one of...*

...those.

Colleen tried the window first, but it still would not open more than six inches.

She went for the door, but it was locked, from the outside.

A chair.

I'll bash it with a chair.

But what kind of attention would that draw to room 312? It would make noise to wake the dead and she would have to gamble that the din of the festivities outside would mask it.

And that they didn't have guards patrolling the Graystone Inn.

The Winchester was lying on the floor by the side of the chair, where it had dropped when Les fell asleep.

They had been stupid to miss it, whoever had taken him while he slumbered, but they had.

Colleen picked it up.

She knew exactly three things about a shotgun: where to put the shells, where the trigger was, and where it discharged. Les had shown her these three things.

Colleen checked the chamber. It was loaded, as it had been when he'd last touched it.

She had never fired a shotgun. She had never, in fact, touched one.

But you didn't need the NRA to figure out the basic principles. You hoisted it to your shoulder, aimed, pulled the trigger, and bang, you're dead.

Or open, if you're a door.

Colleen fired at the door.

No luck.

She fired again, four more times.

Five total.

The door opened.

Colleen looked down the hall. No one there. But surely some-one had heard the blasts; surely someone would be here any moment. Cradling the weapon, she started toward the stairs and tiptoed down to the lobby. It was deserted, too.

Looking outside, she saw the band striking up again and men and *them* dancing together grotesquely.

But Colleen didn't see Les.

The fear Colleen had felt upstairs had given way to courage, the kind a loaded shotgun can impart. Still, she could not leave through the main door—she would have to go out through the back.

Where is it?

Had to be somewhere along first-floor corridor.

Colleen retraced her footsteps through the lobby and passed the elevator.

There it was, the back door, which opened onto the parking lot. There was their car.

It was unlocked. She struggled with the shotgun getting in, but finally she was inside. From the other side of the inn, the sounds of the festivities were growing louder.

Colleen reached for the ignition.

And realized the keys were upstairs.

"Son of a bitch," she muttered.

The next sensation was odor—foul, insidious, originating from something that might have been dead for weeks, but wasn't. It was coming from behind her, from the back seat, in steady pumping breaths, it was...

Jesus, no.

Colleen pointed the shotgun at the back seat and pulled the trigger.

Nothing.

Again.

Nothing.

Les's words when he'd packed the shtgun into the car before leaving Manhattanwere suddenly in her mind:

This shotgun only holds five rounds.

Then that terrible smell was surrounding her.

She felt fur, and then all was blackness.

There was never any published word of the Wellingses' disappearance, nor any word about anything happening in Graystone, Vermont. Nothing at all for another year, not until a small posting on Expedia.

WEEK AWAY

In Some of the Good Lord's Prettiest Country.

Be part of a Great New England tradition.

Be our Guests! Home-cooked food, spirits.

Scenery to beat the band!

Click here for reservations.

Or write Box 1, Graystone, Vt.

THIS LITTLE BUG

This time, I walk.

I start early, emerging from my subway sleep nest by 5 a.m. in order to greet the first commuters. So many busy people in the big city. So many hard-working mothers and fathers. So many young people embarked on their careers. So many big shots, major domos, people of substance and weight, the movers and shakers of society here in and around Boston, Massachusetts.

You see, I walk.

I walk from the Park Street subway down Tremont to Chinatown, then up Washington, past City Hall, through Quincy Marketplace to the over-priced waterfront, back through the banking district and over to the Common and Garden and Back Bay in time for the midday shoppers. At dinner time, depending on the weather, I walk through the Prudential Center and Copley Place. On occasion, I walk through the train and bus stations and over to Boston Logan International Airport, where I comb my hair, walk erect, and act on my best behavior, attracting little attention to myself.

All day and into the summer night, I walk.

I walk and I breathe—always breathing, deeply satisfying breaths, in-out, in-out, in-out, with particular strength on the exhalation, a refreshing vigorous breathing even though I allow myself a smoke every now and then. When I breathe, I feel that familiar yet still-strange tickle in my lungs, and I smile. I know it can't hurt me, what's been living patiently there inside me.

So many thousands go by, an endless river, and I walk.

Some are still wearing their pandemic masks. Others, perhaps fully vaccinated and believing they are immune to COVID but knowing nothing of the far deadlier bug with which I am most intimately acquainted, revel in the so-called freedom that going maskless allows after lockdowns and a year and a half of hell.

Scum, they say, those that speak.

Swine.

Bum.

Get lost. Get a job. Get out of my way. Get bent. Yuck. Gross. Fuck you.

There was a fleeting time early in the pandemic when the public expressed empathy for me and my kind, dropping dollar bills at my feet that I declined to accept and wishing me well. Or was that not empathy but fear? Whatever, goodwill gave way to hostility as the vaccination rates rose, hospitalizations and deaths declined, and Massachusetts opened up.

When you speak and cast evil eyes now, I do not answer.

But it makes me grin, knowing what I know, knowing that you are completely ignorant.

Yes, I am a forbearing and extremely patient man.

It is good to be alive. In my own way, I am having a ball. You may find that difficult to believe, looking at my clothing, my beard, the shoes, the bundle I carry, but it is true. It is good to walk, to have that occasional cigarette, to drink heartily from that bottle and enjoy. It is good to be free, to have my health, such as it is, good to be able to breathe.

It is good to be alone.

It is good to be in the city, surrounded by so many.

I consider all of you my friends. I hate you with a passion that does not abate, yet you are my friends. A paradox, you say. The world is full of them. The sun that rises in the morning must sink in the evening. From the dead of winter the springtime flowers. In the eye of a storm, the calm. Paradox, my friends, the natural order of things.

Or are you so blind that you cannot see?

You will recall the childhood saying that sticks and stones may break my bones, but words will never hurt me.

How true it is.

Your words roll off me, but your physical remonstrances hurt, if not yet actually fractured bones. I have been beaten and mugged, by young punks mostly. I have been chased, cornered, locked up overnight by the cops. I have fought back, but in my own way and on my own terms.

Terms that are favorable only to me, as you shall soon discover. I admit I am not a pretty sight. I do have plans to clean things up.

Still, I know what I am, the nasty side of mankind still living in caves. I myself lived cave-like once, in the not-too-distant past.

And yet, that is not the half of it.

Has it always been this way? you may silently ask yourselves as you pass me by, disgust written on your faces and in the way you cross streets to avoid me. You should know better than that. You with the stylish clothes, the kids and the gas-guzzling SUVs, the 401(k)s and bank accounts, the country clubs and Cape Cod and Berkshire weekends, and the neat, ordered lives that are about to be ripped asunder in ways that will make COVID seem like the common cold—you, my friends, should know better than that.

No one is always this way, or any way. Motion is inevitable, the only constant being change. Didn't Hegel teach us that? Marx and Darwin? Everyone is born. Everyone crawls before walking, burbles before speaking, scribbles before writing. Everyone loves, and in turn feels love, somewhere, no matter how faint or brief or enduring. Everyone has a past, and there is good in that past, and there is bad, too, not always in equal proportions.

I walk.

I walk because I want to be with you, because I have something for you. I walk because of what you, fellow members of this species called homo sapiens, have done for me. I want to pay you back.

Not necessary, you protest? What was due has been paid?

Oh, but I insist.

So I walk, always on the move. I walk into the crowded lobbies of hotels and convention centers, and through the crowds outside Fenway Park. Like the good people at the airport and the bus and train stations, they will return home, whether home be Boston or California or England or India or China or Japan or Australia. They will not know it, will never retrospectively trace it back to me, but they will carry a lasting memory of a so-called homeless man in Boston.

Let me tell you a little story.

I think there are things you should know, the next time you encounter me and the stench of my breath, which you attribute, only partially correctly, to cigarettes and booze.

The story begins, as many do, in the long-ago and far-away. I was a much younger man then, a deeply respected man, if I may be immodest. I was, in fact, a scientist, and I was called a doctor for the PhD I carried after my name. Specifically, I was a climatologist, a widely published and scientifically daring one, and my specialty was the conditions of weather and astronomy that produce glaciers. My theories of orbital inclination (that is, the changing angles with which the Earth over the millennia has faced the sun) had revolutionized our basic understanding of the Ice Ages and I had recently co-authored what was then the definitive text on the subject.

More recently, as carbon emissions rose and the planet warmed and the ice caps began to melt, I established myself as an international respected climate-change authority.

Therefore, I was honored, but not surprised, when I was invited to join Polar 2020.

Chances are you have never heard of the Polar 2020 expedition. There is no good reason that you should have. The pandemic ravaged the earth, Trump was president, Biden hoped to beat him in the election, Putin still blustered, and on and on and on. No, Polar 2020 rated only a small mention in a wire story that ran in a few papers and websites and got no TV coverage that I saw. But this bothered none of the scientists who formed our party, and I doubt it made any difference to the seamen and officers who manned our ship, the RV *Arctic Maiden*, either. Almost without exception, the most significant work in science is conducted in methodical and decidedly non-romantic fashion, hardly the stuff of front-page headlines.

Do not imagine, however, that this was your run-of-the-mill scientific junket.

This was a multi-million-dollar effort, years in the planning, supported by private funds and congressional grants, and it would be many more years before our best universities and scholarly institutions would sift and sort their way through the incredible wealth of data with which we expected to return. Never had there been such a mission planned for the Arctic. Byrd and Peary could only have dreamed of what we were determined to do. The spectrum of interests was, perhaps, for a single mission, unique. There were scientists with expertise in glaciation, zoology, ultraviolet radiation, meteorology, geology, microbiology, internal medicine, immunology—yes, the explorers themselves were to be subjects of unprecedented research. The eventual result, we were confident, would be not only a deeper understanding of the Arctic, but also of mankind itself as it faced its greatest peril in recorded history.

Until, that is, what I am about to relate to you.

So, on an unusually hot day in late June 2020, we left Woods Hole Oceanographic Institution. We departed without fanfare, only immediate family members bidding us farewell. I kissed my wife and three teenage children, promised to FaceTime regularly, and we were off.

Please forgive my immodesty, but everyone on that ship as it sailed into Vineyard and Nantucket Sound and then the open Atlantic did have great expectations. Personally, I, a fifty-two-year-old man, harbored dreams of a Nobel Prize—or at least, finally, a nomination.

The irony of the day's sultry weather presented did not escape us.

In another week we were to be plunged into the northern extremes of Greenland, that most misnamed of lands. True, it would be summer there when we arrived, with daylight around the clock, and afternoon temperatures rising well into the balmy 50s—but Arctic summers are notoriously short, as fleeting and ultimately as disappointing as a former lover's kiss, if I may be so poetic. Within two months of our arrival, along toward the end of August, the mercury would begin to plummet, the snow would begin, and we would be locked into an Arctic winter—granted, one less harsh than in decades before. We planned to stay almost a year, returning in May 2021, when the ice had released what would then have become our captive ship.

From Woods Hole, we put in at St. John's, then continued on to Godthaab, Greenland, where we took on board a handful of Danish scientists who were making the journey with us. From Godthaab, we steamed north, along the shore of Baffin Island, where we observed the icebergs to be multiplying in both number and size. We put in a day and a night in Thule, a truly tiny and dreary outpost, then proceeded north again, until our captain found suitable moorage in a fjord extending like a skeletal finger off Kane Basin. The ice had grown even thicker, and the fog was nearly impenetrable at times. We would safely go no further, our captain informed us, and there was universal assent that Kane Basin suited our various needs to a T.

It took the better part of two days to unload our supplies and equipment and establish our base camp on a sheet of rock overlooking a glacier. Ours was not a geographical expedition, of course—the vastness of Greenland by then had long since been charted and mapped—but an exercise in information-gathering and experimentation that could, for the most part, be conducted from a single camp. Naturally, there would be outcamps and selected journeys inland, of two- or three-week's duration. For these, we had along two dozen Huskies and traditional Eskimo sleds—this at the insistence of our Danish hosts who, for reasons we did not attempt to fathom, were soured on snowmobiles.

The first weeks were a period of industry and good cheer amongst our party, which had taken residence in a series of tents erected behind the comparative shelter of a series of boulders. There is a certain savage beauty to the Arctic summer, and that beauty, combined with the endless day, was like a tonic. For it is summer when the wildflowers bloom, the lemmings and ermine and arctic hare prowl, when whatever other limited flora and fauna there is in this unforgiving territory explodes in crowning celebration of the cycle of life. Then, too, there was the almost daily display of aurora borealis, or northern lights, which paints its ghostly rainbow across the sky like the backdrop to some haunted dream.

As for me, I was intent on rainfall collection, pollen analysis, color spectrometry, ice coring—especially the latter. An entire history of weather is captured in the layers of ice that comprise a glacier, and a simple hand-auger-driven core, although time-consuming and sweat-inducing and muscle-tiring, is worth its proverbial weight in gold. My colleagues were plunged into their various and sundry labors, and there was the unspoken but certain feeling that what we had successfully embarked upon was an expedition bound for inclusion in the ranks of all-time great Arctic ventures, if such is the way to describe a legacy that predates Eric the Red.

Winter's arrival did nothing to disturb the camaraderie that had developed amongst us. If anything, it served to strengthen the bonds that had grown, and which now joined us together like the close-knit family we had in fact become. The snow was virtually non-stop, as those of us who were newcomers to this land had been told to anticipate. The wind was a harsh master, and the temperatures were soon similarly uncooperative. By the beginning of October, it was rare indeed the day when the mercury could be coaxed above zero degrees Centigrade.

But it was not weather, or the onset of the Arctic night (which, as you may know, lasts twenty-four hours a day) that began to change the temperament of our party toward the beginning of January.

No, it was not that. Christmas had come, and we had celebrated it with an evening of old-fashioned caroling and a rare dinner of reindeer steak with gravy, a Danish custom on this largest of Denmark's islands. Those of us who so desired had Zoomed and FaceTimed with our families.

No, it was the discovery at Outcamp 3 that would eventually bring ugly turmoil to Polar 2020.

Outcamp 3 had been set up some four kilometers inland by the microbiology folks, who were in pursuit of various strains of bacteria known only to this region and its equally inhospitable twin, Antarctica. It was little more than a single tent, this particular outcamp, and it was not manned on a continual basis, only as the dictates of microbiology demanded. Dave Heddon was the head of the microbiology contingent, which numbered exactly three, including Dave. He was a subdued man, introspective yet not glum, a powerful, broad-shouldered father of two young boys who looked for all the world like a starting NFL defensive lineman.

But he was a scientist—tops in his field, or so was the glow of his reputation—and he possessed that deliberate and calm way of speaking, so wonderfully rare, that is immediately soothing and almost therapeutic to those who hear it.

And that's how I knew something was up the evening of January 24, when he returned from three days at Outcamp 3.

I was alone in the chow tent, finishing off a cup of freeze-dried coffee, when Dave walked in, his beard twinkling with frost and his boots glazed with ice. In place of that calm voice was an imposter, a voice that fairly crackled with excitement. Remember, Dave Heddon was a man of unusual emotional maturity and control. I had learned that listening to him describe how much he missed his two young boys, but how sacrifices must sometimes be made in the name of science—and now, now he was speaking like a teenager high on weed.

"Out there," he began, sipping on the steaming coffee I had brought him, "I think we have discovered extraterrestrial life."

"What?" I asked.

"What we found by Outcamp 3," he said. "Frozen. And perfectly preserved, or so it would appear."

"What?" I repeated, persisting in my ignorance. "What have you found?"

"Alien life. Twelve beings. From where, is anybody's guess. But definitely not of this world. You'll know that as soon as you see their... their heads."

And then, his voice still tinged with excitement, he went on to relate the events of the last two days at Outcamp 3. How he and one of his party, Joanne White, had set off the first day to gather samples on the agar plates they carried in special aluminum boxes. How they had wandered perhaps 200 meters north of the camp through an unusually strong, snowless wind when they happened upon... shall I call them beings, as Dave did?... and the wreckage of a vehicle they initially believed to be constructed of steel.

"We had reached the peak of a rise," Dave recalled, "and were descending the other side when our lights picked up what we first assumed was another rise, albeit one irregularly contoured. Thinking little of it, we moved closer, our lights stabbing the pitch. As we approached, the rise took on a distinctly different shape. Or shapes, I should say, for there were several.

"The most prominent was a rockpile, roughly the size of a large automobile. It looked as if it may have been erected, however crudely, for purposes of shelter. Off to one side was a circle of blackened stones that appeared to have once enclosed a fire. Moving closer still, we got our first indistinct look at the... beings, four of them, sprawled in various contorted postures around the stones.

"Of course, the term 'beings' had not occurred to us then. Standing from the distance we were, and under such unsatisfactory light conditions, we assumed we had found the remains of earlier human explorers—the frozen cadavers of the unfortunate members of whatever ill-fated party it had been. Many of the early European and American pioneers of this region, as you know, never came home, and were never found.

"And who would have thought otherwise? The forms we were surveying were of human size and appeared to have the human compliment of limbs—two arms, two legs—and they were clothed in mammalian fur not the least bit incongruous for this cruel environment. Arctic hare was my guess. Of the four forms, no faces were visible. Not then. It seemed that their heads were unusually large, but that was difficult to ascertain. They had died in the same position, on their stomachs, faces into the snow."

Dave stopped. He beckoned for more coffee and I willingly obliged him. Never have I been so transfixed by a story as then.

"Wasn't there a feeling of perturbation, observing such a scene?" I said softly. "Even assuming, as you say you did, that they were early explorers of this vast wasteland."

"Indeed there was that feeling," Dave continued. "I don't know how long we stood there, staring, contemplating, trying fervently to put the pieces together, in all honesty more than a little scared. Ms. White and I are microbiologists, Robert, as I need not remind you. Perhaps someone better versed in anthropology or paleontology or medicine might have felt differently, but we, frankly, were most uneasy standing there.

"After an indeterminate period—it probably was a matter of mere minutes, although it seemed an eternity—Joanne and I moved closer. I think we felt it simultaneously—the heat coming from that camp, if camp is indeed what that place was for them. It wasn't a suffocating, tropical heat, but the zone surrounding the beings was several degrees warmer than the ambient temperature. We could feel it on our faces.

"That's when it occurred to me how unusual it was that snow had not drifted over the whole site. Obviously, the heat, whatever its origin, had been sufficient to keep the site clear. Protected, as it were, from the elements for a period of time.

"By this point, neither Joanne nor I were talking. This feeling of perturbation you have alluded to was beginning to intensify. Even before we turned one of them over to look at a face, we both knew something about this site was terribly strange. And I don't mean the fact that death had visited. Certainly, that was gruesome. But this feeling—by the second, it grew stronger. Not fear exactly. No, it was closer to the sort of nervous excitement I imagine Howard Carter felt on first entering Tutankhamen's burial vault."

There was a pause.

"I see by your look I'm having difficulty conveying those feelings," Dave said.

"Hardly," I said. "You are doing an admirable job."

"Naturally, our curiosity was too much to contain. Just as Carter could not control the urge to gaze upon Tutankhamen's visage, neither could we curtail our desire to see the faces of these... at that point, we still believed they were human, you understand. Having some scant knowledge of earlier discoveries of camps, I believed it was possible that we would see a perfectly preserved face. Pained and having suffered, no doubt, but preserved in a condition allowing transport to a more appropriate final resting place—a family cemetery, for example.

"We moved to within inches of one of them. We could see then that its head was much larger than it should have been, but we were too rattled to dwell on that incongruity. It took both of us to roll that one over. The body itself was frozen solid, of course, and it was heavy, and the job was complicated by the poor light. Finally, after trying various positions and leverages, we managed to turn it onto its back. I had placed my flashlight down to free both hands, so it was Joanne who first illuminated the face.

"I was sure I would faint. My knees went weak. For instead of the human face I had been expecting, there was something one only encounters in nightmares. There was no forehead, no nose, no ears—only a single eye, the compound eye of an insect such as the common dragonfly, grossly exaggerated in size. Worse, it seemed as if that eye were still experiencing vision."

"Dear God!" I exclaimed.

"I say that because there was a purplish iridescence emanating from that eye. But it was not a constant color or intensity of color, far from it. For the few seconds we stared at it, it seemed to be changing hue, from purple to blue to yellow—to be pulsating, as if it were electrically charged, or had been irradiated, or was radioactive. Almost like—like it could still see us, whatever it was. Naturally, it couldn't, but that was the overwhelming impression."

Suddenly, I was cold. I drew my coat closer around me, to negligible effect.

"I know how all of this must sound," Dave continued, "like a script to a Hollywood movie, but you and everyone else will have the opportunity to see for yourselves, I am sure. I assume every effort will be made to recover all four beings."

"You assume correctly," I said. An incredible discovery such as this could only lead to intense study and investigation.

I noticed that Dave was tapping his fingers, as if still trying to fully comprehend what he had seen, without great success.

"Where was I?" he finally said.

"You were describing the face."

"Yes, the face. After seeing that, there ensued another period of near-complete silence—nothing but the wind, and the whistling noise it made passing over the rocks. Joanne looked at me and I returned her look, but we said nothing. I am sure you are wondering if I was frightened. In fact, I was, I will admit—but only to a minor degree. Because despite whatever low level of energy remained active within its eye, which presumably was its nerve center, I was convinced it was dead. Frozen, probably for years, possibly for decades, there seemed no way it could have survived.

"So it is understandable that after our initial surprise began to fade, we succumbed to curiosity. From being to being we went, turning each of the four over, examining each, taking mental notes. As near as we could determine, they were identical—the same approximate size, same number of limbs, same compound eye. If, indeed, there were differences of gender or age, they were not discernible from our inspection.

"It was not until after we had examined each of the beings that we happened upon the vehicle. It was secluded on the far side of the rock pile, deliberately, I suspect, to protect it from wind and storms. It would not surprise me to learn that the pile was erected specifically to protect it from the elements in the hope, one might guess, that it might someday be repaired for a return trip home.

"By that point, a hypothesis was beginning to emerge. Namely, that these beings, whoever they were and wherever they were from, had been stranded there by accident or mishap or mechanical malfunction—and maybe by something as simple as running out of fuel. Quite conceivably, they were awaiting a rescue mission that never happened. That would explain why they had built their camp, and why they had died in it. It would explain how they had come to hunt the arctic hare whose fur they made into the coats they were wearing when death overcame them. And it would explain the fires they burned from the few scraps of vegetation they had been able to forage back toward the coast. Because no matter how technologically advanced they were, I was convinced that they were warm-blooded creatures dependent on the interior environment that was their means of transportation. Once that was lost to them, it was only a question of time before they—so fragile as they must have been—succumbed to the elements. Particularly if they were stranded here in the dead of winter, as is my strong suspicion.

"In any event, we found the vehicle—or what I suppose is their vehicle until proved otherwise. If you have ever watched certain movies or TV shows, you may have some conception of what a so-called spaceship is supposed to look like: shaped like a cigar or a pie, large in size. This is nothing like that. To begin, it is in the shape of a perfect cube. It is small, about seven feet per side, with a seating arrangement that maximized all available space, I suspect the four could fit inside with little difficulty. Based on our cursory look, I would hazard that it is made of stainless steel or some steel-like material manufactured in the place they come from. There are no markings, no lights, no windows or portholes, and only the outline of a door. I think other members of our team will be tempted to open it once we have retrieved it—that is, if salvage is feasible with the equipment we have."

The remainder of Dave's account chronicled how he and his colleague had spent another hour at the site, probing and sifting through the snow for other artifacts. Strangely, there were none, none that could be found, anyway—no tools, no lights, no sleeping bags or tents, no food supplies, no utensils or scraps that would indicate food had ever been prepared or eaten at the site. In fact, Dave recounted, the entrails and meat of the hares they had made into coats had been left untouched. These findings, he noted, reinforced his hypothesis that they were fragile beings—beings that perhaps were unable to eat the kind of food available in this sparse environment, if they ate at all and didn't subsist on some form of energy unknown to us. Beings that were of a higher order, unquestionably—but beings ill-equipped to handle Arctic cold.

Seeing that their battery power was running low and recognizing that their original mission of collecting microbiological samples was still incomplete, Dave and Joanne left the site—but not before determining to their mutual satisfaction that they would be able to find it again.

"Truly, it's an awesome discovery," I said when Dave was done.

"I think you understate the case," he said, with a smile. "Next to this, King Tutankhamun would be but a sideshow in the long history of discoveries. Think of it, Robert! Extraterrestrial life, perfectly preserved! Along with the vehicle in which they traversed the universe. There's simply no telling how this could revolutionize any number of fields. Aeronautics. Physics. Biology. I could go on. It will be years before the full impact of this is understood and implemented!"

Needless to say, word of the discovery spread through the main camp in no time.

A meeting was convened the next morning, and all but a handful of our party was in attendance. After allowing Dave and Joanne to retell their story, attention turned to the logistics of retrieving the beings and their vehicle. A crew would leave that afternoon to do the preliminary work, and the hope was that the beings could be brought to base camp the next day, with the vehicle to follow within a week—the latter timetable depending, of course, on its weight, the difficulty of building a suitable contrivance to move it, and the power of the Danes' trusted Huskies, which had proven themselves all winter in whatever tasks had been put to them. It was further agreed that a special tent would be erected solely for the purpose of studying the beings. A separate tent would house the vehicle.

As it developed, recovering the beings and their vehicle took only a few hours, and we had everything safely in camp by dinner the following day. The explanation for this unanticipated expediency was at once simple but baffling: the vehicle, which we had assumed weighed tons, actually weighed less. In fact, much to the amazement of our mechanical crew, we found that three of us could lift it, and a single Huskie could haul it once it had been secured to a sled. Whatever alloy had gone into its construction, it was not iron or aluminum or steel—or any material known to mankind, for that matter, as subsequent tests would reveal.

Almost immediately, the physicians, led by Dr. Bruce C. Hazlett, the expedition's surgeon and medical chairman, began their autopsies. They worked virtually around the clock, fueled, as they were, by the same adrenalin coursing through all of us. They were meticulous in their work, for they well knew that a legion of scientists back in the States would want their own opportunities for research once we had returned with our find. It was slow work, painstakingly documented by extensive notetaking, videotaping, and photography, but by the end of the first week the doctors had learned a tremendous amount—and had been confronted with an equally impressive number of mysteries and inconsistencies.

Dr. Hazlett's team discovered, for example, that the beings' skin was similar to human skin, having the same number of layers and composed of cells similar in structure and apparently serving the same functions—protection from infection, regulation of internal temperature, retention of vital fluids. Our medical staff was able to document the muscles, ligaments, and skeleton, all of which suggested the beings had walked in an upright manner. There were no toes on the feet, and no hair on their heads or anywhere else on their bodies, but as one member of our party noted, those features are already all but vestigial in homo sapiens itself.

I suppose none of us were surprised to learn that Alpha, Beta, Kappa, and Epsilon, as we had taken to calling them, possessed brains nearly twice the size of their human counterparts. Their spines, too, were approximately double human size, with a capacity for twice the volume of nervous tissue. As for the eyes—those haunting eyes, which none save the doctors chose to look directly into for very long—they were indeed the source of radiation, of an intensity, fortunately, that was too low to be of danger to us. Its purpose, however, remained an open question, one that we on Polar 2020 could answer. That would require more advanced technology and specialists we did not have on board.

And so that question and many besides were left to subsequent endeavors.

What did they eat? A particularly vexing puzzle, for there was no stomach or intestines. Did they eat at all, or exist on some nonorganic form of energy? Did they speak, or was communication accomplished in some far more sophisticated mode, as we suspected? They indeed had mouths and tongues, but the muscles of the tongue, the doctors concluded, were only crudely developed, and where vocal cords should have been there was nothing. How did they reproduce? There was no evidence of sex organs and no indication of differences between the genders—if, in fact, two genders were represented.

Alpha, Beta, Kappa, and Epsilon were carbon copies of each other, or so it seemed.

Our technicians were unsuccessful in their efforts to penetrate the quartet's vehicle, for it resisted all attempts to puncture, drill, pry, or bang open. Unquestionably, their vehicle held clues as to the origin and nature of the beings—and what quantum leaps in technology might be possible after the vehicle's secrets we could only guess. It was not too wild to dare to believe that the vehicle might even provide useful to our nation in keeping the edge in the new arms race developing between the U.S. and China.

Alas, those exciting developments were destined to wait until later.

The weeks passed and the excitement over Alpha, Beta, Kappa, and Epsilon subsided. Spring was approaching, and although in that clime spring promises only the return of weak sunlight and temperatures only occasionally above freezing, something that could legitimately be called spring fever had us in our grip. Even excepting our alien finds—they themselves were destined to make the name Polar 2020 a household word, I was confident—our expedition had been a tremendous success, more so than anyone had dreamed during the months of planning preceding it. My own endeavors had borne fruit beyond my expectations, and with no small measure of pride in my achievements, I looked forward to authoring and co-authoring several major papers upon my return to the halls of academia.

It was the last week of April, nearly a month before we had planned to depart Greenland, that Dave and Joanne became sick.

Curiously, they both took ill the same day, and at approximately the same hour, late morning. But beyond that coincidence, nothing about their initial complaints raised an eyebrow. Without exception, all of us experienced sickness since our arrival on the island—and Joanne's and Dave's symptoms matched those of the flu that had spread through the camp earlier in the year. Headache, stomach cramps, fever, annoying cases of diarrhea—yes, their symptoms fit those of an ordinary viral infection. Seeing that their business was microbes, I, for one, simply assumed that Dave and Joanne had contracted their bugs in the course of their work.

By the third day, it was becoming clear that their malady was not commonplace. Instead of improving, or moderating, or at the very least stabilizing, their conditions had worsened. Their fevers had intensified, and with temperatures threatening to break 107 degrees, they had started to have auditory and visual hallucinations. Had we been in an equatorial zone and not an arctic one, Dr. Hazlett said, there would have been a suspicion of malaria. But malaria was not their diagnosis, nor could the doctors come up with one that satisfied them.

What was most disturbing was that their sickness did not respond to antibiotics or any of the other treatments the doctors tried.

At 10:25 p.m. on May 2, after having lapsed into a fevered frenzy that had forced us to bind his ankles and wrists and strap him to a stretcher in the camp's sick bay, Dave died of heart failure. Three hours later, in the early part of May 3, and following a similar period of extreme agitation, Joanne also succumbed. Their deaths plunged us into severe depression. Everyone had been following the course of Dave's and Joanne's health, particularly in their last three or four days, and the knowledge that they were gone devastated us.

What was even more chilling were the fevers a handful of others were beginning to report even as Dave and Joanne lay on their deathbeds.

By May 6, nearly half the camp was experiencing the same symptoms. Whatever the cause, we were witnessing an epidemic we could not curtail. That was indisputable. During an emergency meeting of the remaining healthy crew, it was decided that Polar 2020 must be immediately terminated and we would return to the U.S., more than two months ahead of schedule. In the time it would take to break camp, the sick were to be quarantined and the healthy were to take rigid precautions in the handling of food and water.

Six more expeditioners—I need not name them—had died by the morning we pulled anchor and steamed back out through the ice-clogged waters of Kane Basin. Like Dave and Joanne, the bodies of the deceased were placed in refrigerated storage on the *Arctic Maiden* for the journey to home and proper burial. Autopsies, of course, had been performed on Dave and Joanne, and they were performed on the next six, as well. The manner of death in every case, Dr. Hazlett reported, was heart failure induced by prolonged fever and dehydration. As to the cause of the fevers—that was surmised to be viral in nature, although Polar 2020 lacked the expertise and technology needed to isolate or positively identify the villain virus.

I was hardly the only person as yet unaffected by the disease who began to believe that its advent must be associated with the discovery of the beings—who, ironically, were being kept in the same cold storage as the human dead for the trip south.

True, our first contact with them had been three months before the onset of Dave and Joanne's distress. But as those two scientists themselves would have been quick to observe, some microbes have an incubation period in humans of weeks or months or even years—consider syphilis, as only one example among many, whose tertiary effects may be delayed as long as three decades after contact. Perhaps the beings had not been overcome by cold, after all, I thought; perhaps it had been a virus, one they had brought with them, or been infected with on their arrival here. If so, that virus had remained inactive, but lethally alive, in Greenland's cold.

As might be imagined, we were in regular contact with the authorities during our trip south from Greenland. Our situation, from what I could gather talking to the captain and Dr. Hazlett, was being monitored with growing concern in certain circles in Washington. By the time we had reached the northern coast of Maine, plans had been formulated for a Navy helicopter to fly several of the government's infectious disease specialists out to our ship for an on-site inspection.

We did not blink at this announcement. Naturally, it would be necessary to take the proper steps to ensure our arrival would not contaminate the population at large. These specialists would assist in the planning, we assumed, and no doubt would take tissue and fluid specimens from the shipboard autopsies so as to commence their own investigation without further delay.

Just after noon on May 11, the helicopter touched down on a makeshift flight deck the crew had cleared by rearranging some of the equipment and booms aft of the pilothouse. I was unnerved by who disembarked: men dressed in Hazmat suits and breathing from air tanks on their backs. More disturbing still was what they carried: not equipment for collecting specimens, but military-issue M249 light machine guns. I asked one man why it was necessary to be armed, and he replied that this team by regulation was routinely armed, whether on a friendly mission such as ours, or on a Specials Forces mission in some war.

The men in white spoke briefly with the captain and Dr. Hazlett, then were led below to where the bodies were being stored. In less than five minutes, they returned, but not empty-handed. With the help of several of our crew members, the men in white had brought topside the bodies of the beings, wrapped tightly in canvas. They also carried steel canisters containing autopsy specimens from our human victims. It took little time to load them into the cargo bin of the helicopter, which had kept its door sealed while the beings had been brought up. Next, a line was attached from the helicopter to the space vehicle, which we had encircled with cable and lashed to the deck.

Before we knew it, the helicopter was gone—and with it, Alpha, Beta, Kappa, Epsilon, and their vehicle.

At dawn the day after the helicopter visit, a U.S. Navy frigate appeared on the horizon and broadcast a brief radio message ordering us to remain at our present position, some seventy miles due east of Jonesport, Maine, until further notice. The frigate, the USS *Sam Houston*, then steamed approximately two miles upwind of the *Arctic Maiden*, where it took up a watch it was careful to maintain. Like the *Arctic Maiden*, *Sam Houston*'s captain informed our own skipper that the frigate was to remain in the area awaiting further word from the authorities as to the time, place, and manner of our return home.

Our instructions by now were originating in the highest levels of the Biden Administration, which we learned had mobilized a crisis team of epidemiologists and public health experts led by Anthony Fauci. The number-one concern, of course, was the public-health threat we represented—concern about a possible pandemic on top of a pandemic—and while we on the *Arctic Maiden* were becoming increasingly panicked about our own fate, I think even the sickest among us could appreciate the administration's grave concern. Although we were not privy to the details of deliberations concerning us, this much was conveyed to us through the *Sam Houston*: arrangements were being made to quarantine the remaining members of our party in abandoned barracks at the old Brunswick Naval Air Station, north of Portland, Maine.

A week we waited, conditions on board the *Arctic Maiden* deteriorating almost by the minute. There was one other helicopter visit—to drop supplies of morphine sulfate requested by Dr. Hazlett to ease the discomfort of our most seriously ill—but otherwise we were as disconnected from civilization as we had been in Greenland. It was during this week that morale disintegrated. It was during this week that six more died, and all but two of us began to show at least the beginning symptoms of the disease—the two being Dr. Hazlett and myself.

In their fevered states, the survivors took to wandering the ship, talking to themselves, gesticulating at imaginary foes, uttering vituperative and profane language, accusing their colleagues of the most reprehensible behaviors. Of a more frightening magnitude were the altercations that spontaneously began to erupt among the crew and the scientists. The word nightmare does not adequately describe this week, and I spent much of it together with Dr. Hazlett barricaded inside my cabin, venturing out only to procure food.

On the seventh day, those few sailors who had stayed faithful to their posts abandoned them. Until then, they had managed to maneuver the ship so it stayed roughly within the two-mile radius allowed by the *Sam Houston*. On the seventh day, they shut down the engines, locked their hysterical captain into his wardroom, and left the ship to drift. A group of five then took to a lifeboat, lowered themselves into the water, and headed off in a westerly direction. A storm was brewing but they had traveled a distance when the *Sam Houston* fired a missile that sank them.

So you'd like to know what happened next, wouldn't you? You people who scorn me now as I walk among you, inhaling and exhaling deeply, this most highly transmissible of all germs I carry spreading widely, then doing what it is programmed to do: replicate and kill.

Long story short, I saw the explosion that sank the lifeboat and knew what was next. In a sort of modern take on the *Titanic*, I lowered myself off the ship into another lifeboat moments later. I had barely moved to safety when the *Sam Houston* sank our ship with a second missile.

The storm intensified soon after, which may explain why the Houston could not find me. Or perhaps the captain concluded no one could survive such a storm—a true Nor'easter that sent several vessels larger than a rubber-hulled dinghy to the bottom—and never initiated a search. Whatever, I am sure there was an investigation. That captain's stripes, I bet, have been stripped.

In any event, miraculously I did survive the storm. For several days I drifted, until the lifeboat came ashore at Bar Harbor, Maine, where I broke into a car whose owner, apparently a forgetful sort, had left her pocketbook in view. I stole her cash, enough for the bus trip back to Cape Cod with plenty left over for the inevitable contingencies.

I had hoped my wife and children would be ecstatic when I reached my home, but they were anything but. Federal agents had prepared for every possibility, even the one-in-a-million chance that I or someone else had survived the sinking of the *Arctic Maiden*. Families, friends, and colleagues had been instructed to call if anyone showed up. Police patrolled.

"I'm sorry, honey, I have no choice," my wife said, closing the door.

I was about to plead with her when I heard sirens.

More days and bus rides brought me to Boston, the nearest big city. Easier to hide there, not that I would be easily recognizable now, given how long I had gone without a shave or haircut, or even a shower or change of clothing. I place no trust in homeless centers, however well-intentioned their operators may be.

Let me leave you with a few facts and questions for you to ponder.

The questions first.

Did Alpha, Beta, Kappa, and Epsilon know what they carried? Clearly, they were immune, but did they know? If they did, were they on a mission to destroy a species they held, correctly, to be a threat to Planet Earth—and, with Bezos and Branson and NASA seeking to colonize space, planets, and systems beyond? If they did not, why had they come?

Ultimately, these are esoteric questions. What happened, happened. What is, is.

Now, the facts.

Unlike the coronavirus, this one spreads equally well indoors or out. Thrives in all temperatures, from sub-freezing to extreme climate-change hot. Requires an almost infinitesimally low virus load and overwhelms the immune system quickly. To the researchers, I say: good luck with your vaccines. Pfizer and Moderna got their COVID products in months, but you won't even have weeks with this particular bug. Even if big pharma did, what is the guarantee they could succeed? This one came from far beyond. I would be surprised if the laws of our science applied.

By the way, good luck Fauci and CDC and FDA and WHO.

In my lighter moments, I imagine this virus rejoices, for stripped to its essentials, what is the purpose of any life form but to reproduce, in this case to propagate its RNA so that it sees another tomorrow.

Shall we give it a name? SuperCOVID? The media types would love that, in the brief period before the Apocalypse. COVID-Ultimate? Alien variant? Shall there be a national naming contest before time runs out?

Or how about a reality show! The Virus is Right, say. American Virus. Dire Jeopardy. Dancing with the Extraterrestrials.

Ha-ha.

Lol.

It is important that I maintain a sense of humor.

And keep things in perspective.

Because while this little bug has arguably made me a tad daffy, it cannot kill me, for I am lucky to have developed immunity. The scientist in me knows I belong to a very small cohort—that .000001 or less percent who will survive as our species largely departs the planet, leaving it to heal from the wars and industrialization and hatred and anger that so plague it.

How will I subsist, you may rightly ask?

As I do already: with food from dumpsters. As the population plummets, I will find sustenance from the food left behind in stores and warehouses. Canned goods have a shelf life measured in years. And after that, I shall partake of Mother Earth's bounty, the berries and grains and fish and wildlife that sustained our ancestors eons ago.

Yes, I will be fine.

I may even, should opportunity arise, decide to procreate.

About the Author

This is G. Wayne Miller's 20th published book. He is an author, a journalist, a filmmaker, a podcaster and a visiting fellow at Salve Regina University's Pell Center for International Relations and Public Policy, where he is cofounder and director of the Story in the Public Square program. He also co-hosts and co-produces the national Telly-winning public television/SiriusXM Satellite Radio show, "Story in the Public Square."

Miller has been honored for his writing more than 50 times and was a member of the *Providence Journal* team that was a finalist for the 2004 Pulitzer Prize in Public Service. Three documentaries he wrote and co-produced have been broadcast on public television, including The *Providence Journal*'s "Coming Home," about veterans of the wars in Iraq and Afghanistan, nominated in 2012 for a New England Emmy and winner of a regional Edward R. Murrow Award.

Visit Miller at www.gwaynemiller.com

Curious about other Crossroad Press books?
Stop by our site:
www.crossroadpress.com
We offer quality writing
in digital, audio, and print formats.

CPSIA information can be obtained
at www.ICGtesting.com
Printed in the USA
LVHW102244110422
715956LV00005B/82